RUSSIAN DOLLS

Stories from the Breathing Castle

bitlit

A **free** eBook edition is available
with the purchase of this print book.

COTEAU
BOOKS

www.coteaubooks.com

RUSSIAN DOLLS

Stories from the Breathing Castle

W.P. KINSELLA

Coteau Books

Edited by Dave Margoshes
Book designed by Tania Craan
Typeset by Susan Buck
Back cover photograph by Stuart Davis/Vancouver Sun
Printed and bound in Canada at Friesens

Library and Archives Canada Cataloguing in Publication

Kinsella, W. P., author
     Russian dolls : stories from the breathing castle / W.P. Kinsella.

Issued in print and electronic formats.
ISBN 978-1-55050-695-2 (paperback).--ISBN 978-1-55050-696-9 (pdf).--
ISBN 978-1-55050-697-6 (epub).--ISBN 978-1-55050-698-3 (mobi)

     I. Title.

PS8571.I57R88 2016   C813'.54   C2016-906595-2
                                               C2016-906596-0

Library of Congress Control Number 2016957116

2517 Victoria Avenue
Regina, Saskatchewan
Canada S4P 0T2
www.coteaubooks.com

Available in Canada from:
Publishers Group Canada
2440 Viking Way
Richmond, British Columbia
Canada V6V 1N2

10 9 8 7 6 5 4 3 2 1

Coteau Books gratefully acknowledges the financial support of its publishing program by: the Saskatchewan Arts Board, The Canada Council for the Arts, the Government of Saskatchewan through Creative Saskatchewan, the City of Regina. We further acknowledge the [financial] support of the Government of Canada. Nous reconnaissons l'appui [financier] du gouvernement du Canada.

TABLE OF CONTENTS

IN THE BEGINNING
VANCOUVER 1979

Christie's past is like a handful of coins repeatedly tossed in the air. Each time they land, the story they tell is different.

I think of her as Calliope, the Muse of literature. Calliope carries a writing tablet, like I carry a clipboard with a hundred sheets of lined yellow paper. Tonight, Christie wears a dark green skirt and jacket of a grainy material with which one might upholster a sofa.

"Suitable for a power lunch at the Four Seasons," is what I said when she emerged from the bedroom. Not that we'd go there, or ever have power lunches.

I may bury something of Christie's in the garden, dance over it under a full moon, chanting, naked, except for a silver talisman on a silver chain. I will pour blood on the loamy earth. In expectation, I will leave my window open after rain, when the air is pure and biting as ice.

Our apartment is immaculately furnished in chrome, black and white leather, and polished woods. The perpetual thrust of the air conditioner keeps us cool as strawberries in a display case. We are preparing to visit my family. I am wearing a white, short sleeved shirt, for they keep their apartment stifling as a greenhouse.

The preceding paragraph, the description of the apartment and the business about my family, is a figment of my imagination. Or, perhaps, I am simply an unreliable narrator. My family, what there is of it, live in another city far away. They have never met Christie. Probably never will. We do not live in a glass and chrome apartment. We share a very large bedroom with a tiny kitchenette on the second floor of a multi-layered, patched-together, frame house in east Vancouver. Our window overlooks the playground of a private school where teenage girls in green school uniforms play field hockey on warm spring afternoons.

Not long after I met Christie, we went for coffee at a small lunch counter on Hastings Street where I have come to be friends with the proprietor, Jones.

"Damaged goods," he said, when I walked in alone the next day. "Where do you find chicks like that, Wylie?" Jones is probably in his late thirties, a brush cut, bleary eyes, a perpetual three-day growth of beard.

"What do you mean?"

"Only need one look to tell she's seriously damaged goods. My advice, disappear like she's attacking you with a knife. She's running full speed from something or toward something. You don't ever want to find out what it is. She's pretty, but she's trouble."

Jones rubs his hands on his dirty apron. He works twelve-hour days at this tiny lunch counter and barely manages to eke out a living. He has a degree in philosophy from a prestigious university. You don't see many large ads in the newspaper advertising for philosophers.

"I think she may have had a bad marriage," I said.

"Trust me, Wylie, it's more than that. Every kind of weirdo wanders in and out of this lunch counter. Been watching these people for years. I can read them. That girl is carrying serious baggage, trunks and trunks full. I know you like redheaded chicks, and she's cute, knows how to wear blue jeans, but her fucking green eyes can see right through you. Trust me on this one, Wylie."

"Where were you born?" I ask Christie. She smiles across the table at me with a steady cat-eyed stare. "It can't hurt to tell me that. What kind of advantage do you think it would give me to know where you were born?"

"England," says Christie, licking her thin, sensuous lips. It is a very hot summer evening. Christie drinks Diet Coke from a sweat-beaded glass. A cigarette pack, of a green deeper than her eyes, lies at her fingertips. "I'm told Joseph Conrad was in the family woodpile a few generations back." She breathes in smoke, shaking her head to displace a few damp plum-coloured curls from her forehead.

"A few days ago you told me that you've never been outside North America. Why do you lie like that?"

"Wylie, when you ask a question you always insist on an answer."

Why do I not take my friend's advice and disappear from Christie's life? Because, I discovered quite by accident that it is Christie who draws my stories from me. And what stories they've become. For me, she is like an apparition from Greek mythology pulling thread hand over hand from my mouth. She seduces me into spinning the chaff of my life into bright little jewels, some small, some large, word pictures that bubble on the page like flowers boiling in a cauldron. Christie has become the prism that filters and refines my plain words into rainbows. A Muse, that's what she is. And, if I believe it, then it's true. Literature is full of stories of a Tenth Muse. Christie, and whatever comes with her, is mine and I'm not going to let go of her, or it.

"Improbable stories," one editor said of the crap I used to write, though he bought two of them. "Like having a clown at an execution."

THE PHANTOM BOWLING BALL

DETROIT (UPI) – A man died after a 14 lb. bowling ball crashed through his car windshield and hit him on the head. The ball seemed to have come from nowhere, say police. The ball bounced on the hood of the car and shattered the windshield. There are no high buildings or bridges in the area. A $2,000 reward has been offered for information concerning the origin of the phantom bowling ball.

One afternoon in 1975, the phantom bowling ball put on a red garter and lured Jimmy Hoffa to a fatal rendezvous, with promises of ecstasy.

CHAPTER 1

I have always been determined to be a writer. I have also always known that I was not very good. But even not very good writers get published occasionally. I have suitcases full of unpublished manuscripts, a three-inch thick folder full of rejection slips and a slim envelope with a handful of acceptance letters. My feeling was, even as I wrote a new story, that it would still be a failure, but it would be one percent better than the previous fifty stories I had written. I was willing to serve an apprenticeship, but apprenticeships end – and I could not see far enough into the future to envision myself as a journeyman. Years passed this way. Then Christie came into my life.

I was living in a rooming house in East Vancouver when I first met her. *Existing* in a rooming house in East Vancouver would be more apt.

My fame as a writer was limited to winning a contest sponsored by a mimeographed magazine with a maudlin story about a boy and somebody else's dog that brought me a one-hundred-dollar prize.

I knew my way about Vancouver well enough to qualify for a license as a taxi driver, an occupation I pursued half-heartedly when all other doors were closed. I did odd jobs, delivered telephone books door to door, helped out a mover friend on end-of-the-month weekends. I once demonstrated a product in a supermarket – I wore an apron, cooked sausage on a tiny skillet and gave out samples. I continually burned the sausage and people spit out the samples. I was fired after three hours.

Whenever I was late with the rent, which was often, my landlady, a garish old woman named Mrs. Kryzanowski, would threaten to permanently separate me from my room in the Breathing Castle, as the rooming house is known, a warren of additions built on additions, full of occupied sun porches, walk-in closets, and mysterious hideaways, each more lonely than the last.

Under my large, creaking bed with its ancient teak headboard, are those three suitcases full of novels, stories and notes, much of the collection thinly disguised autobiography, written in a strident, all-knowing voice. When I reread that work it does not surprise me that I have to drive taxi to keep my rent paid and my stomach full. That was, until I met Christie.

Two of Christie's favorite words are "Tell me?" Question? Statement? Command? "Tell me?" she repeats over and over as we make love, aching for me to describe to her our lovemaking in the most graphic way possible. Mostly I cannot. My jaws seem locked by some gargantuan headgear. Christie thrashes and cries beneath me. "Tell me. Tell me. Tell me."

"Tell me, Wylie?" she whispers another time, rubbing about me like a heat-seeking cat. Tell me how we met. Tell me about our first time. But reality is too much for me. It turns me catatonic, until, much later, I sit staring at the geography of my keyboard. As I type, coloured flowers appear on the page.

This is another of the kind of story I was writing when Christie appeared in my life. It is a story that was published in a small magazine, but from it you will see why I was not more successful.

THE POWER OF THE UNIVERSE

The spaceship looked like a cross between a footlocker and one of those dun-coloured boxes where mailmen pick up letters and packages mid-way on their routes.

Zinth landed the spaceship in thick foliage on the edge of a downtown park. He unbent himself from the craft. He was about five feet tall, resembling a stick-figure drawing made of pink shower curtain material. He walked through the empty park staying within the moon shadow of trees. It was 3 a.m.

Staring straight up the trunk of a sycamore, he spotted a gull asleep on a high limb. He trained his vision on it, deduced its DNA, and a second later he occupied the body of an identical gull.

As dawn broke, Zinth the gull flew to a dumpster behind a fast food restaurant. As a vital-looking young black man jogged up to the back door Zinth snapped into synch with the young man's DNA. As the black man entered the restaurant, his duplicate turned away from the door and moved off through the downtown streets.

Zinth's assignment was to learn about fuel. He soon discovered that his borrowed body was crying for fuel. He let the part of the young man's brain that craved sustenance, take over. He entered a café and ordered breakfast, surprised at the words he spoke and more surprised at what was delivered to him. He let himself taste a few of the morsels as the young man ate. But Zinth soon turned off his taste buds. While the food and drink were hot, they lacked the hot blood taste so necessary to good food. Apparently insects were not part of this species' diet. There was nothing like a blowfly casserole with a scattering of fire ants for breakfast.

Zinth wandered into a laundromat, which at 10 a.m. was a hive of activity. The box-like white machines that first wet and then dried the cloth articles stuffed into them obviously operated on some kind of fuel. Zinth would watch and learn, take samples.

He noted that after the cloth items were placed in the machines, a magical white powder was poured over them, sometimes from a small box, sometimes from a cup dipped into a large box of magic powder. Zinth noted that the machines were quiet until fueled by metal slugs of some ilk, two usually, sometimes three, and the wet machines would spring to life, hissing and gurgling, vibrating with energy.

Their magical powder apparently remained in the cloth articles for when they were transferred to the wind-box, as Zinth thought of it, the second machine needed only to be fueled by more slugs. He spent over an hour staring at the rows of machines, until a black woman dressed in purple garments glared at him and said loudly, "What you lookin' at?"

Zinth turned his gaze away without replying. Already a plan was forming. He noticed that bolted to the wall was a machine that dispensed small boxes of magical powder, and another machine that dispensed fuel pellets in return for patterned paper, the same kind he had exchanged for his breakfast.

He watched a woman acquire an orange-and-black box of powder, and a handful of pellets. She set the powder and pellets on the counter and began sorting her cloth objects into two piles which Zinth determined had something to do with shades of colour.

He walked casually down the counter until he was behind the woman. Suddenly, he seized the box in one hand, the fuel pellets in the other. He mishandled the stack of metal pellets, grasping three, sending the other three clattering to the floor.

Zinth told his feet to run and as he moved toward the street was surprised at the commotion that followed him. The pellets and magical powder must be of great value, he thought. He had been near the rear of the laundromat when the owner of the pellets and powder began wailing alarmingly. As he made his way down the aisle people pulled at his clothes and attempted to trip him. A big woman gave him a nasty wallop on the side of the head with her clothes basket. As he neared the front of the building a burly man came running out of a compartment, holding a bluish weapon that immediately instilled great fear in his cloned host. The man pointed the weapon at him and demanded that he stop.

When he didn't stop, the long-handled weapon made a loud bark and scraps of metal were propelled into his body doing a certain amount of damage to the chest of his travelling vehicle.

On the street, uniformed police or soldiers joined in the chase, and he barely made it to the dumpster where he had left the gull before they overtook him. As he entered the gull and glided away, his travelling host vanished, leaving behind several confused uniforms looking about for someone to bark their weapons at.

Zinth flew back to his vehicle, not without difficulty as the gull was definitely not built to transport objects by holding them with its rather pitiful feet. He waited until dark before he released the gull and eased his own form back into the spacecraft. As he flew into outer space at double the speed of light, Zinth was proud of himself, and considered it a day well spent.

CHAPTER 2

I was coming down the stairs when I laid eyes on Christie for the first time. She was standing at the door to a tiny room on the ground floor with Mrs. Kryzanowski. The previous occupant had been some sort of psychopath who screamed like a banshee in early hours of the morning, and the previous week threw his toaster through the window into a bed of marigolds. Next day, two young Asian men wearing black muscle shirts forcibly escorted the psychopath from the premises. Mrs. Kryzanowski has powerful friends in what I perceive as the Vancouver underworld.

Christie was wearing tight blue jeans, black, ankle-high cowboy or biker boots, a white, off-the-shoulder blouse and no bra. I froze three steps from the bottom.

Mrs. Kryzanowski, firmly clutching the key to the room, was delivering a lecture about what was tolerated and what was not. With her heavy Polish accent, her speech sounded like coughing. She had pink, leathery skin and sour eyes.

"Rent on the first by noon, or out you go. No hooking, no parties, no loud music." Christie carried a single brindle suitcase that looked like it had been through many owners, all of whom had abused it.

An hour later, I tapped on Christie's door.

The look on her face when she opened it made it clear she thought Mrs. K. had returned to deliver more instructions.

"I'm Wylie. I live upstairs." I said. "I see you've met Mrs. Crazynowsky. Welcome to the Breathing Castle."

Christie had hair the colour of a ripe, red plum, greenish eyes and freckles everywhere. She was smoking a cigarette.

"So what are you, the fucking Welcome Wagon?"

"I live upstairs," I said. "I left all the free samples in my room. I saw Mrs. K. check you in and thought you might like company. I'm going for coffee at a place around the corner. Would you like to join me?"

Christie gave me a baleful look. "So you've come to hit on the new resident." She paused a moment, keeping me in suspense. "You look harmless enough, and I haven't had anything to eat today. But, I warn you, if you mess with me I can be dangerous."

"You're a good judge of character," I said. "I am harmless, at least that's what everyone tells me."

"No one's harmless," said Christie, reaching back to pick up her cigarettes and her leather purse from a tiny insect-legged table.

Christie's voice was low and musical. It struck me that she could be singing. She rattled on, sometimes casually, as if we were old friends, sometimes breathlessly, as if we had only a few moments together and she had to get her whole story told before something unpleasant happened.

"I shared an apartment for a while, but this chick was using and never had any money for rent. Junkies are like that. This was after my old man and me broke up for the last time. Threatened to get me, the son of a bitch. Used to follow me around. I carried a gun to protect myself."

She tapped the oversized leather handbag on the dresser. We were in my room at the Breathing Castle. We'd been at the lunch counter for like two hours. I had coffee. Christie had a hamburger and chocolate shake, raisin pie, coffee, coconut cream pie.

"I got busted for carrying the gun. They didn't care that it was for self-protection, like they were gonna keep that psychopath from killing me. I never appeared in court. There must be a warrant out for me. That was why I sort of faded into the woodwork when the cop car passed us on the street a while ago, on our way back from the lunch counter. Did you notice?"

I nodded, although I hadn't noticed. I am very good at listening to a monologue. Article by article I was divesting myself of my clothes.

Reaching behind her, Christie undid several buttons down the back of her cotton blouse. She let the blouse slide down her arms until, facing me, she was naked from the waist up. Her breasts were small and there were pale freckles on her shoulders.

"Christie is presently living alone," she said in underlined italics, stating what appeared to be the obvious, as she stepped toward me, her small hands on the wide black belt of her jeans.

Christie in my arms, like running barefoot through bluebells.

Christie's warm hands glided delicately over my body. Her tongue traced a path down my belly. Her mouth on me was like hot silk. Behind the plum-coloured curls her eyes were closed.

Later, Christie lit a cigarette and laid it carefully on the edge of the dresser. She put on her blouse, struggling to button up the back, and began her running monologue again.

"I was in the hospital once, women things. Scar." She patted her flat, denim-covered belly. "I should tell you about my operation. Christie could tell you a few things about doctors..."

I watched and listened as she stretched her arms catlike, adjusting her breasts beneath the thin cotton of the blouse.

I was thinking about the time in high school when I asked a girl for a date and she laughed at me.

"What would we talk about?" she said. "You're such a student. I don't go to classes half the time." Her name was Roxy, and she was regarded as tough. She dated jocks who owned cars, and a guy with a motorcycle who often dropped her off at school. I wondered what they talked about. In high school it is sad to be classified as a student.

The monologue came to a temporary halt. Christie gathered her handbag, slung the leather strap over her shoulder, picked up her cigarette from the edge of the dresser.

"Maybe I'll see you around." She turned toward the door.

Once you know what it's like to be humiliated, laughed at, the experience can never again be so devastating. What did I have to lose?

"Christie?"

She stopped, glanced back at me, tossed her head, making her curls shiver like leaves touched by a breeze.

"I'd like you to take off your clothes and come back and lie down with me. I want to really make love with you."

The room was full of the sound of my heart banging in my ears.

She took a drag on her cigarette, moved her head almost imperceptibly as she exhaled.

"I don't think I ever wanted to do anything so much in my whole life. I did everything but ask, didn't I? I can't ask. I mean, what if you said no?" She placed her purse on the dresser and began the ritual unbuttoning.

By the next day, Christie had returned her key to Mrs. Kryzanowski and moved in with me.

I mentioned that I'm not a very good writer. The story I was writing when I met Christie was called "The Spaceship that Crashed on a Cattle Ranch," which began, "'Brovald the midget wrangler was the first to reach the scene of the crash. Brovald was a cousin of Eddie Gaedel, who wearing the number 18, once went to bat for the St. Louis Browns. Tumbleweeds were bursting into flame as far as a quarter mile from the crash scene, which tended to spook Brovald's pony, Tiny Tim.'"

Is that not truly bad?

That night, as Christie slept in my bed, I wrote a new story. I could tell it was better than anything I'd done before.

BUS DANCING

In the desert at night there is sex and there is dancing. Traditionally, buses enjoy the waltz.

Near the oasis where the buses have been abandoned, in the chill night the moon touches a tendril of ground fog, a coyote serenades a dazzle of stars, while from beyond the first slope swells the music of Bob Wills and the Texas Playboys. A waltz. A slow, weary, fiddle-heavy waltz.

She was a school bus wearing a serious yellow and black uniform, warning lights always a watt or two more brilliant than her contemporaries. Precise, military, she had fancied herself having the panache of a Japanese general. On serene spring mornings, bougainvillea like blood splotches beside the road, she would take control of her steering. Her velocity cowing the shrieking children into their seats like a firm push. But buses are only as good as their last tune-up. Eventually, she was sold to a church where for several years she worked only Sundays, after which it took her months to obliterate the odors of incense, varnish and freshly scrubbed children. Finally, she was purchased by a couple from Azle, Texas, who saw themselves as pioneers.

"We have always dreamed of living in a bus in the desert," they said. She quaked. Her tires twitched. There were horror stories told in every bus barn and wrecking yard of what was likely to happen if you were purchased by the young and optimistic.

Her seats were gutted. Plywood flooring added. Propane installed. There was handmade furniture, curtains on the windows. The couple from Azle were happy as they squatted at the tiny oasis where tumbleweeds hissed by in the night, and the wind sawed a tune on distant and rusting barbed wire.

Then, the female pioneer became pregnant.

"We will spend weekends in the bus," they said.

They spent one. Sand and dust have ways of infiltrating closed places, the bus interior became grainy and uncomfortable, too hot in the day, too cold at night. He scrawled "Dust me!" on the insect-legged table. The propane tank developed a leak. Vandals flattened her tires and scarified her fading yellow paint.

Billy Byrd is picking a solo on the weepy steel guitar, as Ernest Tubb sings "Waltz Across Texas."

Skeletal and groaning, the buses rise from where they are drifted axle-deep in sand. They bow, lock together, twirl rhythmically about the oasis, skirting the palm trees huddled above the trickle of water like mothers staring down at a new baby.

Oh, yes, buses are connoisseurs of the waltz. Hank Williams. Ernest Tubb. Bob Wills. Lefty Frizzell. Two steps forward and one back. Two steps forward and one back.

He was a Greyhound, strong and virile, rear-duals, halogen headlights, a cavernous luggage compartment. In his younger days, he travelled to India in search of wisdom and universal truth. He experienced disappointment. He found nothing existential about having boxes of live chickens roped to his roof. Cloven-hoofed goats soiled his plush upholstery. Even now, in the desert, in his declining years, he wakes with a start in the night, the odours of goat and curry fresh to his senses.

He ended his career making six trips a day between El Paso and Juarez, a hundred people crammed in his fetid interior, while he overheated at Customs and Immigration, his springs flaccid, his shock absorbers atrophying. Consigned to a wrecking yard, he was sold for fifty dollars to a ferret-faced man in a sombrero, who striped out his seats, while surreptitiously accepting crumpled American ten dollar bills from each of two hundred illegals.

On their run across Texas his transmission locked at the oasis. The ferret-faced man cursed him in both Spanish and English, tossed a rock which made a suture-like crack on his drivers-side windshield. Heartbroken, he watched his ragged entourage disappear into the moonlit desert. The saguaro watched and nodded. He recalled that in Juarez he had once or twice danced to mariachi music.

He had been fading under the desert sun, wasting into the sand for three years when she arrived. As the time passed he watched as her oil dripped enticingly onto the sand. He longed to touch her shiny black steering wheel. Female buses who long to dance emit a certain musk.

She remained coy until it became clear that she too had been abandoned.

As an orange desert sunset disappears behind the dunes, he rubs her flaking paint and she tells him how good it feels.

"It's been so long," she whispers.

His radiator dilates. He can hear her wheels spinning helplessly in the sand. He fantasizes the smell of scorching rubber. He polishes her sand-pitted side view mirror until she trembles in ecstasy. They kiss. She licks his universal joint, massages his transmission until he imagines his gears are unfrozen, that he is wheeling down the open road lubricated and loose, bugs splattering against his windshield. The buses shudder violently, flakes of rust, like brown snow, fall onto the banks of the oasis. She relaxes her wheels, sighing passionately, remembering a Russian lover, a Skoda in a fur hat and greatcoat with sad, dark brown headlights, and dirty fingernails.

As the sugary strains of "Mom and Dad's Waltz" waft over the hill, the buses twine about each other. Soliciting each other's warmth, they twist and glide across the desert, their shadows blue and eerie, as they dance in the moonlight to a three-quarter-time tune.

CHAPTER 3

"Tell me." Christie's two favourite words.

"Tell me," she repeats over and over, as we make love. Again, she aches for me to describe our lovemaking.

A tiny breeze scrapes the poplar leaves across the screen of my window, gentle as bird wings.

My eyes are full of sweat, my mouth flooded with the taste of Christie. But black memories slide down on me like dirt, locking my jaws, strangling my voice. Christie chants beneath me in the moist evening, "Tell me. Tell me."

More often now, when Christie says "Tell me," I tell. I am so in love that if Christie says bleed, I will slit my wrists.

"Tell me about us living in your room?" Christie says. I tell a story but not the one she expects to hear. Since Christie has become my muse, much of what I write is more whimsical, instead of teaching or treatise.

I spend a great deal of time speculating about Christie's past, about what I do not know about Christie. My friends, the few I have, have grown tired of hearing about Christie and what might or might not be truth.

"Why don't you talk about something else?" my friends say, before evaporating for good.

Unfortunately, I appear to be someone who does not learn from experience.

"My best girlfriend was murdered," Christie says to me one day. She is sitting up in our large, unkempt bed, which smells fragrantly of sex. She is naked. Some of her plumb-coloured hair is long enough to tickle her nipples.

I should mention that I am, in literary terms, a sometimes unreliable narrator. Those who are reading this story for pleasure and entertainment need pay no attention to this statement. However, academic readers, who often derive sexual stimulation from finding a symbol, an image, an unreliable narrator, will benefit greatly. It is true, I have some difficulty distinguishing between what has happened to me and what may have happened to me, and what may happen to me in the future.

"We were living in one large room in the upstairs of a big, square house with white siding," Christie says. "It had many rooms. Not too different from this place. But The Castle is clean, and there aren't six kids and a pig of an old lady in our room. There was a black gas stove with two open burners. The flames were the colour of a bluebird, the burner handles were white porcelain.

"Shirley lived up the street in a foster home. She didn't know who her parents were, which was probably good. She was dark skinned with sad eyes and a rolling gait. 'I imagine my mother was a princess who was kidnapped by evil men,' she told me. 'She managed to leave me at a hospital before the men in dark suits carried her away.'"

Christie paused. "I imagined her mother was a whore who abandoned her in an alley, her legacy a couple of communicable diseases and propensity toward a drug habit.

"Shirley and I walked to school every morning. The day it happened, I slept late. My old lady'd brought a couple of guys home to party with in the middle of the night. Us kids had to huddle on the sofa while she did her thing on the bed. We didn't get much sleep. I told Shirley to go on ahead, that there was no use us both being late.

"On the way to school, a guy beat her to death with a piece of firewood. He did it in the basement of a church, a grungy place with a cement floor and gray benches chained to the walls. It always stunk there because the Boy Scouts used to piss in the drain in the middle of the floor.

"The killer told the police he stood in the doorway to the basement and offered Shirley candy if she went inside with him. If I'd been there, I'd have told him to fuck off and that would have been that. But Shirley was shy, and trusted everybody. Police said he raped her after he killed her, after he splattered some of her brains on the mildewy wall of the church basement. If I'd been with her, she wouldn't have died."

"When did this happen?" I ask. "What city?" My questions resound hollowly, like footsteps in an empty room. Christie smiles sullenly, her green eyes bright with pain. She sometimes looks that way after we have made love.

"There was no trial. They said he was insane, put him away. Fucking diddler, they should have let him out on the street for half an hour, the men on the street would have taken care of him."

Christy is very real. Almost everything I tell you about her will be true, except for the lies Christie told me about herself.

"Tell me something more about your mother?" I ask. We are in a bar on East Hastings Street. Christie stares across the beer-laden table which is covered with a layer of green terry cloth.

"I've already told you too much," she says.

"You've told me virtually nothing. The big white house? Your brothers and sisters?"

"My mother had beautiful blond hair. She was cool as a mermaid. She read *House Beautiful*, and studied art history for three years at a snotty eastern women's college in the States. She knew how to practice gracious living. She knew how to be hostess for a dinner party of twelve."

"That doesn't jibe with what you've told me."

"Why should it?"

"Because I asked a question. When I ask a question, I expect you to either tell me it's none of my business, or give me an honest answer."

"There have to be other options. I believe the answers to questions vary according to the situation in which they're asked. If you asked the same question an hour from now, the answer might be entirely different."

Life with Christie is like living on a Möbius Strip.

EVANGELICAL COAT HANGERS

Delia, a student majoring in psychology, answered an ad for part-time work. The address turned out to be a suburban church, a modern A-frame structure, with acres of reflective glass. A huge parking lot was tastefully landscaped, hidden behind rows of well-watered cedars. In a corner of the parking lot stood two huge semitrailers. A couple of cars were parked by a side entrance. Heat reflected off the tarmac, silence reigned.

Delia knocked, no one answered.

She opened the door and called "Hello!"

A young man appeared at the top of a short flight of stairs. The air smelled of varnish. "I'll be right with you." He ducked out of sight; a moment later, he walked down the stairs, a large key on a string dangling from his hand. "I take it you're here about the job?" Delia nodded.

"You're the only applicant." He led her outside and headed across the lot toward the trucks.

"At least a week's work. The trailers are full of coat hangers; we need someone to sort them into groups of five, tie them together with a twist tie. We'll take it from there."

"Does the church have a thrift store?"

"We do, and that where most of these are headed," the young man, who was dressed in dark slacks and white shirt open at the neck, replied. "There's more to it than that, but you needn't concern yourself."

As he fumbled with the key he began talking about coat hangers.

"Did you know Thomas Jefferson is credited by some sources

with inventing the coat hanger?

"It's that recent?

"A couple of fellows got patents in the 1800s. Wasn't until 1906 that a store in Grand Rapids, Michigan, began displaying clothes on hangers. Wasn't until 1932 that the paper tube to prevent creasing was patented."

"I would have thought Leonardo Da Vinci would have invented them. There were no coat hangers in Shakespeare's day? How strange!" said Delia.

"Someone had to invent the lathe before there could be those solid wood boomerang-shaped hangers." said the young man.

"Curious!" said Delia. "Variations of the lathe have been around since primitive times, and Leonardo did invent a type of treadle lathe, so it was lack of imagination rather than lack of tools."

"What is the one item that can be found in, like, 99+ per cent of all the homes in America? Coat hangers," he said, answering his own question.

"I would have thought guns," said Delia, but under her breath.

"Why would anyone care?" she said aloud. "Are these hangers special in some way?"

"Not now, but they soon will be."

"Indeed."

"By the way, are you washed in the blood of the lamb?"

Delia looked at him askance. "Not bloody likely. Pardon the pun."

"It was a metaphorical question. Revelations 7:14. Are you washed in the blood of the lamb? It means are you saved?"

"No. I don't believe in any of that. Sorry, do I have to be a believer to get the job?"

"Not at all, in fact, you'll be perfect for it. We're testing a new concept."

"And what would that be?"

"I'm afraid it would spoil it if I told you."

"Suit yourself. Do I get the job?"

He finally got the trailer lock open. Immediately inside was a large black garbage bag stuffed full of small black twist ties. The trailer itself was crammed with coat hangers of every ilk. They were not sorted, but thrown in at confusing angles, a total tangle of tens of thousands.

"Sort the wire ones into bundles of five, tie them together. Stack the bundles neatly, someone else will box them. Any that are outsize or made of wood, or like those fat pink plastic ones, set aside. Someone else will deal with them."

"This will take more than a week," said Delia.

"There's no panic," said the young man.

"I should hope not," said Delia.

They agreed on wages and hours and she set to work.

It was an easy job. After a couple of hours, the young man appeared carrying what looked like a banana box, filled it with the little bundles of coat hangers Delia had created and disappeared into the church. On the second day, they hired a teenage boy to work with her. But he couldn't seem to grasp the concept that all coat hangers were not equal. He mixed wire, wooden and plastic, and often tied the bottoms together instead of the necks. He was fired after a couple of hours.

"What do you suppose will happen to someone that stupid?" Delia asked the young man from the church.

"The Lord will provide," he replied.

"You're associated with the Lord, but I don't notice you providing. Though I suppose he could become a postal worker, or a civil servant, or even a low level politician. With his intelligence level he'd fit right in."

On the third day, Delia noticed several more cars parked at the church. At lunch time, she took her sandwich into a quiet room in the church basement that was used as a Sunday school. From upstairs she could hear a loud voice or voices. When she finished lunch, she climbed the short flight of stairs and peered into the church. At the altar, stood a tall, silver-haired man in a flowing white robe. The young man who was her contact stood beside him. As Delia watched, the young man took a bundle of coat hangers from a box and placed them on the lectern in front of the minister or priest, who blessed them long and loudly, crying out for them to be sanctified by the Lord, and to go forth into the heathen world and do the bidding of the Almighty. This process was repeated over and over, the silver-haired man praying and wailing over each bundle for perhaps two minutes. The sanctified bundles were then taken by a woman on the other side of the altar, who put them into another box which, when it was full was carted off by yet another young man in black slacks and white shirt. Delia watched fascinated.

By now, the trailer was half empty. Each day at lunch, Delia checked the progress in the church. The rabble-rousing preacher did not seem to be taking any breaks. He was now wild eyed and dishevelled, appearing to need both a shave and a shower.

On her way out of the church one day, Delia noticed that a cloak room by the side door was crammed full of boxes of sanctified hangers waiting to go to the thrift shop downtown. As she eyed the boxes she could hear eerie sounds.

Like children singing:

"I'm on my way to heaven
We shall not be moved
Like a tree that's growing by the water
We shall not be moved."

Out of curiosity, Delia reached into a box and took a group of five wire hangers, and two wooden ones that were tied together. She took them home and set them on the sofa in her efficiency apartment.

"What's so special about you?" Delia said, then stared around to make sure there was no one to hear her.

"Jesus wept," whispered the wire coat hangers.

"Not so subliminal advertising," said Delia.

"I contain a shard of the true cross," said one of the heavy varnished hangers.

"Whoa," said Delia, "this is a bit much."

They're selling this stuff to a gullible public, she thought. This can't be good. She turned on her tiny TV in time to see the local news documenting people running screaming into the streets. Some totally frightened, some wailing that the Rapture was at hand.

Fortunately, the hangers themselves seemed to know when to speak and when to be quiet. In front of the curious, and especially the media, they were cold and silent. The people who had heard them were dismissed as cranks. Still the hospital emergency rooms and doctors' offices were crammed.

When Delia reported for work the next morning she was met by the young man who handed over her pay cheque, saying that her services were no longer required.

"We've had to recall the one batch we sent out. It's been all over the media. It wasn't the reaction we hoped for. We've decided that unfortunately we are way ahead of our time. It is too much, too soon. Something like this has to be done so that the masses accept what is happening. We shall have to rethink the concept completely."

"I'm sure you will," said Delia. Even from the church door, she could hear the small cacophony of voices from the dark cloakroom. "How do you undo what you've done?" Delia went on.

"We're not certain, but we're working on it."

At home, Delia eyed the hangers. Somehow the ties had been undone. The seven hangers were on the sofa and various chairs about the room.

"You've been cancelled," Delia said.

"Jesus wept!" replied a wire coat hanger with a fervor that had not been present earlier.

"I contain a fragment of the true cross," said one of the wooden hangers forcefully.

"I don't like this one bit," said Delia advancing toward the sofa.

"Mine eyes have seen the glory…" chorused the wire hangers.

"You're all going down the garbage chute," said Delia, reaching for one of the wooden hangers, but something cold seized her ankle and she fell to her knees.

"What is seen is temporary, what is unseen is eternal," hissed a wooden hanger.

"We're on our way to heaven, we shall not be moved," chorused the hangers, drowning out Delia's soft cries for help.

CHAPTER 4

"No one poet grows conscious of the Muse
except by experience of a woman in whom
the Goddess is to some degree resident."
— Robert Graves

I am going to guess at what is about to happen to me. I am going to predict the future. I am going to be happy for a few months, though I'm certain I won't realize how happy until it is over. The happy months will be spent with Christie, and with my typewriter. Christie is not lying when she says she is my Muse. That part is true. Trust me. I will enjoy considerable success, while Christie and I are together editors will not only buy my stories but ask for more.

Then I will lose Christie, and go back to being a failure. I will not have learned a single thing. That is very sad. Critics like to see the main character in a novel learn something about himself. If you strive to be successful and have critics say something positive about your novel, make sure that in the course of your three hundred pages the protagonist learns something about himself.

After Christie is gone all I can do is try to find ways to get her back. I dream of writing a sensational story called "In Care of This Magazine," in which I tell Christie's story and issue a plea to the reader to look for Christie and to write to me in care of this magazine if they see her. But the situation is, I believe, classified as Catch 22. Since Christie is my Muse, my success was due to her. Since she is gone I am incapable of writing a sensational story which might help me find her.

"Where do you live?" Christie asked me as we drank coffee at the lunch counter that first night we met.

"'In my father's house are many mansions,'" I told her. "Isn't that from the bible? In biblical context mansions meant rooms. The Breathing Castle probably has more rooms than the one in the quote.

"Originally a huge seven-bedroom house with wide verandas, lots of gingerbread curlicues outside, sliding panels, secret rooms, a dumbwaiter, disappearing hallways, attics upon attics, inside, it was built in 1897 by a lumber baron to house his large family. It has always been called The Castle. I call it the *Breathing* Castle.

"A few years later the lumber baron built a true mansion for his family. The Castle passed through two owners, one a stockbroker, ruined by the crash of 1929 and afraid there wasn't a tall enough building to jump from in Vancouver, blew his brains out in the gazebo behind the house.

"Repossessed by a bank, the Castle sat vacant and slack-windowed for several years. Finally, it was purchased by an enterprising restaurant owner in the Chinese community, Wang Ho, who rented out every available inch of space in the house and grounds, including the gazebo. I've written a short story about Wang Ho and the Castle. I'll show it to you if you're interested."

Christie brightened at this. "Yes, please," she said."Anyway, after Wang Ho died, the house passed to an already wealthy son, or adopted son, who sold it to a cancerous-looking man named Kryzanowski, flanked by a big-boned, loud-speaking wife. The cancerous Kryzanowski soon cashed in his yellowed soul. The widow moved to another property she owns nearby and manages the Breathing Castle from a distance. But she has spies who report the details of every boiled cabbage, tossed beer bottle, and domestic altercation. Trespassers, transients, loud drunks, sellers of heroin, cocaine, crack, and Mary Kay Cosmetics are not tolerated. Those who cause disturbances or neglect the rent are dealt with swiftly, by a couple of lithe Chinese, experts in several Oriental martial arts, who some say are young nephews of the late Wang Ho.

"The house breathes. I watch it as I approach late in the night, a white cloud rolling across a cobalt sky. Like an animation it rises and falls as it breathes, the windows expanding, contracting, the chimney tipping first one way, then another. Voices filter out like notes of music, through the layers of shingles, voices, stories, lies, truths. This Breathing Castle has told me so much. I'll pass someone in the hall, be invited in for tea, or a beer, or just for the sake of my company. Stories are told. Some are like receiving a sack full of splintered ends of boards from which I am expected to make a solid plank, covered in many coats of varnish. I spin the stories like the Fates spin lives. Others I overhear. I stand in the dark hallways, listen as words slip under doors into the hall along with the yellow glow of forty watt bulbs."

Christie had been listening in rapt silence to my poetic description of the house we now both lived in. "Fascinating, Wylie. But you didn't really answer my question. Where do you live?"

"Two can play at not answering questions," I told her. "Now, I'll show you another story about the Castle. You have to decide what's true and what's not."

TRUTH AND HISTORY

Miss Paskins was one of the only tenants in The Breathing Castle, the rambling, multi-additioned rooming house in East Vancouver where I reside, who remembers the previous owner, Wang Ho. Tenants in a rooming house change with depressing regularity, rootless as corks in their lonely bob through life, the rooming house a beach where they rest between tides.

"Wang Ho lived in the glassed-in sunporch at the front of the house, and rented out every available inch of space," Miss Paskins tells me. We are drinking tea in her tiny room that is stuffed with kitten-faced oven mitts, the arms of her sofa and easy chair decorated with tatted and crocheted doilies. China knickknacks are everywhere, gifts from distant sisters and nieces, perhaps former pupils; Miss Paskins is a school teacher who took early retirement because of 'bad nerves,' brought on in part by a disastrous love affair.

"He could have lived comfortably. He was wealthy from owning a large restaurant in Chinatown," she goes on.

During the housing pinch at the end of World War II, she tells me, the garage was turned into apartments and the many-roomed mansion sliced like an orange into segments, tenants fitted into the segments like Russian dolls, almost one inside the other. Additions were built and attached at odd angles, a row of mail boxes installed in the front hallway, while Wang Ho lived a lonesome life in the sun porch amid stacks of Chinese newspapers and several bamboo cages occupied by thimble-sized canaries.

Even the hen house in the back yard, where he kept a dozen or so Rhode Island Red hens and a dozen more stylish-looking white Leghorns, was converted. "Wang Ho hired a couple of men, illegals probably, to clean it out. He put all the chickens in a gunnysack, live, and carried them off in the direction of downtown; I guess he served them at his restaurant. The hired help put down floors and installed glass where there had been only chicken wire over the windows. The renovated chicken house was rented out to a soldier from North Carolina and his Canadian wife, who had a squirrel coat, and an awful Russian first name that sounded like Dvorjak. She was a Doukhobor, one of that strange religious sect who burn down each other's houses, and hold naked parades – at least the women do.

"The soldier and his wife had to share a bathroom with the family who rented the room behind the furnace. The chicken house had a wood stove and candles; I guess it was romantic for them, being newlyweds and all. Yes, Wang Ho rented every space that could be rented, and at top dollar. There were no nosy building inspectors in those days.

"After the housing shortage cleared up in the mid-50s, Wang Ho went back to having chickens again. Kept them right up until he died."

The hen house still stands, forlorn and neglected, used now to store garden tools, rusted unrecognizable items that may have fallen off automobiles, appliances, and goods abandoned by tenants who have skulked away in the night leaving ugly objects, unpaid rent and the odours of poverty. The present owner of The Castle, a Mrs. Kryzanowski, is required by law to keep the orphaned possessions for several months before they are trucked to an auction or the city dump.

"Wang Ho was very tall for a Chinese, and he always wore grey – long-sleeved gray sweaters over grey shirts, and baggy grey trousers. I don't know when he ever ate. He kept tea in the sun porch, but he must have eaten at his restaurant. He was very gentlemanly, always bowed to me when I paid the rent, and he loved to show me the canaries he kept in two, tall, bamboo cages in the sun porch. There were six or eight of them, yellow as dandelions, most of them no bigger than my thumb.

"One evening when I came to pay the rent, Wang Ho looked very sad. He was sitting in an old, overstuffed chair, and there was a stack of purple airmail letters on the chair's arm. There were orange-coloured, foreign-looking stamps in the corner of each envelope and vertical lines of Chinese characters on the fronts.

"You look like you've had some bad news," I said to him. "'Yes,' he replied, cool as you please. 'I have just been informed that my wife is dead.'

"Well, you could have knocked me over with a feather. I didn't know Wang Ho had a wife. He told me then, that he not only had a wife, but a son. He also told me he was sixty-one years old and had been in Canada for thirty-five years.

"Why didn't you bring your family over here?" I asked. I mean, he was a businessman, he could have afforded to.

"'Ah,' he sighed, 'the time was never quite appropriate to have my wife join me.'

"It was less than a month later that Wang Ho asked me to marry him," Miss Paskins goes on. She is in her mid-seventies, with ermine-white hair and a pink face. Her eyes are a pure, sky blue, and her small nose twitches like a rabbit's when she is excited. Miss Paskins has never married. She dresses immaculately in pinks and blues, stylishly but inexpensively. "I considered the matter for forty-eight hours and I told him yes." Miss Paskins looks as though she could play an all-American grandmother on a TV series. "That was the biggest mistake I ever made. He always behaved like such a gentleman, I thought he could be trusted."

This is not the first time Miss Paskins has told me this story. We have been tea-drinking companions for over three years. Miss Paskins is a basically honest person and she thinks that what she is telling me is both truth and history. Much of her story is neither.

32

If I am to be honest, it was greed that propelled me to investigate, in order to establish what I call "The True History of Wang Ho." In the beginning, I didn't doubt Miss Paskins' story, but having, in the days when I actually held steady employment, several unpleasant experiences with a branch of government called the Public Trustee, an agency that looks after, or appropriates would be a better word, the estates of people who die without any known next of kin, I decided to investigate to see if Wang Ho's relatives in China had been cheated out of his estate. If he, indeed, owned a successful restaurant in Chinatown, then his estate would have been substantial.

I began by consulting ancient copies of the *Vancouver City Directory*. Thirty years ago, coverage of Chinatown, or even of houses owned by Chinese, was not very accurate. Most directory personnel were Caucasian, the Chinese were perceived as secretive. Early listings for The Castle described it merely as "Occupied." In a later directory the owner's name was shown as Wang, O. Sometimes his name appeared in the alphabetical section, more often it did not. While most Caucasian names were followed by occupation and name of employer, no such listings appeared after Wang, O. One directory, in what I guessed to be the year before Wang Ho's death showed simply "R'st'rt" after his name. I was now forced to spend money.

At the Land Titles office I checked the ownerships of The Castle. There I discovered something surprising. From 1939 to 1975, the Castle had been owned by On Ho Wang Low, café owner. Going back to the directories, I discovered a listing one year for a Wang Low, Prop. Green Garden Restaurant. The Green Garden was one of the oldest, largest and most successful restaurants in Chinatown.

"We were engaged for almost two months," Miss Paskins has told me several times. "We drank tea together in the late evenings. We agreed vaguely on a spring wedding. At least I suggested spring and Wang Ho didn't object.

"'I'd like to see your restaurant,' I said to Wang Ho more than once. 'There are certain formalities to be observed, dear lady,' was his reply to me.

"And then came the day when I found out what kind of man he really was. It was a Saturday and a young man came knocking on the door of the rooming house and inquiring about Wang Ho. He was Chinese and was wearing a beautiful blue suit and a cream-coloured Panama hat. 'I am from the Department of Immigration,' he said. 'I am inquiring about the gentleman who owns this building,' and he rattled off a long name that had Wang Ho in the middle of it. 'Could you tell me, please, the approximate date of his death?' 'He's as alive as you and me,' I said. 'He went off to work just an hour or so ago.' "'Ah, there must be a misunderstanding,' the young man said. 'The department has had inquiries from his wife in China who reports receiving a letter a few months ago reporting her husband's death.'

"'But I thought the wife was dead,' I blurted, obviously more upset than a stranger should have been at hearing such information.

"The young man smiled sadly. 'Not an uncommon practise among immigrants,' he said. 'When they want to, ah, start a new life without any complications.'

"Well, I never spoke to Wang Ho again," Miss Paskins assures me each time she tells the story. "And he never tried to contact me. I guess that man from Immigration talked to him at work. I mailed my rent to him after that, even though we lived in the same building."

As I've intimated, my motives were not solely to see that justice was done. I imagined my liberating the restaurant profits from the Public Trustee; I imagined a grateful family arriving from China to oversee the operation; I imagined them awarding me a ten percent interest for my trouble. Even a five percent interest, I decided, would enable a would-be writer, with two suitcases full of unpublished manuscripts under his bed, to write full time and not have to drive taxi, wait tables or teach remedial English. I imagined I might eventually settle for eternal gratitude and free food at the restaurant.

I ventured into the Green Garden about three in the afternoon, the quietest time of day for a restaurant, and asked to see the manager.

"That would be Mr. Tang," a hostess in an aquamarine-coloured Chinese-silk dress informed me.

A few moments later, a middle-aged man in a business suit appeared, smiling from a round, unlined face. His hair was a combed iron-gray. I carried a large loose-leaf binder. I wanted to be mistaken, at first, for a salesman.

"I'm studying the history of East Vancouver," I told Mr. Tang when we were settled in his office, pointing at my notebook. "I wonder if you could tell me a little about the original owner of the Green Garden, Mr. On Ho Wang Low?"

"You have done some research already," Mr. Tang said, still smiling. "The gentleman about whom you inquire was known only on legal documents by the name you mention. His true name was Wang Ho, but there was an unfortunate misunderstanding with an obstinate immigration official. All his life in Canada he had to use the other name where legal matters were concerned."

As we talked, I kept revising my estimate of his age upward, from forty-five, to fifty-five, to sixty-five, to close to seventy. I asked Mr. Tang a number of times during our talk if he were related to Wang Ho, but he politely evaded the question, as he did my inquiries about the disposition of Wang Ho's estate, though he assured me that the government had no hand in the running of the business.

I then broached the delicate matter of Wang Ho's engagement to Miss Paskins.

"I suggest you might well have a future as a detective," Mr. Tang said. "The incident you describe is, to the best of my knowledge, known only to the parties involved and myself. I would like to do my best to erase your negative opinion of Wang Ho and to acquaint you with the truth of the situation, but in order to do so I need your word that the information will not be relayed to Miss Paskins."

I promised.

"To put it simply," said Mr. Tang, "what was involved was a misinterpretation of pleasantries. There are, you will agree, in every culture certain phrases exchanged in conversation, polite mouthings which are virtually meaningless?"

I nodded my agreement.

"For instance, when we met in the foyer, I acknowledged you and inquired of your health, and you inquired of mine. Such acknowledgements are always answered in the affirmative, unless one or the other of us are about to meet our ancestors. Even then we usually state our health to be adequate at the particular moment. Do you agree?"

"I do."

"Then you will allow me to explain further," said Tang. "In some oriental households, politeness and custom require that if a guest compliments the host on possession of a certain item, a painting perhaps, or a vase of distinction, the host will bow and say, 'It is yours, my friend.' The guest will in turn bow and say 'You are too kind.' The exchange is meaningless in the context of that society, but a stranger to such customs might assume that the object of his admiration was indeed a gift, and, at the end of the evening attempt to leave with it."

"What would happen if such a mistake were made?"

"Oh, the guest would be allowed to depart, but later on an elder of the community would call, probably with a good translator, and explain, with many apologies, that a mistake had been made."

"Are you saying that Wang Ho's proposal to Miss Paskins was not a proposal but was misinterpreted by her?"

"You are entirely correct."

"But how?"

"I, though much younger, am from the same village as Wang Ho.

There was a custom in our village. I am uncertain whether it was practiced in other villages, for we were isolated and travelled little. But in our village, if you called at the home of a spinster woman, and if you were an eligible male, you complimented that spinster woman on her demeanour and her dress, and added, even if she were very old and you were very young, or vice versa, 'Would you do me the honour of becoming my wife?'

"The spinster woman would acknowledge the proposal by saying 'You are too kind. I shall eventually let you know of my decision.' And the conversation would carry on. You see, everyone in our village also understood the rituals of courtship, so such a proposal of politeness could never be misinterpreted as the real thing."

"Then it must have come as a terrifying surprise to Wang Ho when Miss Paskins accepted his proposal and announced their engagement."

"An understatement. And, you must realize, Wang Ho had no network of family and elders to fall back on. He confided in me because I was from the same village."

"But why didn't he go to her himself, explain what had happened?"

"The logical thing to do, of course. But Wang Ho could not stand to lose face in such a manner. There is an ancient saying, 'It is better to be thought a rogue than a fool.'"

"Then Wang Ho's wife really was dead?"

"That is true. Otherwise he would never have made even the polite proposal."

"And the man from Immigration? I recall Miss Paskins' recitals that Wang Ho only denied bringing his wife to Canada; the son was never mentioned. Perhaps you once owned a brilliant blue suit and a Panama hat?"

"You give me too much credit," said Mr. Tang, smiling, making no denials. "Perhaps the man in the Panama hat acted out of love, or gratitude, or perhaps the fine clothes were his reward for playing a role."

"Thank you," I said. "It is always a pleasure to learn the truth."

"A truth perhaps," said Mr. Tang. "No one ever knows *the* truth. If you consider carefully, I have had almost thirty years to prepare a defence for Wang Ho. Is my story any more plausible than that of Miss Paskins? There is another ancient saying, 'History is determined by the one who lives to tell the story last.' In which case, I wish you a long and prosperous life."

CHAPTER 5

"I owned a business once." Christie told me one day, referring to herself in the third person, as she often did.

"Really?"

"Yeah, and it wasn't an escort service or a massage parlor."

"Why would I think that?"

"Well, you have to admit I've told you some pretty odd shit."

"So, what kind of business?"

"Legitimate as all hell, and it came about by accident. I had this girlfriend about my age. She was rich by my standards, which meant her parents had a house and she had a room of her own. Maria was dark haired and stocky, not terribly pretty. She looked like her mother, who spoke virtually no English and spent her days cooking wonderful foods.

"Her dad was Italian and he operated a small cement contracting business. He was crazy about Maria, thought the sun rose and set on her. He was nice to me, too. It was like being in another universe. I have no idea who my father was, all the creeps my mother hung out with wanted to cop a feel or get into my pants.

"Maria and I were trying to figure out what to do with our summer. We sat around her room, playing music, drinking Cokes, smoking. We talked about looking for jobs. Her dad came home one evening complaining that he couldn't get a crew of labourers, temporary help for his busy summer season.

"That night Maria got some cardboard, made two little signs, TEMPORARY HELP WANTED. ASK ME! In the morning, she phoned many of the boys who had finished school with her, got a couple of nibbles. In the afternoon, we took the bus downtown, walked around business neighborhoods where we thought people might be looking for work. Lots of guys wanted a chance to talk to a couple of fairly cute chicks. Bottom line, at seven next morning, a crew of eight guys showed up at Maria's home. Her dad was thrilled. The crew worked out. That night her dad took us out for dinner, gave us each a hundred dollars, five twenties in a little manila envelope. We were beyond thrilled.

"That night Maria said to me, 'There must be lots of guys like my Dad who need temporary people.' We stayed up half the night planning. We took our $200 and had a thousand business cards printed. We called ourselves Foremost Temporary Help. We used her dad's business number. We had fifteen hundred flyers printed on the flimsiest of paper, proclaiming our services. We used what was left of the money to run an ad in the daily paper advertising for temporary help. I manned the phone while Maria walked around the city all day, handing out business cards and flyers to businesses and giving a flyer to anyone who looked like they might need work. The next day we reversed positions.

"We were just in the right place at the right time. Within two weeks we got our own phone, rented a tiny office in a very old building downtown. We couldn't believe how much money we were making. We billed our clients double what we paid our employees. There were temp agencies around, but they were lazy and waited for business to come to them. We had to hire her dad's accountant to keep track of things for us. Next thing we knew we had a staff, while we both drummed up business. We rented a storefront in a poor part of town, set up fifteen folding chairs, where people could sit around and wait in case someone called in a job for them. I think it's the happiest I had ever been.

"By the fall we were a going concern. We shared all the duties, worked real long hours, but the success was piling up.

"Then one day everything changed. It was lunch hour. I was

alone in the shop, sitting at a battered old desk at the back of the storefront, when three huge guys came in. Black men wearing the black and silver jerseys of the Oakland Raiders football team. They looked around at the empty chairs, they studied the job notices we had on a large cork board on the right hand wall. They had their names and numbers on the backs of their uniforms. EMERY 15, BROWNE 22, CARVER 47. It was Emery who approached me. The other two flanked him, one on each side.

"'Can I help you?'

"'We is defenders,' said Emery, in a voice like static.

"'Defenders?' I said. 'We get calls for bouncers, crowd control, once in a while we need a body guard. Is that what you have in mind?'

"Emery shook his head. 'What we aims to defend is you young ladies.'

"'From what?' I said stupidly.

"'From us.' said Emery, looking first right, then left. The rest of what we came to call the Oakland Contingent, nodded.

"I was outraged. 'You're trying to shake me down? Never!'

"'We is reasonable men,' said Emery. 'What we thinks is you should hire us for say $10 an hour each. You could call us your body-guards. We'll drop by every Friday and collect our wages. You can write us off as security…'

'You're out of your fucking minds,' I shouted. 'There are police, there are laws…'

"'True enough. But we is only askin' nicely for jobs. We just want to protect you nice young ladies from all the bad things that might happen if you was to go without security. This place could get smashed up real bad.' His cohorts nodded. 'There could be a fire, old building like this would go up in a minute. This ain't a very nice part of town,' Emery advanced a step, placed a huge, meaty black hand flat on my desk. We've seen you workin' late in the evening. Now, Christie, unless you have someone lookin' out for you, terrible things could happen to young girls like you and Maria.'

"He used our names! This wasn't a joke. I became more furious.

"'Fuck off and die!' I shouted. He was about to speak again...

"I was smoking a cigarette. I jammed it into the back of his ham-like hand.

"He yowled and took a step backward. His cohorts each took a step forward.

"'You is gonna be real sorry you did that.' He was nursing his scorched hand.

"I was terrified but I wouldn't back down. 'No, you're gonna be sorry you tried to extort money from me.'

"At some unseen signal, Browne and Carver turned and made their way toward the door. Emery looked at me with stony eyes.

"'I'll see you again, after you've had time to consider. You gonna be very, very sorry for what you done.' Still nursing his hand, Emery followed his friends from the storefront. They each cast giant shadows.

"I was on the phone to the police before those huge shadows had disappeared. I was surprised at how quickly the police acted and how interested they were. A Detective Borowski ('call me Wanda,' she said) walked in the door not twenty minutes later. She could see how shaken up I was, and was really kind and reassuring. She was dressed like a street missionary, not like I thought a detective should be – jeans, a creamy blouse, a jacket with a shoulder holster clearly visible. She had dark hair and eyes, looked like how Maria might look in ten years.

She sat across from me and took notes as I told her the whole story. When I finished she half smiled.

"'I deal with scumbags of varying degrees every day, you'd probably be surprised at how many there are. What we have here are either the stupidest, most arrogant assholes in the history of the world, or else they are just three big dumb guys who set out to scare the crap out of you. I don't see many criminals who wear Oakland Raider uniforms with their names on the back. They are gonna be really easy to find. My guess would be they're Americans who just arrived here and for some reason think because they're in a foreign country that there are no laws, or no laws that apply to them. Black people aren't exactly plentiful in this part of town." She smiled at me. "'Have you got somebody to see you home?

"'Maria, my partner, should be back any time now. I've already called her Dad and he's coming to pick us up.'

"'Good,' said Detective Borowski. 'These guys shouldn't be hard to find. We'll have a talk with them. Right now we can't charge them with anything. I believe you, but it would be a he said, she said thing. 'We were only joking' and so on. But we can make their lives pretty difficult. If they give us the slightest static, we'll escort them directly to the border, if they're not citizens. If you see any sign of them again, call us instantly. This is so brazen, I can't believe it's anything but a really bad joke, but until we establish that, we'll take it very seriously.'

"She wasn't the only one who took it seriously. Maria's dad called three of his regular employees away from their dinners, they arrived carrying sharpened cement hoes and pointed trowels. When they saw I was okay, they set off to search the neighborhood.

"That was the way it stood for a couple of weeks. We carried on with our business. The police kept a close watch. Detective Borowski came by several times. There had been no sightings of what we had come to call the Oakland Contingent.

"Then one afternoon Maria disappeared. Went out to pick up sandwiches for lunch and never came back. She was almost an hour late and I was beginning to worry when Emery walked through the door. He had waited until I was alone.

"'You're next,' he said, showing rows of flashing white teeth. Even indoors he cast a huge shadow. Then he was gone. I phoned Detective Borowski and within minutes the street was crawling with police. A fretful day passed. There was no sign of Maria, no sighting of Emery or the Oakland Contingent.

"After forty-eight hours the attitude of the police changed. They started looking closely at me. I was the only one who had ever seen the Oakland Contingent. I was the last to see Maria. They dug into my horrible past, found a social worker who was willing to say I was 'somewhat disturbed,' that as a minor I made accusations against my mother and other people, all of which were unverifiable.

"Detective Borowski became an enemy instead of a friend. Even Maria's dad became distant. The police pointed out that I would profit handsomely from Maria's disappearance.

"'If you want me to,' I said to Detective Borowski, 'I'll sell the business to one of our competitors, give all the money to Maria's dad.' She pretended she didn't hear me.

"I was brought in for questioning. They played good cop, bad cop with me. They sent in a team that scoured our work place from top to bottom. They claimed they found traces of blood in our little storage room. Detective Borowski suggested I get myself a good lawyer.

"I ran. Hitchhiked out of town. Worked at a coffee shop in Thunder Bay, finally made it here, roomed for a couple of weeks with that chick I mentioned, then came here. That's the truth."

I told my friend Jones Christie's story about the Oakland Contingent.

"And you believe that shit?"

"Why shouldn't I?"

"For one thing, I suspect she's a local. Her name's probably something like Irene Callaghan and she comes from a posh home, likely in North Vancouver. Probably went to private school until she got in with a bad crowd, did a lot of bad shit, finally dropped out and disappeared. She's got junkie eyes."

"Christie never does drugs. She takes a drink, but so do you and I."

"She could be shooting up in your fucking bed and you'd never know it. When it comes to that chick, you have a blind spot a mile square."

"She's my Muse," I said lamely.

44

"About that…" but a customer came in to the lunch counter and Jones had to go to work.

That night, with Christie's tale of crime and violence still echoing in my mind, I gave my head a shake and tried to think of something fanciful. My fingers flew over the typewriter keys.

THE INSECT

"Don't swat me, I'm an angel," said a tiny female voice.

Busby, behind the blue-tinted glass of his corner office, was approaching, arm raised, holding a folded newspaper, about to flatten what he thought was a very large-winged insect fluttering against the window. It had appeared seconds before from nowhere, as if it had flown in through the glass.

Busby held the newspaper in striking position, but eyed the insect more closely.

"You're pretty small for an angel," he finally said.

"We come in all sizes."

"Why are you here?"

Busby and his partner Arbuckle, had started an industrial parts service right out of college. They were in the right place at the right time and their sales had doubled every year for the past six years. They were both multimillionaires and their prospects seemed unlimited.

Busby noted that though the wings were disproportionately large compared to the body, the insect did indeed appear to be an angel. Only about four inches tall, almost certainly female because of the voice and pale blonde hair.

"Are you a guardian angel?" he asked, lowering the newspaper.

"You could say that."

"So what are you guarding me from? I can't imagine that I'm in any great danger." Busby was thirty-one, handsome, tall with black hair and piercing brown eyes. He was beautifully dressed in a two-thousand-dollar suit. He turned his swivel chair toward the window, sat down.

"I need to rest," said the angel. She fluttered to his desk, landing next to his pen set.

"Consider this," she said, folding her wings, taking a deep breath. "Your partner, Arbuckle, whom you trust, has for the past two years been directing one percent of gross sales to an account in the Cayman Islands that bears only his name."

"And you know this how?"

The angel sighed. "He can't help it that he's an accountant. He keeps meticulous records. They're locked in his personal safe in his office. I have the combination here." The angel pointed a wing tip at her head.

When she told him, Busby noted the combination on a legal pad.

"What should I do?"

"You could call the police," said the angel, "raise a terrible kafuffle, send him packing, press criminal charges, ruin a number of lives. Or you could, since you are smart enough to realize that Arbuckle's financial acumen is responsible for eighty percent of the company's success, simply point out that you know what's going on and that he should set up a similar account in your name. The company can afford it, no harm no foul."

"Hmm," said Busby, "I would have thought an angel would have ethics."

"You would just be correcting an oversight in your favour," said the angel ambiguously.

"I see your point," said Busby.

"There's more," said the angel.

"Like what?"

"Since you ask, Miranda, the woman you're dating, is planning on getting pregnant so you'll have to marry her. Should that happen you would find out almost immediately, what you've known subliminally, but haven't quite assimilated, that she is greedy, shrill and dictatorial. She also drinks too much and that will only get worse as time passes."

Busby looked sceptical. He really liked, perhaps even loved, Miranda, who managed a furniture store. He had considered proposing.

"Oh, yes," the angel went on. "She's not from a suburb of Chicago, but from rural Kentucky, and she has a trailer full of white trash relatives waiting to move in with you, as soon as she packs away her bridal dress."

"That can't be true. She's not like that," Busby said, but without conviction. Did angels lie? he wondered.

The angel sighed again. "Like a typical man all you can see is that she is very good in bed. Besides, there's a red-headed girl in the shipping department who would be perfect for you. Her name is Belinda, she's kind, sweet-tempered, and will make Miranda look like an amateur in bed."

"I'll think about it," Busby said, his mind reeling. He glanced around the office. "My secretary is due any second, I don't think she'd understand us talking."

"Behold!" said the angel.

Busby beheld as the angel folded her wings and appeared to become a small porcelain statue next to his clock.

"I love Behold!" said the angel. "It commands a certain amount of attention. Your secretary won't even notice me. She has other things on her mind. She's in love with your parts manager, but he's married. They spend their lunch hours in her car at the back of the parking lot engaging in oral sex."

"More than I wanted to know," said Busby.

"I'll be quiet as a statue," said the angel, as the door opened.

Keep calm, Busby told himself repeatedly. Investigate thoroughly, don't do anything rash. Still, a partner stealing from him, a girl-friend planning to deceive him. Late in the night he visited his office building, and using the combination supplied by the angel, opened his partner's safe and found everything the angel had said would be there. He left a message on his girlfriend's phone saying he'd been called away on an emergency. He went home and shut off all his communication devices, as he tried to decide what to do. He couldn't very well tell his banker, or anyone else, that an angel had warned him about his partner's misdeeds.

He was being battered personally and professionally, like a boxer pummelled by an ambidextrous opponent. He paced and thought, paced and thought, especially about Miranda. She did tend to be bossy. She did drink a little too much at social events. She had insisted he take off his wristwatch before coming to bed, something he had never done in his life. He did it for her but he resented it. Small things add up, he thought.

He contacted a detective agency, paid a large sum for an immediate investigation. Within twenty-four hours, her Kentucky roots had been confirmed. That was that. He left a message on her phone, telling her what he had discovered and suggesting it was better if they didn't see each other again.

Now, what to do about Arbuckle? He dismissed the angel's suggestion, for dishonesty was not in his nature. Confrontation appeared the only option. It was not pretty. Arbuckle was more upset that he had somehow obtained the combination to his personal safe than about what he had found there.

"I'll never be able to trust you again," said Arbuckle.

"You can't trust me? You're the one who's stealing."

"That's just the thing," said Arbuckle, "I'm not stealing. If you follow the cash trail, there is none. There is no actual account in the Caymans, there is not one cent of company money missing. I'm suspicious of some of our executives, nothing concrete, but that scenario about the Caymans is something I've shown to our head of security. I've discussed with him how I, or you, or any top executive could pull such a thing off. He's working on changes to our financial security systems."

Busby was speechless. Things were going from bad to worse. Arbuckle offered to buy him out. A huge sum of money, standard agreement not to work for a competitor or start a similar business for five years. Arbuckle must have been thinking of such a deal for some time. Busby apologized, but he knew it was useless, and worst of all, he couldn't explain that an angel was responsible for the misinformation. He briefly wondered if he were having a breakdown. Had he imagined the angel? No, she had given him the combination that only Arbuckle knew.

"We need to talk," he shouted, as he entered his office. The porcelain angel sat benignly on his desk beside a gold clock.

The angel unfolded her wings, stretched, fluttered to the top of a filing cabinet.

He told her what he had discovered about Arbuckle.

"So what am I, a forensic accountant?" she said. "I just reported what I saw. That data even fooled an expert like you."

Busby had no answer.

What if he'd been wrong about Miranda too? He visited the shipping department, spotted the red-headed girl. The angel had been right, the girl made his mouth water. Belinda had a tinkling laugh and a smile, with dimples, that could stop traffic. However, to his surprise, she declined when he suggested coffee or a drink. She declined again the next day when he asked her formally for a date.

"Sorry, I'm seeing someone," she said, smiling that heartbreaking smile.

He knew better than to push the matter. "If you ever change your mind, you know who I am," he said, feeling like his stock portfolio had declined fifty percent in a day.

He confronted the angel again.

"I said she was perfect for you. And she is. I didn't say you'd be able to have her. I have no control over that sort of thing."

"Then what was your point in coming here," Busby demanded. "So far, on your advice, I'm being forced to sell my business, and my love life is a shambles."

"Better now than later," said the angel. "Everything will work out in the long run."

"That's the best you can offer?

"Give the redhead about a year."

"Why didn't you say that originally? I'm beginning to think you don't know half as much as you let on."

"What I know and don't know changes from day to day."

Busby picked up his newspaper. "I should have swatted you that first day." He thought the angel looked slightly worried. Instead of pursuing his idea, Busby tossed the newspaper on his desk and stomped off to lunch.

As he ate, he imagined that when he returned, he'd find his secretary waiting. "I'm sorry," would be her first words. "I killed this big insect with your newspaper, but I somehow broke that little glass angel that sat on your desk. I swept it up and put it in the trash. I'll buy you a new one."

"That won't be necessary," said Busby. "Where is the insect?"

"I don't know. I flattened it against the glass, but it just vanished."

When he did return everything was tranquil.

"You look unhappy," said the angel. "Perhaps this would be a good time for me to move on, I've done about all I can for you."

Busby glared. The angel fluttered toward the window and, as Busby took a half-hearted swipe at her, she glided away. She floated against the glass and then through, leaving a residue of a few red stars that faded like fireworks.

Had those stars been in the shape of a trident? Busby blinked, thinking it was probably only his imagination running riot.

CHAPTER 6

C hristie sets down my manuscript.
   "Why do you write like that?"
"Like what?"
"With that tone of voice. It's like a kid telling dirty jokes to his little brother, emphasizing the dirty words in case he misses them. You're not like that. Your writing shouldn't be either."
"How should I write?"
"Like you talk. You tell stories that are queer and funny, because you see the world filtered through something, it may be flames or water or just a dirty window, but it distorts the cruel, the stupid and the pretentious, until I see the world with your strange vision. Isn't that what writers are supposed to do?"
"Give me an example."
"Remember the story you told me about the cat licking your ear?"
"That's not really a story, that's an anecdote."
"That's your problem. It's funny and weird. Write it down and you'll have a story. I don't want to read any more about space ships and dancing buses. Or fairies or insects or whatever you call them."
The next afternoon, spread out on our tangled bed, the shrieks of the grass hockey players filtering up through the leaves, a story came to me, something I'd been thinking about for a while but never had the nerve to write.

OUT OF THE PICTURE

I have the privilege of doing most of my writing in a sunny corner office overlooking the Pacific Ocean. On the long back wall of my office are a number of oil paintings, mostly by the famous Cree artist Allen Sapp. Sapp paints his memories of reserve life in rural Saskatchewan a half century ago. His paintings are realistic. Though I sometimes write of magical happenings, I have little tolerance for abstract art, something I believe I inherited from my Grandfather Drobney, though I never called him Grandfather in any language. He was simply Drobney, to one and all. A few days ago, I rearranged the oils on my wall to make room for a new acquisition, though the painting was not new to me, for it hung in my home when I was a child.

My family have always been secretive. The past was treated as something to be discarded, like out-of-style clothing, something once disposed of, never to be thought of again. Family history was seldom discussed. Baba Drobney told me she was the seventh daughter of a man who owned a small winery near Dubrovnik in Yugoslavia. Other than that and the oil painting, I know little about either side of my family. And I realize I have been equally uninformative. I have withheld from my daughters what little I know about my parents and grandparents.

Drobney died before I was old enough to start school. I was an adult before I visited his grave and saw his tombstone – ARON DROBNEY 1847–1939 – where I learned both his first name and the fact that he lived to be ninety-two. I remember him sitting in a rocker in the kitchen of our drafty farm house, a bright afghan around his knees. He had a full head of iron-gray hair, a walrus mustache of the same colour, and flashing black eyes.

After the Depression ended, and with the advent of World War II, prosperity slowly returned to Canada, and it was my vivacious Aunt Lichta who got custody of the family portrait. Lichta was my mother's sister and lived with us until I was seven years old, as did the rest of my mother's family, along with the portrait, an oil, painted by an artist who Aunt Lichta named as one of the Canadian Group of Seven, which meant nothing to me at the time.

The artist did not ordinarily do portraits, Aunt Lichta said, but Drobney, my grandfather, when he wanted something could be very persuasive, and over one thousand pre-Depression dollars was a great deal of money for a struggling artist in the 1920s, those halcyon days before my grandfather became like everyone else in North America, more or less insolvent.

Aunt Lichta's second marriage was to a man who became a federal member of Parliament for Alberta, and who, when his career was over, was appointed to the Senate. The Canadian Senate has no political power and is a dumping ground for political hacks, faithful fundraisers, and defeated incumbents. But the pay was excellent, the duties non-existent. Aunt Lichta and her husband lived out their lives in Ottawa, where she became famous as a hostess.

I remember, in the late Sixties, seeing a photo in *Maclean's* magazine, taken at some diplomatic function, where the senator, sleek and gray as a Rolls Royce, was flanked by his wife, Lucille.

Aunt Lichta was in her sixties then, a tall, striking woman with hair the pure white of hoar frost. In spite of always having an extravagant European accent, she somehow must have thought Lucille a more Canadian name than Lichta. Foreignness has not always been a virtue in Canada, though a recent prime minister's wife delighted in acknowledging her Yugoslavian ancestry.

Once, when I was quite young, I remember my Baba Drobney being very angry with my grandfather. He had gone to a neighboring farm owned by a Czech named Weisocovitch, and they had gotten into the dandelion wine. Drobney could be heard singing loudly in his own language as he crossed the meadows toward our home. He was unsteady and mumbling when he entered the kitchen.

"Go to bed, you old fool," Baba barked at him in English. Everyone except me and my father spoke several European languages – Slovenian, Serbo-Croatian, German, Romany. Though I never noticed, Aunt Lichta told me years later that, at Baba's insistence, only English was spoken when either I or my father was present.

Drobney stared at us bleary-eyed.

Baba Drobney rearranged me on her ample lap.

"In his family was Gypsies," she said, the foreboding dripping down her chin. Then, after a pause to let the gravity of that situation sink in, "Worse, was Romanians." She paused again to let me reflect on how bad that must be. "In Sarajevo, we had a cat. He named it Nistru," she went on. "'For that river used to run by my door as a boy,' he said. Nistru is a Romanian river," said Baba Drobney ominously.

Apparently Yugoslavians and Romanians did not hold each other in high regard. "If I'd only known," said Baba Drobney, shaking her head. Despite this, she and Drobney spent sixty-two years together, and as far as I know, were extremely happy.

The portrait – by the time I was old enough to comprehend, one person was already gone from it. My first memories of the painting are of it hanging on the bulging calcimined wallpaper in the dark inner hallway of our farmhouse. The house I grew up in was made of logs, the cracks chinked with white plaster by my father, who was a plasterer by trade. The upstairs was unfinished, and the wind whistled eerily through the gaps between the unpainted boards at each end of the attic. A colony of bats lived in that attic, oozing out at dusk on summer evenings to hurtle about the farmyard like black clots in the feathered twilight. Baba Drobney – whose yellowish-white hair, when combed out of its normally worn coiled braids, hung down to her waist – refused to set foot beyond the screen door after sunset in summer, and strongly warned my mother and my aunts not to venture outside for fear of getting a bat in their hair.

"A bat in the hair prophesies an early death," Baba said darkly.

In the portrait, Drobney had one arm across his chest as if he were clutching something unseen, the other hand, fingers spread, was poised above his right leg. A colourful vest was visible beneath his dark suit.

"Drobney once owned a thousand taxis in Ontario, Jamie. Your mother grew up in a stone mansion before everything went poof," Baba confided in me, as she patched the knee of my overalls. "We had servants before everything went poof."

Drobney stared out of the painting as if the artist were offering him an insultingly low price for something. Beside him on an ice-blue love seat sat Baba, looking more benign than in real life, smiling secretly, perhaps pleased by the expensive, peach-coloured gown she wore. To the right of them, my tiny mother, Mariska, sat on a red velvet chair with insect legs. She was very beautiful in a pale blue dress, her cheeks rouged, her blond hair coiled in a French braid. Though an adult, her feet did not even come close to touching the floor. Behind her stood my curly-haired Irish father who was destined to die young.

Behind the love seat stood my tall, beautiful Aunt Lichta, smiling as if the portrait had been her idea. Next to her was a younger sister, Rose, looking slightly scared. On the left, stood my uncles Waldemar and Jaroslaw, and Jaroslaw's wife Katarinka. Uncle Wald looked exactly like Drobney, only younger.

Everyone knew about the empty space in the portrait, except me. And because everyone knew, the space was mentioned occasionally, sometimes seriously, sometimes in a joking manner. I came to understand, without ever being officially told, that in the original painting someone named Percy had been beside Aunt Lichta.

When Drobney said "Percy," there were many cees between the r and the y.

The women were more tolerant, wondering sometimes, when Drobney wasn't present, where Percy might be now. My uncles punched each other on the shoulders and snickered when Percy's name was mentioned.

I came to realize that Percy had been Aunt Lichta's husband, someone she met in Ontario, when the family was still prosperous. Before everything had gone poof, and they had, with my father's help, purchased one-way train fare to Alberta. Percy was what was called a remittance man, someone who had brought some kind of embarrassment to his wealthy family in England, so was banished to the colonies with a financial allotment which permitted him to live well but not regally.

After Percy had, as Drobney sometimes said, let his bristles grow, a reference to Percy being a pig, and after he and Aunt Lichta were divorced, Drobney took the painting back to the artist and insisted that Percy be obliterated from it.

"He is no longer part of the family," Drobney raged. "I can no longer look at his snout without wanting to burn the portrait. The others I love," shouted Drobney in his extravagant European way. "Him, I want OUT!"

So Percy had been painted into oblivion.

When I was a little older, just before Aunt Lichta left the farm to live in Edmonton, where she met her second husband, I begged her to tell me what Percy looked like.

"I can do better than that," said Aunt Lichta, "though you must promise never to mention this to Drobney." Going to her closet, which smelled of dried rose petals, she produced a small photo. Percy was younger than I imagined; dressed in a variety of tweeds, he had straight blond hair slicked back off a high forehead, a long, thin nose with a pale mustache beneath it, thin lips and a receding chin. My mother had let slip once that Percy wore a monocle, but it was nowhere to be seen in the photo.

"He did," said Aunt Lichta, smiling sadly as she answered my question, "but it wasn't an evil monocle like the Germans wear. I believe even Percy's mustache was tweed," she added, and laughed prettily.

One evening when we were seated around our large oilcloth-covered kitchen table, eating supper by the light of two coal-oil lamps, someone mentioned the portrait. Drobney congratulated himself for having Percy painted out of the picture.

"I suppose if I died you'd have me painted out," said Baba, not entirely joking.

"Of course I would," shouted Drobney. "Everything should be as it is," and he stared around the table hoping, I'm sure, that someone would contradict him. Aunt Rose scurried to the stove to fetch more turnips.

"Then everyone in the picture should be wearing overalls, like we are now. And why aren't I in the picture?" I asked.

Everyone in the room wore bulky sweaters and bib overalls, a far cry from the finery of the portrait. I didn't realize until years later just how poor we were. That winter, we lived on turnips from the root cellar and eggs preserved in stone crocks of alum. What must my father have thought when he suddenly became responsible for seven members of my mother's family, when the stony and worthless quarter section of land he farmed produced barely enough for our own livelihood. My uncles Waldemar and Jaroslaw couldn't find work but at least they helped out on the farm. If one of the chickens looked as though it was definitely going to expire of natural causes, it was killed and we enjoyed chicken soup, liberally laced with turnips, for a meal or two.

That night, after I was put to bed, there was a heated discussion, parts of which drifted to me where I lay bundled in a down comforter in what had once been a pantry attached to the kitchen. The discussion was about whether, when there was money, if there would ever again be money, should I be painted into the portrait.

"Jerry and Kitty," Baba Drobney said, referring to my aunt and uncle, "will have children. Wald and Rose will marry. What if Mariska has ten brothers and sisters for Jamie. Children, no. Future inlaws, maybe," she declared with some finality. There was argument, especially from Aunt Kitty for her future offspring. But Baba stood fast, won her point, and the subject of my being painted in, when and if prosperity returned, was never broached again.

I tried to learn why Baba and Drobney had chosen to emigrate to Canada.

"Drobney thought it was a good idea," my mother said.

"I heard the streets of Canadian cities were paved with gold. Ha!" Drobney barked, when I got up the courage to ask him.

Once, when Baba was rocking me to sleep, at a time when I was almost too big to fit on her lap anymore, she hinted that Drobney had been in some kind of difficulty with the Yugoslavian government, and that large sums of money were involved. I share a birthday with Josip Broz, code-name Tito, the man destined to rule the conglomeration that became Yugoslavia. Apparently Baba was hell-bent on my first names being Josip Broz.

"If your grandmother had been here when you were born you'd probably be Marshall Tito O'Day," my father said several times over the years, "but she was in Toronto then, and she's not as persuasive by mail as she is in person."

The Drobneys were not poor when they came to Canada. They settled in Toronto in a large stone house close to the University of Toronto. The house still stands, long ago converted into a warren to house students. Not many years ago, on a visit to Toronto, I drove my wife past the property. "That's where my grandparents lived when they first came to Canada. It's where my mother was living when my father came to patch the plaster in the upstairs bathroom. That was before they moved to Saskatchewan and tried to become farmers."

Drobney, who had been a horse-trader in the old country, became a used car dealer in Toronto, one of the first. Then he discovered the taxi business. It is said that at one time fifty percent of the taxis in Toronto bore a white line down each side with Drobney Taxi in fat white letters on each door. Drobney's mistake was that he believed in his new homeland. In Dubrovnik, he had kept his wealth in a money belt, under the floorboards beneath his and Baba's bed. In Canada, he decided to trust a bank. When the Depression came, not only did people stop riding in taxis but the bank failed. Drobney lost everything.

My father and mother, Baba and I, were the last to leave the farm. Lichta was the first. She got a job in Edmonton as governess to the children of a wealthy lawyer. She married the lawyer's younger brother, the aspiring politician.

After the war, Uncle Waldemar went back to Yugoslavia and after a few years stopped writing. I suspect Uncle Wald was gay. I always meant to ask Lichta about that. Jerry and Kitty moved to Winnipeg, where he became a bus driver. Timid Aunt Rose married a timid Alberta farmer named Stefanichan.

And one fall, while we were still on the farm, Drobney announced that he was going to die, and sixty days later he did. In his final days he lay in bed, his hands raised in front of him, braiding imaginary rope for the horses he had long ago led through the streets of Dubrovnik.

On golden Indian summer days, Baba helped Drobney to a rocker on the sunny south side of the house, where fist-sized marigolds glowed along a path bordered with whitewashed stones.

Drobney sat in the sun, his right hand poised as it was in the portrait. He mumbled the word, "Nistru, Nistru."

Whether he was referring to the river or the long dead cat, I never knew.

After her second marriage, Aunt Lichta wrote asking if she could have the portrait. It was Baba's decision. No one offered any objection, so she agreed.

Baba wrapped the portrait in a blanket, tied it with binder twine and drove by horse and cart eight miles to the highway where she put it on board the east-bound Western Trailways bus. That was the last time I saw the portrait for over forty years.

Aunt Lichta turned out to be the only member of the family I kept in close touch with, other than my parents. I visited her whenever business took me to Ottawa. My parents produced no brothers or sisters for me. Aunt Rose and the timid Stefanichan had several children, as did Jerry and Kitty in Winnipeg.

One of Rose's daughters dropped in on us a few years ago. She was a dark, sullen girl of nineteen, named Lily, who had decided to call herself Desiree and become an actress. She was disappointed that, as a writer, I didn't know any movie stars, more disappointed that I didn't know anyone who could get her into local TV or radio. She departed after a few days. Aunt Lichta said she became a hairdresser and married a boy who was training to be an auto body repairman.

About a year before she died, I received a letter from Aunt Lichta, her beautiful handwriting suddenly spidery and uneven, asking that I be certain to call on her the next time I was in Ottawa.

"Do you remember the portrait that used to hang in the hallway at the farm?" Aunt Lichta asked me.

"The one your first husband had been painted out of?"

"You remember."

"That was what made it memorable."

"I've kept up the tradition," Aunt Lichta said.

"Having people painted out when they…"

"Die. Or lose contact like your Uncle Wald. Drobney was a very strong personality. You have no idea. Even now I don't recall him as Papa or Father, but as Drobney."

"Baba was no slouch herself when it came to strong personality. She was the one who made me a writer. Remember her stories that always began, 'Knocks at the door a stranger?'"

"The messages of childhood are strongest," said Aunt Lichta. "They are engraved," and she touched her head, her hair still the purest of whites, but cottony now, not healthy-looking.

"My children think I'm crazy," she went on. She had two sons with her second husband, one a corporation lawyer, the other in the diplomatic service in Finland. "But they weren't there..."

"And I was?"

Aunt Lichta smiled. She stood up slowly from the antique settee in her living room.

"No one knew about what I was doing until after your mother passed away two years ago. After she was gone I had her removed. Clyde handles my finances now and he had a fit when he got the bill. I had to confess.

Aunt Lichta kept the portrait in an expensive leather carrying case. It was a shock to see it again. It was smaller than in my memory, but still large. The furniture was dominating now, the settee, the red-velvet insect-legged chair where my mother had posed. A youthful Aunt Lichta was the only human figure left in the portrait.

"Take it with you, and finish the job when I'm gone," Aunt Lichta said.

I promised I would. "Childhood messages," I said, kissing her frail cheek.

As I've said, I have the privilege of doing most of my writing in a sunny corner office overlooking the Pacific. There are a number of oil paintings on the walls of my office, all realistic.

Now, among the landscapes is an interior scene, a studio, a blue love seat in the foreground, a rose-coloured chair with insect legs to the left. The room is finished in dark panelling, several gas lamps burn in the background. There are old-fashioned oil paintings on the wall of the studio.

A few months after she died, I had Aunt Lichta painted out of the picture. I also had the portrait X-rayed to confirm something I had long suspected. The artist in Vancouver who did the work charged enough that he didn't feel the need to ask questions, after I assured him the artist's name was a coincidence, that he was a relative of mine and certainly not one of the now-world-famous Group of Seven.

The picture of the empty studio is quite astonishing. Visitors often remark on it because it is the only one of my paintings that doesn't have at least one human figure in it. When I stare at it, Drobney's words, "Everything should be as it is," echo over a half century of my life.

Sitting, writing, at my large oak table, watching the fog-coloured waves of the Pacific, I feel happy and secure. I am delighted that my family is gathered in the room while I work, not just in memory, not hidden the way dead people usually are, but available if I choose to make them so. Baba Drobney, my coal-eyed Gypsy grandfather, my parents young and beautiful, and all the rest should I choose to resurrect them, even Percy the remittance man, who I feel more sympathy for as I grow older. The Drobneys were not an easy family to marry into.

And, finally, if I decide to, I may reveal the secret of Drobney's raised hand, for the demise of Percy was not the first alteration to the painting. The X-ray revealed that under Drobney's hand was a large orange cat. Nistru, named for a river in Romania.

They are all there, sturdy and smiling, in case I need them.

CHAPTER 7

Christie wakes with a start. We've only been asleep for like an hour after making love. I hold her close. I can feel her heart pounding.

"What did you dream of? What is it that scares you so?"

"Christie is afraid if she tells you, you won't love her anymore."

"Nothing can change the way I feel about you."

"Let's see if that's true. For years I have had a recurring dream about being crushed by a giant flatiron. The diamond-shaped, foil-coloured iron wielded, I believe, by my mother. I am small as an ant and the iron forces me face first into the snuffy soil until my back is level to the surface, and though I wriggle and struggle and try to rise, the job is done too well. I smother. Gorge myself on chocolaty loam and enter forever a chasm of silence.

"Or, I walk in a tunnel that drips slime. Other vile water whirls at my knee. What sport a psychiatrist would have with this dream. And I've talked to a few over the years. The tunnel goes on forever, no welcoming light or lost loved ones at the end. My secret is I know there is a side door to the tunnel and I know its sinister name."

Christie begins to sob quietly.

"I tried that door one morning when I was seventeen. The night before was the shortest night after the longest day. Dazed and drunk as dawn's eyelids fluttered, I stumbled into a car outside an all-night cabaret. There were three men in suits and loosened ties. The car still smelled of the showroom. I was barefoot, my hair covering half my face like a shadow, wearing jeans, a soft blue sweater, nothing else. I'd been to a party. Somewhere in the past I remembered throwing one of my boots at a bedroom wall, scratching a face, cursing, feeling a stunning slap.

"In the car I tried to speak, bargain, but my tongue was clotted, everything except the scream of the radio, the smell of newness, far away.

"They gave me ten dollars each, forced the money into my hand, rotated about the interior of the car like children playing musical chairs, while I remained on my knees, hands on the plush upholstery, throat full.

"They left me standing under a streetlight that shut off with a snap as I swayed crazily, the pink glow of dawn on the pavement.

"At home, deciding to do myself what no one would do for me, I noosed my neck. I would step through that convenient side door, escape the body in which I was trapped, escape my senseless life, escape my mother. I stood on a pail in the cellar where mold iced the black dirt walls. Roped to a rafter, I stepped into air. The pail clattered and rolled in a slow, dizzy circle.

"I pictured Mother finding me, blue cold as a butcher shop carcass. I wanted to bring her pain, to see the horror reflected in her dry, toy eyes. But, she heard my fall. Though I knew I should be dying, I listened as she came clattering down the broad, board stairs to where I twirled, bulge-eyed. I could smell her perfume as she cut me down, the knife a glint in her freckled hand.

"Like rumpled dolls we sat on the crumbling concrete floor, hugging, crying, sobbing our love, making promises.

"But even as I smelled her smoky sweat, and our tears mingled, I knew I'd try that door again and again until I was admitted.

"At school the next day, I wore her high-necked white blouse to hide the rope burn."

We sat in silence for a minute after she finished her story.

"It doesn't matter to me, Christie," I tell her. "I love you, nothing can change that. No matter how hard you try to drive me away."

"There's more," she sobs. Again and again I see myself dead, curled on the bed like a baby, barely as big as a pillow, like a bird so much smaller in death than in life. I look in the mirror. I can see Mother on the bed behind me. Does that mean I'll never be able to escape her? My head feels like a kaleidoscope flashing bright crazy patterns, and for some reason I remember one of the happy moments. We were alone as usual, we children, in a room in a drafty house. It rained, a terrifying thunder and lightning storm. The windows fogged as the temperature dropped and the cold waves of water washed across the window, while thunder rolled and lightning zig-zagged across the sky, molten.

"When the storm finally ended, we children crept down the stairs and out into the overgrown backyard. The storm had scattered rose petals across the grasses like a black-clothed flower girl. We gathered the wet flower petals and papered our faces with them, where they dried like scars. All down the left side of my face and neck they clung, sticking and blending with the pink skin. I looked like I was badly scarred. Or, like the scars I have always known existed had moved from within to without. Perhaps I had seen the angel of death. Perhaps I had actually been burned.

"Once, I simply took all the pills that were in my room, in my purse, in my pockets, washed them down with straight whiskey. I'm going to sleep for such a long time, I thought. Only it wasn't the way I wanted it to be. I didn't just go to sleep. The room kept spinning, spinning and I felt so sick, but I couldn't move.

"You confessed to me, Wylie, that you attract suicidal women. What you mean is you are attracted to suicidal women. I know their stories. One felt worthless because her father hated her. Another felt guilt because her father loved her too much. One never knew her father but felt she must have done something to drive him away. One read Sylvia Plath and put her head in an oven. After giving birth, another refused a blood transfusion. One drank turpentine to keep from giving birth."

She pauses and turns her head, looking me directly in the eye.

"If you love me, let me die. If you love me, help me die. But that's just too dramatic."

Christie is pale, as if she is wearing a white mask. Her wide-open eyes are the colour of green satin and equally expressionless.

"We should let ourselves out that convenient door," Christie continues. "Use the door while we are still completely in love, before the little resentments begin gnawing at the relationship like fanged rodents, before days begin dawning clear and cold, somehow improving vision, magnifying faults until they stand out like cavities in front teeth. But Wylie, you will die an old man, the odours of medicine, age and decay surrounding you."

I shake my head. "What you're talking of is sometimes called limerence," I say, "but it's psychological bafflegab, and I don't for a moment buy it. And I don't think you do either. You're testing me when you need to trust me."

"I feel suspended in time like space debris," Christie says.

"Teaching you to trust is like teaching a mermaid to do the splits," I say, allowing myself to smile a little.

"Christie wants to trust you. Christie wants to be real to you. But I always wake up alone. Everyone I've ever loved has left me alone. Am I real, or just a dream?"

"Trust me, you're *my* dream," I tell her. "And I'll never leave you alone."

Christie holds me with a desperate strength I hadn't known she possessed.

Death on my mind. Christie is finally asleep. I sit at my typewriter, stare at the keys. Finally, I begin to type.

MURDEROUS WAYS

I got one shot off at the target, then Rand called my name, loud and urgent. 'Mariel,' he called. I whirled around and the gun went off. He had been right behind me. There he was, falling back, his chest opening before my eyes.

"What did he want? I guess I'll never know. I couldn't find anything amiss, but I knew Rand well enough, long enough, to recognize in his voice, not terror but genuine alarm."

That's what I'll tell them, the police. Oh, they'll give me a hard time. They'll be suspicious but sympathetic at first. There's no phone at the shooting range. I'll have to drive Rand's truck out three miles to a gas station and call 911. Hard time won't be the words for it, once they snoop around and find out about our relationship, once they know who Rand is.

But no matter what they think, what they suspect, they'll have to have evidence, witnesses. There will be no witnesses, only Rand and I know what went on between us. It was an accident. I killed my lover. The police may even choose to keep our relationship quiet after they recognize Rand. I'll just be a young divorcee who Rand, in all his kindness and public spirit, was teaching to shoot because I needed protection.

My ex had threatened my life, had stalked me for years, left obscene notes in my mailbox, threatening messages on my answering machine. This is true. I have the tapes, the notes, a restraining order. Why would I want to do harm to someone I love? Even if our love was illicit. What a strange, archaic word. Like mistress. No one is a mistress anymore. Though I considered myself Rand's mistress. I used the word in front of him all the time.

Three weeks ago, I woke with a shudder in the middle of the night, moonlight blue across my lonely bed, one of those 3 a.m., end-of-the-world, blood-surging wake-ups.

I'm going to kill my lover, I thought. At the same instant I knew how and where I was going to do it. The shooting range. My red-bearded lover. I thrill to bury my face in his beard, I love it when my own scent is there, his beard damp from our lovemaking. Rand is six-foot-four. I'm five-foot-nothing. He jokes he could carry me in his pocket. My hair is crow-wing black; I can tuck the end of it in the back pockets of my jeans. I know how sexy I look in tight jeans. I know how sexy Rand thinks I look in tight jeans. Sometimes when we're alone, at the shooting range or in the woods, I'll kneel on the damp grass and love him with my mouth. Afterward he likes to stare at the stains on my jeans. "They are reminders," he says.

Other times, after we've been shooting, we make love in Rand's truck, the heater on, the windows fogged, the leather seat cold on my back, the smell of grease, gasoline. Rand's belt buckle clanging against something.

I'm going to kill Rand.

I've had one of those revelations that anyone who wasn't blinded by love, by lust, by eternal hope, would have recognized years ago. The revelation is so trite I hesitate to repeat it. Rand, though he may love me – he has to love me, I couldn't have given him five years of my life if I didn't think he loved me – is never going to leave his family.

I wouldn't be planning to live on if I didn't think he loved me. If I didn't think he loved me, I'd be careless. I'd pick up his gun, the .44, from the shelf at the firing range. I'd fire it into his chest, watch the surprise in his dying eyes, then place the cold barrel against the centre of my own chest, against my heart.

Rand is famous. Though people here in Wyoming either don't know about his fame, or don't care. Rand Sutherland is an outsider here in Wyoming. His ranch is between Glenrock and Douglas, off the beaten track, the house with the blue-tiled roof not visible from the highway. His land is fenced with tightly strung rows of barbed wire, or bob wire as the locals call it. The gate to his ranch is electrically controlled, the cattle guard rumbles ominously whenever a vehicle crosses it. I've only been to Rand's ranch twice, both times when his family was away, once to Disneyland, another time when his wife's father died in Pennsylvania. My whole little basementless house on one of the back streets of Glenrock would fit in Rand's bedroom. We made love in his bedroom all afternoon – I couldn't stay overnight because the ranch foreman and his family live only a few hundred yards away.

Rand engages in the most unlikely of occupations. My huge, red-bearded lover, who prefers riding a horse to driving, who loves guns, stringing fence wire, branding cattle, writes a syndicated column on food and wine, which appears weekly in about seventy newspapers all across North America. The column appears under the byline Sebastian T. Rand.

"Sebastian sounds all English, upper crust and snooty," he explained to me shortly after we'd met. "I was still Randy Sutherland when I sent out samples of my column. I'm completely self-taught. My degree is in political science from Rutgers. I'm an Easterner through and through. One of the things I ask my editor at the syndicate is read each column to be certain I haven't let any Wyoming creep into my language."

I met Rand six years ago. My ex contracted to do the haying on Rand's ranch. I fed the men, kept them supplied with water, occasionally drove the truck hauling bales. Rand hopped in the cab with me one afternoon.

"I need a little of that air conditioning," he said. He was bare to the waist. There were clover seeds in his chest hair. Each of his hands would make three of mine. I inhaled involuntarily. The odours of sweat, leather, clover, were overpowering. My impulse was to stop the truck and throw myself into his arms.

"Actually, I don't care diddly about the air conditioning," he said, picking up one of the water bottles from the floor of the cab and taking a long drink. "I don't think I've ever seen a woman with such beautiful hair. I wanted to see you close-up."

"Are you impressed?" I asked. I pulled the truck to the edge of the field, into the shade of a few aspen that drooped over the fence.

"Better believe it," he said. He smiled. His front teeth were white and square, his grey eyes cool and friendly.

"I'm Mariel," I said.

It was two years ago that we began shooting. It was a way for us to be alone. Rand's wife was from the East and did not like guns. My daddy says I started shooting while I was still in my playpen. Rand, in another life, once trained as a police officer. I've never been a target shooter. He teaches me gun handling safety by what he calls police methods.

Rand pulls the truck into the empty parking lot of the firing range. Gravel cracks ominously under the tires. The October sun is gold and red like the leaves still clinging to the white-stalked birch that shade the tiny trailer that serves as a clubhouse.

All the way out here, the words "A good day for dying" keep threading through my mind, piercing like tines of sunlight. Was it Hemingway who said that? It must have been.

I can smell the leather of Rand's vest. I light a cigarette, inhale deeply. Rand glances across at me. I've been sitting against the passenger door, punishing him, letting him see how sullen I am. In happier times, I'd be crowded against him, our hands entwined. I'd have my face against his chest, breathing in his odours, my hand between his legs feeling the hardness of him beneath the denim. The corners of Rand's eyes crinkle as a smile begins.

A good day for dying.

We get out of the truck. There is a faint smell of burning leaves, of sunshine, of winter hiding just beyond the mountains. I inhale again. There is something so thrilling about smoking a cigarette in the crisp outdoors.

Rand leans over and unlocks the sheet metal trunk that is welded into the box of the pickup. I stand back a few paces, cigarette in my left hand, right hooked in the watch pocket of my Levis. With the toe of my right boot I toy with fragments of crushed rock. The trunk has three locks, for it is filled with Rand's guns. I wait for him to pull out the .22 pistol, extend it my way, handle first.

I'm preparing my argument. I am going to insist on using a heavier gun today. Pick a fight if I have to. I remember the weight of the .44, the rush of the discharge, the thrilling tingle up my arms. A good day for dying.

"You've been shooting pretty well the last couple of weeks," Rand says, holding the lid of the trunk open, staring inside, speaking over his shoulder in my direction.

A good day for dying.

"I think you should shoot something larger today. You've earned it. Climb up here and take your choice."

I draw heavily on my cigarette. Rand wants me to quit smoking, but not really. He thinks it is really sexy. He kisses me like I have diamonds hidden in my mouth. I toss the cigarette onto the gravel, rub it under my boot. My heart is melting, my insides aquiver. I feel such a sense of tenderness toward Rand. I place my hands on the tailgate of the truck, vault into the box. My murderous ways waft off like the smoke I have just exhaled. I reach into the trunk for the heaviest gun.

CHAPTER 8

Christie came into money, wants to buy me a new electric typewriter. She doesn't work, we are seldom apart. Where did the money come from?

"No," I said emphatically. "This old Royal is about the same age I am. Besides, I think with my fingers resting on the keys. You know what happens when you do that on an electric?"

Christie sulked. It's not like I don't let her buy me things. One evening when we were window shopping our way home from the Church Key Lounge at three in the morning, I admired an expensive suede vest in a men's store window. The next evening Christie brought it to me. She was always coming home with clothes or books for me, proud as a cat dragging a still-fluttering bird over the threshold. Yet, when I bring her so much as a flower, she is uncomfortable.

"You've never learned to take graciously," I complained.

"Graciously! Fuck graciously. The counselor in the joint taught Christie all about gracious living. Would you believe she learned how to arrange artificial flowers and set a dinner table for eight. Christie is capable of entertaining your boss at a dinner party."

"You've never been in jail."

"How would you know?"

"I just know."

"Weren't you ever a child?" Christie asked me. "You never talk about your childhood. What did you do with yourself? What was your first job?"

That got me to thinking, and I recalled the day I decided I would make storytelling a career.

THE BLUEBIRD CAFÉ

Saturday mornings, not even a teenager yet, I would ride the street-car in the cold prairie city where I grew up to the *Journal* building downtown. I would buy thirty newspapers at five cents each, stash them in a dirty canvas bag with a strap that went over my shoulder, and head east to sell my papers for ten cents each to pedestrians, and clients of the many cafés on both sides of the main drag, including one at 97th Street that posted a sign: "Off Limits to Military Personnel." More than thirty years later, I can still feel the unpleasant weight of that canvas strap on my shoulder. I always imagined that I would someday work for the *Journal*. I used to read each edition religiously, imagining my own byline on the more prominent stories.

The money for selling papers was good, considering me and my friends received twenty-five cents per week allowance. A dollar-fifty was a lot of money for a twelve-year-old. An ice cream cone cost five cents, donuts were two for a nickel, a chocolate bar was seven cents, recently raised from five. However, there were disadvantages. I was too proud to pack a lunch, so by mid-afternoon, when I had sold most of my papers, I was so ravenously hungry that I blew a lot of what I'd just earned. I could get a fried egg sandwich for twenty-five cents, or ham for thirty, not much but it still cut into my profits.

One afternoon, I completely lost it and paid seventy-five cents at a place called the Bluebird Café, for the most delicious meal I had ever eaten – four plump pork sausages, each lying in a drift of mashed potato, covered in a savoury red gravy. There was sliced bread and butter and two vegetables, but it was the sausage and red gravy that won my heart.

The Bluebird Café was a new business in a very old building next to a furniture store. It had been created on a small budget. Instead of a false ceiling, a dozen white globes lit the room, each at the bottom of at least a twenty-foot pole. High above in the dimness a stained tin ceiling could be seen. There were a dozen stools with red leather seats in front of a greyish counter. Four tables of mismatched wooden and chrome chairs were scattered about; the whole place sat about thirty. The sign outside read "CANADIAN AND JAPANESE FOOD."

The war was a recent memory to everyone; I couldn't imagine anyone wanting Japanese food. There was a Japanese girl in my sixth grade class, an anomaly in a class of white kids, the children of war veterans, a couple of whom had lost their fathers in the war. Masako was tall and straight as a flower stalk. She wore long pale dresses that were simply coverings for her body. She sat shyly in her seat, and kept to herself at recess. I had never spoken to her.

I became obsessed with sausages and gravy. I dreamed of them while I hawked my papers, and no matter how thoroughly I promised myself to go straight home, my stomach led me straight to the Bluebird Café, where I squandered half my earnings. One week when I went to pay my bill, Masako was at the cash register. We exchanged shy greetings. She explained that her parents owned the café and she helped out after school and on weekends.

The next week, at the Bluebird Café, I observed something quite odd. As I sat at the counter, waiting for my order, occasionally spinning in a circle on the stool, a very old Japanese man entered the café and took a seat two stools to my right. He was tiny and thin as a broom, with pumpkin coloured skin and a few squiggles of straight white hair. He wore a black overcoat that appeared to weigh as much as he did. He gave Masako his order in Japanese.

My meal came and I dived in. A few moments later, Masako delivered a bowl of hot vegetables and a pot of tea to the old man. He ate silently and deliberately, though I thought I detected restraint; it was as if his hunger was great, and he wanted to eat much faster. As I watched, the old man took from his overcoat pocket a small black-lidded jar filled with a black liquid and brush about eight inches long, wrapped in a cloth. He undid the lid of the jar and after dipping the brush in the liquid – apparently, it was ink – wrote very slowly with a steady hand on the back of the bill.

Masako was stacking plates behind the counter as I made my way to the register. As she passed, she picked up the old man's bill. She stared at it as I counted out my change. I could see the delicate black characters he had inscribed on the back of the bill. "Is that his signature?" I asked.

"No. It's a poem. In Japan, he was a renowned poet." She turned the bill toward me. There were three lines of up and down writing, each character drawn in exquisite detail.

"What does it say?"

She stared at it for a long time.

"Do you read Japanese?"

"Of course," she said, her eyes flashing. "In the camps there was nothing to do but learn Japanese."

"I'm sorry," I said. I knew only vaguely of the Japanese internment camps.

"He lost everything because of the camps," she said. "His home, much valuable land, all taken away. He has only his talent and his pride left. He pays for his meal with a poem. My father collects them. He says in Japan they are better than money." She kept studying the poem. Finally, she read:

"In a dense thicket
black rabbit huddles softly
pink nose aquiver."

The poem was as delicate as the drawn characters, but there was so much more. The old man paid for his meal with a poem. What a concept. I had written several stories, including one called

"Diamond Doom" about a murder in a baseball stadium that earned me an honourable mention in a YMCA contest.

Electric eels seethed through my blood. He paid for his meal with a poem! I pictured myself plunking down a story in payment for a plate of savoury sausage. The possibilities were endless. How long could I eat in exchange for a novel? My future was decided.

CHAPTER 9

Christie is reality. Everything else is filtered through a rainy windshield. Writing about Christie is like stumbling on a five-ton ice cream cone. I love ice cream, but where to begin, where to begin?

Christie, as I mentioned, had her own unique way of distorting reality. She talked about herself in the third person. "Christie is sad. Christie is drunk. Christie wants to be loved."

"Why do you talk about yourself in the third person?" I asked.

"I have an extra pair of eyes up in the corner of the room watching what Christie does. I like to talk about me as if I were somebody else. Of course, I am somebody else, but if I'm far enough away from me, maybe I won't hate what I see so much."

I've been talked about in the third person all my life. My family. If we had many close friends Christie might do it to me too. My mother and my ex-wife used to talk about me in the third person while I was present, sitting in my mother's living room, on one of the box chairs with tatted doilies on the arms and crocheted headrests meant to keep my hair from soiling the hundred-year-old upholstery. When I was single, I used to bring girlfriends to that jungle of an apartment where my mother and my maiden aunt patrolled, like gentle, elderly tigers. If the three women talked about me in the third person while they were getting acquainted, I would later drop the girl off at her home, letting her get out of the car herself, and would never call her again. My mother is still friends with my ex-wife and several old girlfriends. They must have enervating afternoons discussing what has become of me. A sort of negative fan club.

Christie is a muse, I'm sure of it. A muse has been described as "an aid to the author, sometimes the true speaker." That is how I feel. Christie doesn't even have to be present, though my best ideas come when she is. But I start to think of people I have eaves-dropped on, usually at the lunch counter where my friend Jones philosophizes. I never used to do anything with those conversations, but since meeting Christie some of them have turned into stories.

OVERHEARD CONVERSATION

You'll never believe what fucking happened to me, Angie. I mean this is like fucking weird. I met this guy last night in Hanrahan's, long legs, dark eyes, long black hair, nice leather jacket and boots. I figure there's a good chance he's a biker. You know my weakness for leather types. He's not, but that has nothing to do with the story. We have a few drinks, dance a few times. He's horny as all getout. Grinds his pelvis against me and I fucking near come right on the dance floor.

"I take him back to my place and one thing leads to the only thing, you know what I mean. His name's Doug, and he's from back east, just out of jail. He's jumped parole and figures he's wanted so he sort of slides down on his chair every time the cops stroll through Hanrahan's.

"Anyway, we're doin' the deed, and ain't it fine, when all of a sudden he stops and just stares down at me. I figure it's kind of romantic that he likes to look at me. I got that little red lava lamp by the bed and it makes bubbles up the window blind and in its light both of us look like we're sunburned.

"'Son of a bitch,' he says, 'I gotta tell you something. This is really fucking strange, but I can't get it outta my head. When I was in the joint out in Alberta there was this guy who looked exactly like you. I mean exactly. He was a little guy. Same red hair, same blue eyes, same freckles, same husky voice...'"

"'I got an identical twin brother,' I say. 'He run off when he was sixteen and nobody's heard from him since.'"

"'His name Danny?'"

"'Yeah. God. Must be the same guy. We got different last names. I been married once. So what was he in for?'"

"'Can't get over how much you two look alike. It makes me feel funny.'"

"'Yeah? You ever been, like, this way with him? He swings both ways, least he did last time I seen him. I walked in on him one time and he was down on his knees doin' to this guy who worked at the 7-Eleven on the corner what I was doin' to you a few minutes ago.'"

"'Yeah, well, I guess, maybe. Jesus it makes me feel creepy.'"

"'You ever really get it on with him?'"

"'Nah. He done me a couple of times, like you say. I mean a guy's got needs and all that, especially in the joint.'"

"'Ain't no skin off my nose,' I tell him, and I start moving my ass. I mean I'm fucking horny. But this guy, big tough hard rock con, he was in for armed robbery, is grossed out because my twin brother gave him a blow job in the joint.

"Geez, he got off in about a dozen strokes, and he was dressed and out the fucking door in couple of minutes. He said he was headin' for Montreal and I believe him.

"I wonder how Danny is? I forgot to ask Doug the name of the joint he was in. He never did say what Danny done to wind up in the slammer."

CHAPTER 10

"Christie has never been loved so good."

It is late afternoon. Earlier, at Christie's urging, I finished a long story. I let Christie read it, and she liked it very much. We celebrated by making love, long and slow, the voices of schoolgirls playing field hockey drifting in and out our window with the breeze.

"Christie, I've told you almost everything about me, all of which I admit is not very interesting, at least until you somehow put your magic touch to it, but you've told me almost nothing about yourself. Where do you really come from? What are you hiding from?"

"I can't imagine why you'd want to know. Christie isn't very interesting either."

"Let me be the judge of that."

"Have you ever heard of Salmon Arm?"

"It's a small city somewhere in the interior of B.C."

"You're smarter than I thought, most people think it's a disease. I grew up there in a trailer trash family, pretty well raised myself. Ran with a bad crowd, got knocked up when I was sixteen. Give the guy credit, he married me. Would have been a lot better if he hadn't. Our honeymoon was him on a three-day bender in a motel in Kamloops, and me trying to keep out of his way. Second month we were together he got drunk, kicked the crap out of me. I lost the baby at five months. But he wouldn't let me leave, said he'd kill me if I ever left him. Bet you could write a country song about that, call it 'I Got Boot Tracks on my Cheekbone.'"

Christie laughed, reached across me for her cigarettes on the bedside table.

"I did leave, in the middle of the night after he'd gone to sleep drunk. Took my little suitcase, the grocery money, walked to an all-night gas station, offered to pay a trucker to bring me to Calgary. He didn't want money, he wanted a blow job. I had to get to Calgary. I spent two years there, afraid of my shadow. Moved to Edmonton for a better job. Walked right into one of my old man's cousins in the West Edmonton Mall. He tried to grab me, I ran, ducked into a clothing store, hid in the middle of a rack of clothes for over an hour, afraid to even peek out. That night I was on a bus to Vancouver. I saw Mrs. Kryzanowski's ad for a room to rent in the newspaper. The rest is history.

"And, yeah, I look over my shoulder every fucking day, my old man and his friends come to Vancouver sometimes. I'm afraid to get a job in case I run into one of them. I believed him when he said he'd kill me if I ever left him.

"See, not very interesting. What would you call it, a cliché situation? I bet there are a thousand chicks right here in Vancouver running away from ignorant, drunken stumblefucks like my husband."

"Christie, you don't have to be afraid," I said. "I'll take care of you now."

"Yeah, until that SOB finds me and kills both of us with a tire iron." She burst into tears. "Christie is sorry. She doesn't want to put you in danger. Christie is bad for you. I can never get a divorce without that fucker finding out where I am."

I held her close. Calmed her down.

"Things aren't always what they appear to be," Christie finally whispered. "Have you ever noticed, when we're out walking, how I suddenly become a window shopper each time a cop car rolls by?"

"I have."

"Yeah, well, maybe before I left I went out to his toolbox in his truck, came back to the trailer and gave him three hard whacks to the head with his big claw hammer. Maybe Christie is wanted for a lot of things, by more than my old man and his friends."

"But what about the other stories? The business back East. The others?"

"You're such a fucking mark." Christie says, giggling like a little girl.

The story I finished that day: We were at an outdoor cafe on Granville Street. At the next table, a man and two women had finished their food, were drinking coffee and smoking. He was stocky with long red hair and a bushy red mustache. One girl was a rather beautiful blond, fresh faced, with piercing blue eyes. The other girl was slimmer, with dark brown hair; when she got up to get napkins from a counter, she walked gingerly as if she was in slight pain.

"Tell me their story," Christie whispered in my ear. "There's something odd going on there. Look at the blond girl's eyes. I know that look. She's a risk taker."

RISK TAKERS

Jee was not her real name. And I never knew her last name, though it was Van de something, or Vander something – she was from a Dutch immigrant family. "Never mind," she used to say, "you couldn't pronounce it anyway."

The valley east of us was farmed by established Dutch immigrants who came to Canada after WW II, the fertile delta land used for dairy farming and for market gardening. Jee, though, had come to Canada only five years earlier, when she was twelve, she told me. She said her father had been in some kind of trouble in Holland and that relatives had paid the family passage to Canada so they could make a new start.

"Ha," Jee said derisively at that point in her story. Her father had worked on a dairy farm, but apparently lacked whatever skills were required for such work, and was fired.

"He was lazy and stupid," Jee said. He then stole a cultivator, but was not even a good thief, for the RCMP caught him towing the cultivator behind his ragged pickup truck, only a mile from his former employer's farm.

"Now, the asshole's in jail," Jee said.

We were both new arrivals in a community of tiny, rundown cottages and shacks about a mile outside a small city east of Vancouver. It was a rural slum occupied by the poor and the shiftless, designations that were not interchangeable, my mother insisted.

"There is nothing wrong with being poor," she said, "it can happen to anyone, Cathy," by which she meant us. Until a few months before, our family, my mother and father, myself and a younger brother, lived in a small rented house in a quiet neighborhood in East Vancouver. Then one Sunday afternoon in March, my father died of a heart attack, after which Mother explained that while we had lived comfortably, we had lived month to month. There wasn't even enough money to pay the next month's rent. There was an insurance policy with my father's union, but the company and union were stalling and the union rep said it could take another year before Mother saw a dime.

Mother got a part-time job with a janitor service in this small city and we moved into a basementless, mildew-smelling cottage, amidst a cluster of shacks and cabins outside the city limits. The rent was twenty dollars a month. We had no indoor plumbing, a wood burning stove, and we carried water from a community spigot two blocks away.

"Her name is Markje," a market gardener's daughter told me on the school bus one morning. "She's stuck up. Thinks she's too good for the rest of us," the girl hissed into my ear. "And her living out in Darktown." She stopped, embarrassed, realizing that I, too, lived in Darktown.

I was surprised the market gardener's daughter even talked to me. The area we lived in was called Darktown because the original inhabitants had been a few black people who came to the coast from an all-black town in Alberta in the 1920s and set up their own community. Over the years most of the blacks and their descendants found employment with the railways and integrated into Vancouver. It is said some of them are the landlords who collect rent on these dilapidated buildings, occupied now by the really poor and truly shiftless.

Jee's long, lemon-coloured hair touched the back pockets of her jeans, which were faded to an existential blue and held to her wide hips by an expensive black belt with a heavy buckle sporting an embossed marijuana leaf. The principal spoke to Jee about the marijuana leaf, saying it was unacceptable for school, just as it was unacceptable for her to carry her cigarettes in the front pocket of her jean jacket, the top of the red cigarette pack peeking out like a pocket handkerchief.

"Fuck him and his creepy rules," said Jee. "He's from the valley, everybody from the valley is Dutch Reformed Church, like Christian Fundamentalists, only stricter and creepier. My mother reads her Dutch Bible as if it's going to put food on the table. And my old man, when he's home and when he isn't using one of the family as a punching bag, puts on a suit every Sunday and acts so pious shit wouldn't melt in his mouth."

Jee was everything I was not. She was pretty and sexy, with almond eyes and full lips. I have plain black hair and a very dark complexion with a few seed-like freckles on my cheeks and nose.

"There were black Russians in your daddy's family," Mother explained. "Your grandfather had the blackest eyes I've ever seen."

It didn't matter how little I ate, I was still plump. I would have looked better if I could have afforded to dress like everyone else, but I wouldn't ask Mother for clothes money, I took whatever she scrounged at the Goodwill store. I tried for an after-school job, but there weren't many, and I lived so far from civilization.

Jee had arrived in Darktown only a few weeks before I did.

"Second day I got on the school bus, that big bastard Cory DeJong sat down beside me," she told me after we became friends. "First he grabbed my tits and I told him to fuck off. He sat back and looked surprised like these little Christian girls in their skirts and sweaters let him twist their nipples every morning. Then the son of a bitch leaned across me, pinning me to the wall of the bus, and shoved his hand down the front of my jeans, pushed my panties aside and had a finger inside me all in one motion. I shrieked, but nobody paid any attention except his friends who were all staring.

"Maybe these plain looking Christian girls do let him fuck with them, I thought. I wiggled like I was getting off on it. 'You don't need to hold me down,' I said. 'Move your arm and I'll do you, too.' He did.

"I reached over and unzipped his fly, his erection was just dying to escape his jeans. His buddies across the aisle were watching and drooling, their eyes glazed with lust. I took hold of his cock, nice and gentle until I got a good grip on it, then I bent and squeezed and pulled and he screamed like he was being fucking murdered. He leapt into the aisle, screeching and tears running down his cheeks, trying to stuff himself back into his pants. 'Anybody else want a turn?' I said to the boys across the aisle. That was the first and last time any of them fucked with me."

That story was true; it was confirmed to me by several other students. I wondered, though, about some of the other things Jee told me.

"I steal," she said. "Five-finger bargains, all my clothes." We were walking the back roads after school on a sunny, lazy spring day; there was calm water in the ditches while crocuses and daffodils spangled the right of way and the smell of warm tree sap filled the air. Jee took a deep drag on her cigarette.

"You know, you don't have to stop and give yourself up just because some security creep tells you to. Like the day I grabbed this belt." She fingered the heavy buckle with the marijuana leaf. "Just as I stepped out the door of the store, this old lady lays a hand on my arm and says, 'You better come with me, young lady.'

"Well, I gave her a push and beat it across the parking lot. For an old lady, she could move right along, but I got away with no sweat. Unless the security staff catches and holds you, the police don't put a high priority on shoplifting calls. You don't see a police car, siren wailing, on the way to chase down a kid who snatched a lipstick and ran. You ought to come with me sometime," Jee said. "You need some cool clothes."

She was right, I wore a plastic belt that was cracked and falling apart, and my jeans were the on-sale kind, with plain pockets and no rivets or sexy inseams.

"There's nothing I ain't seen," Jee said on another occasion. "On that fucking dairy farm, the five of us lived in one room with a bathroom tacked on as an afterthought. It came furnished with a few sticks and a picture of Jesus on each wall. Living in a place like that, you learn about sex quickly, not that I didn't know before. Our place in Holland wasn't much larger. They'd wait to have sex until they were sure us kids were asleep. But I'd out-wait them. For all her Bible reading and all she said about Papa being lazy and stupid, when he'd go down on her she'd fucking freak. I felt sorry for her because she couldn't scream out the way she wanted to. She'd take a mouthful of pillow to keep from yelling. Then she'd go down on him, for like hours, and he'd sigh and groan and say the sweetest, sexiest things to her. Seeing them like that made me realize what kept them together."

I had little idea of what she was talking about. Sex education in the schools was only a rumour, and there were no red-hot videos to watch on a VCR after school. While my parents, when my father was alive, were civil with each other, they did not show affection in public – my presence, or my brother's, being considered public – and it had never occurred to me that they might actually engage in sex at their advanced ages. What went on in the night behind their closed bedroom door was never a subject of speculation for me.

Many of the things Jee said shocked me. I tried not to let on, but I felt my face blush furiously. I was not quite able to picture the sex acts she described; they were just out of my vision like animals hidden in a thicket.

But there were some things Jee didn't share with me. A girl at school told me that Jee's father had been out of jail for some time, but had not come back to his family and was rumoured to have returned to Holland, perhaps had been deported because of his imprisonment. The girl said she thought that Jee and her family, as non-citizens, would be scheduled for deportation, too. But maybe the authorities didn't know where they were.

In the washroom at school, I commented on Jee's new lipstick, on the fact she always had cigarettes. "I got to fend for myself," she said. "The old lady doesn't have a dime. The church pays the rent, gives her a few dollars for food. Everybody else in Darktown is on welfare but she's afraid, and maybe with good reason, to get involved with the government in any way."

I'd seen Jee in the hall at school talking animatedly with a boy, one of the hoody types with a car that he drove at high speed up and down in front of the school at noon hour, wheels churning dust. Jee had her fingers on his bicep, leaning in, allowing her knee to rub his leg. When she left him, she had a pack of cigarettes three-quarters full. We went to the washroom, locked ourselves in a booth and lit up. "Those creepy types are the easiest to con," Jee said. "They're not shy, they think they're God's gift to horny girls. 'Come for a ride,' he said to me. 'Give me your cigarettes,' I said, and rubbed my tits against him, just one touch to let him know I was serious. Easier than taking candy from a baby. I got bus fare from him, too. We'll go into Vancouver after school. You need some clothes and I need some make-up. The great thing is, I can con him again tomorrow, and the next day, these creeps who think they're irresistible, who think every chick who makes eye contact with them is dying to suck their cock, are the easiest to rip off."

"Don't they catch on and become dangerous after you rip them off a few times?" I wanted to know.

"Not likely," she said, "They're marks. Their egos are too big, they consider being ripped off foreplay. Steve, the guy I was talking to today, is cute in a James Dean kind of way. I'd trade him a blow job some noon hour for a carton of cigarettes and bus fare for a week."

In Vancouver later, we strolled through a department store while she pocketed a lipstick I'd admired, stashed some perfume for herself and eye shadow for both of us. She was brazen about stealing, never skulking, or looking suspicious. She never glanced around to see if someone might be watching her.

"This is something you'd look really good in," she said in the clothing department, a few minutes later. She took a bomber jacket of soft brown leather off its hanger and held it up in front of me; it had silver buckles on the sleeves and shoulders. The price tag was astronomical.

"Go wait at the bus stop two blocks over," Jee said as we rode an escalator toward the first floor. Outside, she handed me the cosmetics.

"That jacket's got an electronic gadget on it, it'll shriek like a dying rabbit when I hit the street, but I'll be running full out when I activate the detector. I'll see you about the time the bus is due."

"Jee, you don't have to..." I began, but she was swallowed up by the lights of the store.

I paced around the bus stop for what seemed like forever. Just as the bus was pulling up and as I was trying to decide whether to catch it or wait for Jee – the bus only ran every two hours – she came bounding out of the park across the street, and pushed into line in front of me.

"Everything's cool," she said, "I think I lost them. There was a young guy chasing me, but I hid under a parked car." She pointed to an oil stain from the thigh to the knee of her jeans. When we were settled at the back of the bus she produced the bomber jacket from under the bulky sweater she was wearing.

"We'll take a rock and smash that tag off it," she said.

"I can't take it home," I said. "How would I explain it?"

"Say I gave it to you. Something I've outgrown. I'll come by if you want and show your mother how much taller and broader across the shoulders I am now. I'll tell her I've grown six inches in the last year."

Jee had an answer for everything. The explanation worked. My mother was on her way to work and wasn't really interested in what kind of jacket Jee was giving me, just one less item for her to worry about.

School let out for the summer and Jee and I, both unable to find jobs, spent a lot of time just hanging out. It was mid-summer when we met Frank and Angie. We were at the local café, spinning around on the counter stools, nursing Cokes and smoking, when they came in. They got out of a telephone company truck, one of those big white ones with blue lettering, with a hydraulic ladder on the back.

"I'm on call twenty-four hours,".Frank explained later. "If there's a storm I have to get up at 3:00 a.m. and repair the lines after trees fall on them or the wind blows them down."

Frank and Angie walked into the Drop Inn Café and took one of the two tables in the center of the room. There were four booths down the outside wall and ten counter stools. They ordered large Cokes with ice. We could feel Frank staring at us. He was stocky with a red complexion, heavy red hair to his collar and a matching walrus mustache. His eyes were a deep-set green-brown. Angie was very slim, wearing tight jeans and ankle-high black motorcycle boots, and a well-worn denim jacket. Her hair was a shining bay colour, worn very short in a pixie cut. Her features were delicate, her skin clear and pink, with blue eyes and a pinprick of a dimple to the left of her mouth.

Jee glanced over her shoulder a couple of times, once she spun slowly on her stool, boldly returning Frank's stare. As they were lighting cigarettes she stepped off her stool, her long hair swishing side to side making a quiet sensuous sound, and moved toward them.

"Got a cigarette?" she asked

"Sure," said Frank, taking the pack from his shirt pocket and holding it out to her. As Jee took a cigarette, Frank said to her, "Why don't you and your friend join us?"

We did.

"I see you're a collector," Frank said, staring at Jee. She shrugged her shoulders not understanding. "You've got cigarettes right in your pocket there." He pointed at her jean jacket, "yet you're smoking mine."

"Yeah," said Jee, smiling easily. "Other people's taste better. I like to stock up. One of my great fears is that I'll run out of cigarettes."

"Used to be mine, too," said Angie, "then I met Frank, and now he takes care of me."

I realized when Angie spoke, she had a breathy, child-like voice, that she was barely older than us, maybe eighteen. Frank was twenty-five at least, maybe closer to thirty.

"How long have you two been together?" Jee asked.

"Couple of years," said Frank. "I found her hitching on a back road out near Aggasiz prison; she looked to me like a dangerous escaped prisoner so I picked her up, took her captive and we've been together ever since. We got married three months ago, the day she turned eighteen. We got ourselves an A-frame way back in the foothills, no neighbours for two miles. We're renting but we've got an option to buy if it stays private. Privacy's very important to us."

I didn't really like Frank, though Jee seemed to, and Angie did little but smoke and smile her little tic of a smile when someone said something that interested her. I didn't like the way Frank looked at Jee, or at me, for that matter, there was something commanding about his stare, something vaguely frightening, yet I wondered if I could resist it if it were turned full on me. I also didn't like the way he treated Angie, as if she were his personal property, something bought and paid for.

"I do most of Angie's thinking for her," he said at one point, while Angie nodded agreement. "She pretty well does what I tell her."

I kicked Jee's foot under the table but she scarcely glanced at me, her eyes were locked on Frank's face, as she pulled smoke deep into her lungs.

"You should come visit us some time," Frank said when we got up to leave.

"I thought you liked privacy?" I said.

He scowled at me, and I felt my heart rate increase.

"We make exceptions." He gave us directions, drew a little map on a napkin. "Or you could visit Angie during the day. She gets a little lonely up there sometimes, and she's got all the latest records.

I set up a charge for her at the record store." He pointed across the street at the blinking sign The Platinum Disc.

"There's something creepy about them," I said to Jee, as we walked out of town. "I didn't like the way he stared at us, at you."

"I think he's sexy," Jee said.

"Well, I do, too, in a kind of dangerous way."

"And imagine being like Angie, having your own house, getting to stay home all day and play records, being looked after, not have to rip people off for bus fare, or bum cigarettes."

"Everything has a price," I said, but left it at that, not adding that I wondered what price Angie was paying.

We did visit though, a couple of afternoons later. It was nearly five miles. As we walked, the bush got denser, the sky more sheltered, and the public road turned into a trail which ended when a private road began; the only visible tracks were of Frank's telephone company truck. The private road was heavily posted. NO TRESPASSING. NO HUNTING. PRIVATE PROPERTY. PATROLLED BY SMITH AND WESSON.

The private road was damp and mossy. Willows grasped at our hair as we walked and ferns plucked at the legs of our jeans as the road narrowed. Ropes of moss dangled from cypress branches. Cheeky columbines, Indian paintbrush, and some waxy yellow flower grew in the centre of the road. We came round a sharp bend into a clearing and there was the A-frame, brown as sand. Its windows, running from floor to the pointed peak of the building, gave off a bluish light, a cloud reflected in the topmost triangle of glass.

We were at the back of the building. There was a large deck, newly stained, furnished with white wooden chairs and a white picnic table. We walked up the four stairs, crossed the deck and peered into the living room through the sliding glass doors. We had to put our hands on either side of our faces to deflect the light. An expensive black leather sofa faced us. There was a stone fireplace in the background. The deck narrowed and continued around to the front of the house where a new red Datsun was parked, and the spot where the telephone company truck usually rested was clearly defined. In front, a heavily forested hillside rose at a harsh angle. The front was also glass panels with a large cedar door in the middle. The kitchen was to the right of the door. We could see Angie at the sink doing dishes and listening to music at high volume from a new hi-fi set in the living room.

She was startled when we tapped on the glass but seemed happy to see us. Inside, the smell of cedar prickled my nose. Angie offered us coffee, or a choice from an assortment of soft drinks in a startlingly large refrigerator, but before we could make a choice she interrupted to say, "No, why don't I make us drinks? There's this drink Frank taught me, a daiquiri, it has lime it in. I'd never seen a lime until Frank came home with them. It's delicious."

Angie got out three small glasses and a glass pitcher into which she measured white rum and lime juice, stirred in sugar, then took the pitcher to the fridge, which on command dispensed crushed ice into the pitcher. A minor miracle to us – in Darktown, an apple box nailed to the wall outside a north window served as ice box, fridge and food storage unit.

"Take it easy," Angie said, after Jee drained half her glass in a swallow. "It tastes like fruit juice but it's got a kick to it." It was my first taste of liquor and maybe Jee's, too, though she would never admit it if it was. The three of us smoked and sipped daiquiris.

"Do you get lonely out here, so far from everything?" Jee asked.

"No. Frank takes good care of me. We need to be off by ourselves. Sometimes we get…pretty noisy."

She smiled her tic of a smile indicating with an upward movement of her head, the upstairs bedroom. Earlier we had been given a tour of the house which stopped at the foot of the stairs.

"I haven't cleaned up there yet," Angie said. "Besides, there are things up there you guys shouldn't see." She smiled mysteriously. "At least until we get to know each other better."

We had two daiquiris each and listened to Angie's records. The drinks seemed to make Angie more talkative. Jee's cheeks flushed and she laughed more loudly than usual. For me, the room seemed occasionally to fall off its axis; instead of feeling happy, I felt anxious and a little depressed.

"You're welcome to stay until Frank gets home," Angie said. "He'll be here about five."

"No. I have to get home," I said, before Jee could argue, though it was a lie, my mother would be at work until midnight.

"I should start dinner," Angie said. "Frank's teaching me to cook." She laughed. "I've had some real disasters. Frank gets…annoyed when that happens, and…" She smiled her curious little smile again, and bent to pull an orange mesh sack of potatoes from a cupboard drawer.

Jee dawdled on the walk home, hoping, I'm sure, that we'd meet Frank. I walked fast, breathing the ferny air, often getting a half block or more ahead of Jee.

"There's something eerie about both of them," I said to Jee later in the evening. We were sitting on the rickety steps outside the cottage when I lived. My mouth was furry and I had a slight headache.

"I think they're great," Jee said. "Imagine having a sexy guy like Frank to take care of you. It would be like heaven."

"There's something mean about him," I said.

"Guys are like that," Jee said. "I wonder what's upstairs that she wouldn't show us? Fuck movies? Sex toys. There's this whole store in Vancouver sells crotchless panties, oils, creams, and fucking dildos big as your arm. One of the DeJong twins brought a catalog to school full of pictures of vibrators, leather panties and bras, and photographs of naked girls with their hands tied, giving blow jobs. You were sick that day, remember? So you didn't see it. I wonder if…" but Jee's voice trailed off.

"Whatever it is, I wouldn't want to see it," I said, which wasn't really true, but I felt somehow obligated to argue.

"You're sure a spoilsport, Cathy. You'll never take a risk, you'll live in a slum like this for the rest of your life. You're not a leader, you're a follower. Actually you're not even a good follower."

"Thanks a lot. But what's any of that got to do with whether I like Frank and Angie?"

"It's your attitude. You go with me when I steal smokes, make-up, clothes. When do you ever risk anything? Frank's a risk. All guys are risks. Angie took a risk and now she taken care of for life."

I couldn't articulate my fear, and I told myself that maybe that was all it was, fear. So I said nothing more.

At Jee's insistence we visited Angie again a few days later.

"Frank was real pissed off I didn't insist you guys stay for dinner," Angie said. "He must have just missed you. He even drove back to look for you and we went into town that evening hoping to see you guys at the café."

Jee and Angie had daiquiris again. I drank Orange Crush over a full tumbler of ice cubes. It was while I watched them laughing, chattering, smoking, or rather when Angie went to the fridge for the pitcher of daiquiris that I noticed what it was about her that made me uneasy. It was the way she walked with an exaggeratedly correct posture, like an old person with fused discs. She moved carefully as if she was in pain, something that thrilled as much as it frightened me. However, Angie showed no signs of pain as she threw herself into Frank's arms when he came through the door. She had been barefoot when we arrived, but after a while, in preparation for Frank's arrival, she put on her black boots and a creamy satin blouse that tucked into her jeans, showing off her tiny breasts. I noticed that she made a point of not inviting us up to the bedroom while she changed.

"Frank likes me to look a certain way when he gets home," she said, "and he doesn't ask that much for all he does in return."

After leaping into his arms, Angie kissed him passionately, wrapping her legs around his waist. Frank gripped her denim-clad ass with his stubby-fingered hands that had little tufts of red hair at each knuckle. Frank did most of the cooking. He was mildly impatient with Angie's ineptness in the kitchen.

"Can you cook?" he asked Jee at one point, after Angie had sliced a tomato up and down instead of crossways.

"Try me," said Jee ambiguously, a little drunk, as was Angie.

We ate on the deck, steak and French fries, a feast for me and Jee. Frank had changed into Bermuda shorts and as I watched, the red hair on his legs was turned golden by the sun. Afterwards, we sat around drinking coffee and smoking. Frank brought out a bottle of Southern Comfort, along with thimble-sized glasses. I refused because I didn't like the aftermath of the daiquiris on the previous visit. And I knew liquor would make me lose some control, and I didn't feel this was a situation where I could afford that.

Later, as the sun was setting into the forest, as Angie returned from the washroom, Frank pulled her into his lap in the big, white deck chair. He kissed her for a long time, arranging her body, his left hand gripping a breast, not fondling but clutching, his right caressing her satin blouse over her belly before settling into the crotch of her jeans, his big hand spreading her already open legs.

I felt terribly uncomfortable. Like a spy. I glanced at Jee, who, a forgotten cigarette burning uncomfortably close to her fingers, stared at them as if conjured. I could see that Angie was responding; she had one of her small hands down the front of Frank's shorts. They were kissing ferociously now, Angie thrusting her pelvis against Frank's big hand.

I scraped back my chair and stood up. Frank broke the kiss, smiled at us past Angie's head as she melted into his neck.

"I was going to offer to drive you ladies back," he said, "but it appears we have a situation here."

He stared boldly at us while continuing to rub Angie's crotch. Jee took a deep drag on her cigarette. "How about if we see you early evening tomorrow at the café? Unless, of course, one or both of you would like to join us upstairs?"

He heaved himself up out of the chair, Angie nestled in his arms, licking his neck. He stared searchingly at us as he walked into the house. I took Jee's hand and pulled her away.

"No, thank you," I said, speaking for both of us. Jee frowned at me as I led her down the steps to the grass and in the direction of the road.

Jee was sullen on the walk home.

"You could have gone if you wanted to," I said.

"And leave you sitting, or to walk home by yourself."

"Would you have if I wasn't there?"

"I think so. The idea's so scary, and so exciting. And Frank's so sexy."

"I don't think so."

"Different strokes," said Jee.

"What would three people do?"

"If you have to ask you've got no business being there."

"You're so experienced," I said nastily. "Seriously, how could you know?"

"Instinct," said Jee. "Instinct, and willingness to take risks."

Frank and Angie were at the café next evening.

"Sorry about last night," Frank said, "but a call from nature always takes top priority."

Angie smiled her little tic of a smile. Frank treated us to sundaes, pineapple for me, chocolate for everyone else. Then we walked around the small shopping district.

"Let me buy you each a little present of apology," Frank said. He seemed to know exactly what pleased us, a carton of cigarettes for Jee, eight packs of twenty-five, an expensive lipstick for me. I almost went for a shade called White Peach that would have set off my dark complexion, but at the last moment I remained traditional and chose Ripe Raspberry.

A few nights later, Jee and I hung around the café until closing, both hoping that Frank and Angie would show up. At the same time,

I was scared that they would. We walked off into the night, breathing the cool, damp air, hearing the gravel crackle under our shoes, the occasional scuttle of an animal in the underbrush. An almost full moon illuminated our way. We giggled, smoked, walked, drawn it seemed to Frank and Angie.

When we got to the house, everything was dark, the moon reflecting off the topmost triangle of window. We walked around the building. The Datsun and the telephone company truck were cold and dewy. A raccoon clacked across the deck while we stood statue-like on the lawn, staring. We watched the house for a long time, imagining we heard things, groaning, crying, the more violent sounds of love.

The next night, the Saturday of the Labour Day weekend – we'd begin our final year of high school on Tuesday – we tried again, only leaving the café earlier. As we neared the clearing, the glow was like a sunrise, a forest fire.

The house was totally illuminated, and the sounds ensuing were not like anything we'd heard, or imagined. We stopped just out of view of the house. I thought the sounds were of a bird, or birds, clattering, flopping, crying out to escape. Jee gripped my hand. We advanced across the lawn to the edge of the deck. The night was yellow and black. Every light in the A-frame was on. Music was playing on the hi-fi, Donovan, Rita Coolidge, loud enough to carry to the edge of the deck but not overpowering.

We glanced at each other, inched up the steps to the deck, straining forward trying to make out what was happening. The glass doors were wide open. Frank had his back to us. Angie was bent over the arm of the black leather sofa. She was naked from the waist up, her face against the leather seat cushion.

Her arms were tied behind her back. Frank was wielding a belt or a length of leather strap, bringing it down hard across Angie's ass, the backs of her legs. Her ankles were tied with a leather thong. It became clear as we watched that this was not a punishment inflicted in anger, for the strokes of the strap were often a half minute, even a minute apart.

Frank was talking to her, constantly, though we couldn't quite make out what he was saying, for he was speaking in a measured, almost conversational voice. There was the sound of the strap striking, her cries and whimpering, the soothing music, the unintelligible words Frank spoke, then the strap again.

After we'd watched five or six strokes, Frank talked for a longer time, as if he were making a serious argument, as if Angie was in a position to do something, anything. He bent close to Angie to hear something she said. He nodded. He set the strap down, and reaching under her undid the zipper on Angie's jeans. He pulled them down a few inches at a time until they were bunched about her knees.

Still talking to her, he picked up the strap, and at that moment the record ended and suddenly we could hear Frank's voice clearly, even though he was speaking toward the interior of the house.

"Let me hear it, baby. Tell me how much you want it. Show me how much you want it."

Angie was crying, whimpering, babbling, but I know I saw her raise her ass an inch or two in response to Frank's words.

"That's it, baby, that's it," he crooned, then brought the strap down twice in succession, once across her bare ass, the second across the backs of her thighs.

Angie screamed, and we could make out, "No more. No more," as Frank began talking to her again.

Jee let go of my hand and strode across the deck toward the open door. I followed, my heart hammering. But they were so involved they didn't see or hear us until Jee tapped loudly on the glass wall beside the door.

"What's going on?" she said, her voice ragged.

When Frank turned I expected the worst. I thought he might begin flailing at us with the belt. But if he was surprised, he didn't show it. He gave us a sly, knowing, half smile.

"Everything's cool," he said. "We play a lot of games. We get off on it."

But it was Angie's reaction to our arrival that stunned us. Eyes wild and swollen from crying, her face pushed into the leather of the sofa cushion, she screamed, "Get away from us!"

Her voice was shrill and full of tears, like a child throwing a tantrum.

"Get away from us!" she shrieked again. "You've spoiled everything. This is why we live so far from people. You've spied on us. Get away, leave us alone."

We retreated to the deck. Frank followed us to the door.

"It's cool," he said, the strap still dangling at the end of his arm. "You best go now. Everything will be cool tomorrow. She'll be okay. I'll have a talk with her. Maybe we'll see you at the café."

As we walked into the darkness the music came on again. Donovan singing about San Francisco and flowers. For a long ways, we'd hear the strap like a car backfiring, we heard it until we were so far away it must have been only memory.

"Wow!" said Jee.

"It's sick," I said.

"I've never seen anything so incredible," Jee said. Her breath was shallow and I'm sure I could hear her heart beating. Her step slowed as she lit a cigarette, and even over the sound of our footsteps I could hear the force with which she pulled the hot smoke into her lungs.

Later, as I recalled the scene on the deck, I wondered if Jee had been alone, would her purposeful stride toward Frank and Angie have been to intercede or to join them?

"I don't want to see them again," I said to Jee the next afternoon. "Surely they won't have the nerve to show up at the café."

But, as we walked toward the café after school a couple of days later, Frank's truck was parked at the curb.

"Wait here," Jee said. I did, though I should have gone with her.

She straightened her back, walked to the window of the truck, leaned in, her breasts on the window ledge. I remember she was wearing a raspberry-coloured sweater. A moment later, she stepped back, walked around to the passenger side, opened the door and got in. The truck eased away from the curb. She didn't even wave.

"I said to him, 'Whatever you do with her I want you to do with me.'"

We were in a cubicle in the school washroom. Jee lit cigarettes for each of us.

"You didn't."

She smiled. She unbuckled her jeans and moving cautiously sat down. I saw all that I needed to. I thought my heart would burst from my chest.

"I stayed overnight," Jee said. "I'm gonna, like, work for them."

"Work?" I echoed stupidly.

"Like housekeeping. That's what I told my old lady. What she don't know won't hurt her."

There were so many questions I couldn't bring myself to ask. I refused to go with Jee to the café in case we ran into them. I was the outsider now, they couldn't be themselves around me. They had too many secrets.

Jee relayed an invitation to dinner from Frank and Angie.

I couldn't make myself say the words. I just kept shaking my head.

Then they were gone. Jee was spending at least three nights a week with Frank and Angie and often missing class. Frank dropped her off at school on the mornings she did attend.

In mid-September, she didn't come to school on Friday or again on Monday.

Monday night I walked the lonely miles to the A-frame, only to find it scary and silent. Leaves crunched under my shoes as I walked across the empty deck and peered through the fading light into the vacant living room. The empty house creaked ominously in the night. In the light wind, tree branches dragging against the eaves frightened me.

"Acht, gone nord. Work. Work housekeep," said Jee's mother, shrugging her shoulders, when I went to their house the next day.

A few days later, I saw a telephone company truck parked by a house under construction. I leaned in the passenger window, the way Jee did with Frank.

"Do you know what's become of Frank?" I asked, "Stocky guy with red hair, big mustache." The driver was dark and thin, eating a lunch of fish and chips, wrapped in newspaper.

"Took a transfer way up north, place called Hundred Mile House, way out in the wilderness."

I hoped Jee might write, or even Frank. I'd visit if they asked.

Last week, I took a worn-out black shoulder bag of my mother's, one she would never use again, from her closet, filled it with empty cartons, newspapers, junk and took the bus into Vancouver. In a clothing store on Robson Street, I tried on a pair of Levis. Leaving my old unstylish jeans and the purse behind in the changing booth, I admired the fit of the new ones in the mirror. "I want to see how they look in daylight," I said. No one stopped me as I stepped into the street and kept going. Jee would have been proud of me.

CHAPTER 11

She doesn't like me, does she? Jones said as he poured me a coffee. We both knew he meant Christie. "She knows I know she's a fraud."

"How can you say that? She's had a bad life, right from the get go."

"The odour of fraud about her is stronger than frying onions. Wylie, she's a user, a con artist. You cannot believe anything she tells you. I repeat, anything."

"If she's such a user, what could she want with me? I don't have any money, property. My assets consist of my clothes and a second hand typewriter."

"She's taken your heart. That's worth more than any amount of material goods."

"I've given it to her. She refuses to let me support her. She pays half the rent."

"Right, and where does she get her money? I've never seen that chick do a day's work in all the time you've hung out with her."

"It's a secret. A perfectly logical explanation. Well, mostly logical."

"She could be an actress if she wanted to. She plays the victim to the hilt, and she plays it well. 'Poor me.' that's her mantra. And you swallow every tale she tells you. Trust me, Wylie, I was born being able to suss out a phony. And your Christie is a phony through and through."

"You know I don't care what you think. She inspires me. She says something to me, looks at me, touches me a certain way, and I rush to my typewriter and write better material than I've ever written in my life. You have to agree with that, you've seen the drivel I was writing before I met Christie."

"I have to admit you've improved a hundred percent, but my guess is it was just time and patience and practise. I don't believe for a moment that Christie had anything to do with it."

"Alright," I said, reaching into the manila folder I always carry. "Read this, compare it with "The Spaceship that Crashed on a Cattle Ranch," tell me Christie didn't have anything to do with the improvement."

KISSING PETTY

There is a famous book of photography, published years ago but still in print, called *Joys and Sorrows*. I am in it. I am one of the sorrows. I am seventeen, on my knees, fists clenched, facial features distorted in grief. I look younger than seventeen, a wide sunburned face with red hair in a brush cut, a pear-shaped body. I am wearing an unattractive short-sleeved shirt with alternating horizontal stripes of kelly green and white. There is a jam-like smear of blood under and around my mouth.

The very next year I grew, shot up like kudzu, a full eight inches to six foot two, thinned down and stayed that way. Now, in middle age, my red hair has turned white as powdered snow, my always-ruddy complexion is pink as a baby's. I scarcely recognize the stocky, suffering child in the photograph taken by a local journalist who happened to be in the right place at the right time. I look at the agonized face and realize how lucky I've been since that summer. My life has not contained a lot of anguish. A college degree, a rise to executive VP in the oil industry, a long marriage, two children who now have degrees, marriages, children of their own.

The photograph is my posterity, my claim to fame. When they were young, my children marveled that the kneeling stranger with the contorted facial features was their father. Each carried the book to Show and Tell. Not that I haven't spent an inordinate amount of time thinking about that day and the months that preceded it. As my life oozes on, I continue to wonder if there wasn't something I could have done to prevent the tragedy of that day.

I joined the Drama Club to be near Petty. Petty's name will always be a mystery. Like most of us in that industrial city, her family came from Eastern Europe. I always assumed Petty was short for something. I remember a couple of boys teasing her, saying that her real name was Petunia, and they brought up the name of a cartoon character of the era named Petunia Pig. There was a Chinese girl in our school whose name was Pretty. Pretty Pong, and I was told her sister's name was Heavenly Pong. I remember Petty giving those boys a luxuriant smile without giving away any information. The smile was enough for them. They let her alone. If that had happened to me, I would have been humiliated, and the nickname, whether it was Petunia or something else embarrassing, would have stuck to me like lint to velvet.

The finale of our year in the Drama Club was a one-act play festival. Earlier in the year, I had done my acting by starring as Falstaff in an excerpt from Shakespeare so I was allowed to direct one of the festival plays and star in it if I chose to. Through a complicated selection process I won first choice for an actress for my play and I chose Petty. The play, a melodrama, was set in a mining town, a one-industry town not unlike our own; the hero was a handsome young miner who rescues the local waitress from the clutches of a conniving banker. I could have played the hero, but who would have believed me in the part? I chose instead a tall, pale young man, who I thought would look convincing in coveralls and a miner's lamp, and who I hoped I could persuade to project his voice. I played the restaurant owner, a middle-aged man, so I could be on stage for the whole production and feed lines to my actors when they got in trouble. During the inevitable happy ending, as the pale young man, who turned out to be a better actor than I'd anticipated, was kissing Petty, I was blustering about tossing the evil banker out the back door into a snow drift, wishing all the while that it was me who was holding Petty in my arms. There was one scene in the middle of the play where, after both hero and villain have departed, Petty crosses the stage to me, takes my hand and says, "Mr. Stockton, I need to talk to you," then leads me onto the apron where she pours out her troubles. My character's name in the script was Shiftlett or something close to that, but each actor slurred the word so we changed it to my real last name. With Petty's warm, soft hand in mine, I was in heaven. That brief walk and the scene that followed were the highlights of the play for me.

The four weeks of rehearsals were conducted mainly in school stairwells, but twice, when the weather was too beautiful to stay indoors, we walked across Bainbridge Avenue, the main street of town, to a small park where the students convened at lunch and before and after class. Because smoking was not allowed on school property, students who smoked had to cross the street to the park. Sometimes I'd go there and stand around just so I could watch Petty smoking. She rode a bus in from a nearby suburb and was always at the park when I reached school in the morning. I began arriving earlier.

I dreamed constantly of Petty falling in love with me, I dreamed that Petty's gorgeous eyes had X-ray vision that could see through to the smart me, the kind me, the loving me. Then I'd look in the mirror, at the chubby, pear-shaped kid with cheeks that looked like I'd just come in from a blizzard, and the dream would fade away. Petty was usually with a group of girls all dressed in the uniform of the day, blue jeans and denim jackets; they would stand around in the leafy sunlight and gossip, giggle and smoke. I was continually relieved that, while Petty dated occasionally, she didn't have a steady boyfriend, though she was sometimes seen walking with a heavyset boy named Carl Brost who was centre of the football team. Many of the girls were as good as married, wearing their boyfriend's school jackets, necking in front of the lockers in the school hallways, disappearing into their boyfriend's cars at lunch hour, the cars clunking off toward a make-out spot down by the river, or if the boyfriend's car was inoperative, as they often were, the couple melted into the oak grove behind the park, the girl carrying a blanket from the car. But Petty was available. There was always hope for a miracle.

What did Petty have? She was beautiful, but not spectacularly so, her long hair was golden, her complexion clear with a darkish tinge. Her eyes were chameleons, appearing blue in some light, green in others, gray flecked with gold at other times. She had a good figure, but she exuded such an aura of goodwill, of energy, of high spirits, that her looks became immaterial. There is such a fine line between sexiness and sluttiness. Other girls could have dressed the way Petty did and been dismissed at a glance as attention seekers. Yet Petty could wear a demure skirt and high-necked blouse and appear sexier than the braless girls who wore mini and micro skirts that showed practically everything. And Petty could wear tight Levis with a man's white shirt, the tails tied in a knot across her belly, without appearing cheap. I concluded that Petty was born with presence, with charisma, with class.

My own family was unspectacular. Both my parents were second generation Americans; my father's family was from Ireland, my mother's from Yugoslavia. Dad worked in the pulp mill. He'd bring home beer with his Friday paycheque and he and mother would drink after we kids were supposedly asleep; they would get loud and dance up a storm, sometimes by themselves, sometimes with friends. But that was it. They were never abusive. We were never neglected. Yet, they had no ambitions beyond the next pay day. I had ambitions, vague though they were at the time. I wanted to better myself. I wanted to live the life in magazine ads – new cars, beautifully furnished homes, world travel. On Saturdays, I earned a few dollars shoveling shavings off the roof of one of the pulp mills outside of town. With my earnings, I joined the High School Investment Club. I took a First Aid course, learned how to apply a tourniquet, put a splint on a broken limb, and how to administer CPR – a process that could literally bring someone back from the dead, though I believe it had another name in those days, perhaps artificial respiration.

There was no budget for the school drama festival, costumes were whatever each actor could come up with. I remember helping to fashion a miner's lamp for my leading actor from a soup can and a pickle dish. Petty appeared in a waitress uniform, pale yellow with brown trim, with a matching cap, like nurses used to wear. She drew laughs from the audience that I hadn't even suspected were in the script. Petty won Best Actress, and, because of her performance, I won as Best Director and our play was chosen Best of Festival.

After the festival, the drama teacher invited the participants to her house for homemade chili. There was dancing, and eventually singing. I danced with Petty to a dreamy waltz. Petty was wearing a soft white jacket and a dark green skirt. As the dance ended we walked through French doors onto the huge deck and stood at the railing staring into the azalea-scented darkness. Petty lit a cigarette. Something else about Petty – she made everyone around her feel at ease. Shy and tongue-tied as I was, I was able to talk and even joke with Petty. Our shoulders touched. I was already planning that after I kissed her I would ask if I could see her home. Another few seconds and I would have been kissing Petty. But we were interrupted by the football player, Carl Brost, who wasn't a member of the drama club. He came stomping onto the deck in his work boots.

"Thought I'd give you a ride home," he said, ignoring my presence.

"Whatever gave you an idea like that?" said Petty, keeping her voice perfectly friendly, but letting Carl know he was interrupting a private party in more ways than one.

But we all went inside and eventually Petty did leave with Carl because he lived in her neighborhood and, of course, I didn't have a car.

At lunch hour a few days later, Petty and Carl Brost were arguing about something in the park.

As she was walking stiffly away, Petty spotted me. "Mr. Stockton, I need to talk to you," she said. Taking my hand in hers she led me toward the school. Petty, holding my hand. Petty, not embarrassed to be seen with me. Unfortunately, my bliss lasted less than half a minute. The traffic light was green. A dozen kids were loitering about the light. Petty led me into the street. And then she was gone. Snatched from my grasp like a handbag torn away by a thief. A car had come through the red light at full speed and struck Petty, tossed her backward across the hood and into the windshield. Then, as the car was braking madly, the scream of tires like a dying animal, her body fell to the pavement after being carried about ninety feet. I saw it all in slow motion, have continued to see it all the years of my life; her body on the hood of the car, then falling, the terrible sound of her head hitting the pavement. I'm told that from where I stood I couldn't have heard that sound, but I wake to it in the night even now.

Everyone was stunned. The odour of burning rubber filled the air. The car had finally stopped a few yards beyond where Petty lay in the gutter. Everyone seemed frozen in time except me. I wanted Petty back, I wanted to erase the past few seconds, I wanted to feel Petty holding my hand, leading me toward a wonderful unexpected future. I ran toward Petty.

The four boys in the car were all from the school. The car, a blue and white two-tone Ford, was driven by a marginal thug named Beale. He eventually served six months in jail and lost his license for a year. I attended the trial, watched him at the defence table wearing a brown suit, his hair cut short, while his lawyer whined about Beale's underprivileged childhood and how a momentary mistake in judgement shouldn't affect his whole life. I've been told he later worked as a gas jockey, and at seasonal construction work, and that he died a few years ago of lung cancer. I don't believe in divine retribution. I hope he was unhappy each moment of his miserable life on earth.

The boy in the front passenger seat, a friend of Petty's, rolled down the window, and reaching awkwardly around, tried to grab her clothing as she struck the windshield. He missed. If he'd caught her clothes it might have saved her life. He apparently had a conscience. It is said that even though he was only a passenger, he never drove a car again, that he became a drifter and drank himself to death before he was thirty.

What could Petty have wanted with me? Was it a problem she wanted to discuss with me? Was it something more?

"Mr. Stockton, I need to talk to you." Petty's last words. What was she about to tell me? Had Petty's beautiful eyes really seen beyond my body, had she seen the smart me, the funny me, the kind me, the me who was crazy in love with her?

The first thing I did when I reached Petty was to feel for a pulse, first her neck, then her wrist. Nothing. She was so much smaller than I remembered, so limp, so much heavier in her unconscious state that I would ever have imagined. I tried to recall everything I had learned in my First Aid course. I positioned Petty, turned her gently onto her back, tipped her head back, held her nose, pressed my mouth against hers, breathing puffs of air into her, ignoring the blood that was trickling from her mouth.

I worked feverishly, minute after minute, sweat pouring into my eyes, dripping like rain onto Petty's beautiful face. After what seemed like an hour, the ambulance arrived. It was seconds after that when my photograph was taken by a local reporter who just happened to be passing the accident scene, the flashbulbs of his awkward silver camera crackling like popcorn. In the photo that appeared in that book, there is a splotch of white in the background that is recognizable to me as the coat of an attendant who is kneeling over Petty, perhaps attaching an IV to her arm. In the bottom right hand corner is the flared leg of Petty's jeans, a stockinged foot sticking out. The impact had separated Petty from her shoes.

The school flag flew at half-staff the remainder of the term. There was a smear of blood on the windshield of the death car. I saw it afterward. I have often wondered who washed it off.

CHAPTER 12

Lovers often end up telling each other everything. What passes for courtship is really two monologues, two oral histories. When one, or the other, or both have revealed everything, silence sets in and the relationship winds down like a child's top spinning ever more slowly. Christie's questions pried open doors I had closed and sealed. Yet, I could ferret nothing pertinent from Christie. While she told me more than I wanted to know about someone, it seemed unlikely to me that the someone was her. Her tales were like kaleidoscopes, whirling, whirling. Everything she said was filled with contradictions.

Christie loved children. She entertained them in cafes, fussed over them in parks and department stores.

"Have you ever thought of having a baby?" I asked.

"Increasing the number of people you love won't make you care less for any one of them," Christie said. She was sitting on my big teak bed, wearing jeans, a glittery t-shirt, leaning forward, her hands on her ankles.

"You didn't answer my question."

"I tried it once but I didn't like it," Christie snapped. She took a deep breath. "Christie's baby would have been five last month, if she'd lived. I lost her when I was seventeen."

So that part was true. Or was it?

"I'm so sorry," I said, "it was thoughtless of me to ask. You've told me the story, I should have known better."

The Muses, they say, are often unable to distinguish between truth and fantasy.

"You told me when we met that you were twenty-six. You don't have any stretch marks."

"You don't have to have any fucking stretch marks to have given birth to a dead baby at six months." She threw an ashtray at the wall as she slammed out of the room. "And I'm allowed to lie about my age, all women are allowed."

What could I say? I was very nice to her for the next several days. Maybe the bad marriage story was the truth.

Jones was not impressed. "You know those signs on construction projects, the ones that say, DANGER EXPLOSIVES? That's what Christie, or whatever her name is, should wear around her neck instead of jewellery. She's gonna do something really weird, weirder than you can even imagine. She's gonna rob a bank, kill a couple of innocent people. Wouldn't surprise me if she murdered someone, I just hope it's not you. At first I thought she was just eccentric, a pathological liar. But she's more than that, she's cunning too, and crazy. Don't you notice, Wylie? She's crazy as a bed bug."

"I'll cop to eccentric. Is that your opinion as a PhD in philosophy?"

"I don't need a PhD to recognize a head case. I see her in here almost every day when you two come in for coffee. I see the way she looks at you. That's all I need for my diagnosis."

I changed the subject by regurgitating an anonymous quote about philosophers in general: "There are three kinds of deceiver – those who deceive themselves but not others; knaves, those who deceive others but not themselves; and philosophers, those who deceive both themselves and others."

"Write about who you would like to be," whispered Christie. We were lying in bed, tangled up in each other's arms after making love.

"I don't think it would make a good story."

"Try anyway. Be someone you know you could never be."

"Well, I have a law-abiding heart. I seldom take chances. I'd like to be someone totally without a conscience."

When I got up and went to my typewriter, nothing came. Eventually, though, my fingers started to move.

KEEPING A PET WOLF

Sister Veronica was so desperate for a convert that she accepted Rostashewitz, the one-eyed wino, without stopping to consider that his conversion might not be entirely genuine.

Actually, Sister Veronica was not entirely genuine herself, not that she had hidden motives or engaged in any fraudulent practices. She lived off the interest from an inheritance, rented a storefront just off East Hastings Street, with seating for twenty-five on yellow, varnished folding chairs. There was a small altar, a nondenominational cross on the wall. In the back was a kitchen, manned by a retired logging camp cook named Pop, who prepared the evening meal in return for use of one of the six small bedrooms upstairs.

Pop was stringy, arthritic, and not the least religious. In return for free room and board he allowed himself a certain amount of pretence, along with an occasional "Amen" or "Hallelujah."

Sister Veronica was in her mid-thirties, blonde haired, blue eyed, with a wide open pink face. She could have been beautiful, but she did not allow herself to wear worldly clothes. As a girl she had always admired the appearance of the Grey Nuns, and when she started her own mission she had a tailor create dresses resembling those of that order, except that each had a band about two inches wide on the right sleeve, the orange of a robin's breast.

Although Sister Veronica came from a long line of religious fanatics, she had not studied theology. She had a degree in interior design with a minor in philosophy from a two-year community college.

Vancouver may be the only city in North America with an overabundance of missions. Winos can be choosy. Pop was not that good a cook, Sister Veronica not a spellbinding preacher. Therefore, the Sisters of a Merciful God Mission was usually empty. Only the real troublesome winos, the ones who had stopped removing their clothes when they performed bodily functions, the mentally discouraged, the total lunatics, ever graced Sister Veronica's mission.

Sister Veronica liked to walk through the streets of Vancouver's skid row early in the mornings when the weather was often sunny and cool, the air not yet polluted by barroom exhausts and traffic fumes. She would always linger for a while at The Corner, a dismal concrete triangle on East Hastings Street at Carrall, where the unfortunate slumped on stone benches, or on the concrete-block-covered earth, many crushing brown-bagged bottles to their chests as if they were precious pets.

She would speak to the derelicts in a breathless, whispery voice.

"Do you ever give a thought to the Kingdom?" she asked rhetorically, but her feathery voice floated away like a lost butterfly. "This life has not been kind to you, but all is not lost. It is not too late to prepare for your eternity in the Kingdom."

Those conscious enough to hear stared at the concrete as though it was a tabloid with a story and pictures about King Kong being found alive and well in Crete.

One morning, as she moved disappointedly away from The Corner, she spotted Rostashewitz, his hands cupped about the head of a parking meter, as if he were holding a horse by the ears, while he vomited into the gutter.

Rostashewitz was an obscene whisper of a man, with wild, receding hair showing a freckled, sunburned scalp. His face was like a dry river bed covered in patches of blue stubble that looked like tacks driven through his cheeks from the inside. His right eye was simply gone. A runaway, spying on the world from the leafy branches of an aspen grove, or sold as a transplant in order to buy liquor. Perhaps, these many years later, the eye, still bloodshot, glaring from a beautiful girl's face. Rostashewitz's eyelid was apparently sewn shut.

Rostashewitz was born a wino waiting to happen.

"You're gonna grow up to be a rotten drunk just like your old man," Rostashewitz's mother hollered at him a half dozen times a day, every day of his life, until, when he was nine, she was arrested, along with her boyfriend of the moment, a lank black man with a pink shirt and a black sombrero with a silver band. They were busted for holding up a 7-Eleven store with a toy gun, escaping temporarily with fourteen dollars and six packs of cigarettes.

Surprisingly, Rostashewitz cleaned up rather well. Showered, shaved, dressed in clean clothes, he was much younger than Sister Veronica had first supposed. No older than she. Within two days, Sister Veronica had taken Rostashewitz to her bed. Under the covers, Rostashewitz snuffled and growled while Sister Veronica wailed in ecstasy. Upstairs in his monk-like cell, Pop, even though he did not believe in the supernatural in any form, whispered a prayer for Sister Veronica's redemption.

"Harboring a man like Rostashewitz is like keeping a pet wolf," Pop told Sister Veronica, though he could see her blue eyes were lit with love, and he could tell she barely heard him. "For years he may cringe and lick your hand, perfectly domesticated, but just once give him the scent of blood and he'll tear your arm off. A wild animal is always a wild animal no matter how you may dress him up. A perfumed wolf in a tuxedo is still a wolf."

Sister Veronica was no stranger to gospel hall evangelism. As children, her parents had participated in the crusades of Aimee Semple McPherson, she of the piercing black eyes and ephemeral white gowns. And Sister Veronica, as a child, had learned to sing hymns on street corners and rattle a tambourine with the best of them.

She married early. A blustery, black-haired man named Coogan, with whom she discovered early on that she enjoyed every lascivious pleasure of the boudoir, including having her pink ass slapped as she was climaxing.

Coogan, a musician of sorts, did not love God. He denied His existence. "If a god did exist, I would fight him tooth and nail, for he is cruel and inhuman and does nothing to protect his followers, who are so stupid they truly deserve to be called sheep."

Sister Veronica was properly horrified, but continued to believe that her God at least protected her, and that He had probably sent Coogan to test her faith.

Coogan eventually met a tall, French-Canadian girl at the club where he played banjo. She not only enjoyed having her ass slapped; she had a wealthy father. Coogan became a thing of the past and Sister Veronica went back to her snickering tambourine, until her parents died and she discovered that their evangelism had been more profitable than she had ever imagined.

"Is it possible to overcome an entire lifetime of sin?" Rostashewitz asked Sister Veronica the first morning, as she was leading him back to her mission, his mouth full of feathers, his throat full of bile, his stomach rolling like a freighter in high seas.

"It is never too late," Sister Veronica replied, squeezing Rostashewitz's grimy hand.

The morning sun turned Rostashewitz's single eye red.

In the bathroom of the mission, Rostashewitz took a swig of Aqua Velva aftershave. He rinsed the fur off his teeth and swallowed it down. His stomach burned like fire and his head cleared slightly. A hand-painted sign in the window of the mission, fly-specked and water stained, read "Sisters of a Merciful God." Above the door were the words HELPING HANDS along with a rather grotesque hand amputated at the wrist. The artist had ingested certain hallucinatory substances while working as repayment for board and room.

Rostashewitz took another swallow of aftershave, swilled it around in his mouth like a wine taster, swallowed.

"I've drunk worse," he said to the yellowed mirror, trying fruitlessly to straighten his ugly, lopsided nose.

"You smell good," Sister Veronica said when he emerged. "So fresh."

"My specialty," said Rostashewitz.

"I'm not exactly what I seem," Rostashewitz said, after he had shaved, bathed, been fed and had changed into clean clothes he picked out at the Thrift Shop next door to the mission.

"I lost this in 'Nam," he said modestly, tapping the spot where his eye used to be. "I came here on the bus from Seattle. I'm not a bum. I have a disability pension from Uncle Sam. What happened was I had a room and enough money for food, but right after I cashed my cheque two guys mugged me. I had no money for rent so the landlord locked me out. I slept in the park, in doorways. I didn't eat for days. Occasionally, a lonely bum would share his wine with me in order to have some company. I was too proud to beg. I'm not used to drinking much. I'd been on the street for three weeks when you found me.

"My cheque will be in next week," he went on. "You know if you could front me a few dollars I could get my possessions. When the cheque comes, I'll pay you back, pay for my room, and make a donation to the mission. Uncle Sam isn't cheap. He knows how much an eye is worth."

It was so easy Rostashewitz had to restrain himself from going on a spending spree.

Rostashewitz faithfully attended the service each evening at 6:00 p.m. Sometimes he was almost alone.

As a public speaker Sister Veronica was a plodder. Her theology may have been accurate, though no one cared. Her voice was breathless, almost whispery, her delivery unpolished.

Rostashewitz had always had, somewhere deep in his belly like a swallowed marble, an ember of ambition. As he watched Sister Veronica preach so ineffectually to a handful of dozing derelicts, he felt that ember stir, then spring slowly to life. He was going to need every ounce of guile to pull this off. He needed to be sober. A fifth of vodka ingested sparingly, disguised by Aqua Velva, was his solution.

"What we need is an outreach program," he said, after they had made noisy love in Sister Veronica's brass bed. "Most churches don't have any idea what goes on in the inner city, and their parishioners have lots of money for good causes.

"If you and I – I have a little expertise in public speaking from when I was in the Marines – were to tell them about the people we are trying to help, they'd feel so guilty they'd have no trouble supporting the mission."

"While the mission is not meant to break even, it is more draining on my finances than I ever dreamed," Sister Veronica admitted.

"Then you'll let us give my idea a try?"

"Would it be the Christian thing to do?"

"You bet."

Even as he moved ahead, the new developments in his life bothered Rostashewitz. Could it be that he had a calling? He took to preaching like a fly to shit. Preaching was exactly the same as telling his mugging and non-existent pension story to a sympathetic mark, only instead of one gullible person he had between five and fifty as an audience.

At the mission, Rostashewitz honed his speaking skills. He loved to slam the lectern with his fist, at the same time raising his voice to emphasize a point, stirring recognition in at least some of the pickled brains that lounged on the wax-coloured folding chairs, their odours quietly polluting the air. Word got around that Rostachewitz was at least an interesting speaker. Attendance gradually increased.

Rostashewitz loved the word outreach, it had so many connotations. He convinced Sister Veronica to buy him a suit from an expensive downtown clothier, again promising to pay her when his cheque, which had mysteriously gone astray, finally caught up with him.

He wrote a letter to the Veteran's Administration in Washington, D.C., stating his Marine rank and serial number, his pension number and asking them to locate his cheques and forward them to him at the Sisters of a Merciful God Mission. He let Sister Veronica edit the letter and loan him a stamp. Rostashewitz dropped the letter through a sewer grating at the corner of Gore and East Hastings.

The fundraising for Outreach began with an Anglican congregation not far from downtown, an affluent neighborhood a short bus ride from skid row.

Sister Veronica was so sincere, so honest-looking in her dowdy clothes and lack of makeup. Rostashewitz lounged inconspicuously in the background. Sister Veronica set up each church visitation, and spoke briefly each time, but it was Rostashewitz who delivered a ringing plea for funds to help the helpless, infirm and underprivileged. His spiel consisted of religious cliches delivered in an loud, authoritative voice.

Rostashewitz was not hesitant to speak of his own recovery. He told an elaborate tale that soon developed a life of its own about Sister Veronica plucking him from the jaws of death and depravity, finding him, a broken man, near death on the streets of Vancouver, and nursing him back to life, her gentleness, her faith a shining light to lead him to the truth and the Kingdom. Rostashewitz improved the story each time he told it.

Word got around. People in business suits dropped in for the experience, mainly to be entertained, to be able to tell their friends they had had supper at The Mission, as the place was beginning to be known. The visitors happily paid five dollars for a meal of potatoes, mashed turnips, and a hamburger steak compound composed of equal parts onion, cereal, and meat. They made ten and twenty dollar contributions to the plate Sister Veronica passed around as Rostashewitz was winding down his sermon. The money, of course, would be used for Outreach, that wonderful word that meant everything and nothing.

As he preached, greed staring out of his eye like a green budgie bird, he watched the tens and twenties fall into the collection plate. Flames roared up through Rostashewitz's chest. Sister Veronica had fronted him his nonexistent pension money for four consecutive months. In another month he would wangle a partnership with signing authority for the bank accounts. Then he wouldn't need her anymore. His ambition soared. He was surprised no one could see the flames burning, his ribs translucent through his white shirt.

Rostashewitz's single eye glowed rat-red as he slammed his fist on the lectern to emphasize a theological point. On a varnished chair to his right, a dowdy Sister Veronica smiled benignly, the sweet smell of Aqua Velva stimulating her nostrils.

CHAPTER 13

Christie and I walked into an arcade on East Hastings Street. Dark, whirring sounds, like being inside a giant clock, lights flashing.

"I want to play," says Christie.

"Shouldn't we wait until we get home?"

"Fuck, Wylie, you know what I mean. Don't be cute."

I took out a fiver and went to get change. The goddess of quarters, sitting on a stool, high up so she could keep her eyes on the whole establishment, and make it almost impossible for some punk to rob her, glanced down at me. She was maybe eighteen, jeans and t-shirt, eyes not quite focused, obviously high on something, but not so high she couldn't make change. As we made our way back toward the machine Christie wanted to play, she said to me. "That chick's interesting. What'd you call her, the goddess of quarters? You should write something from her point of view."

"Why don't you?" I challenged her.

The next day, while I was trying to write, Christie interrupts me: "Give me a couple of pages of your yellow paper. There's something I want to write down." We are in our apartment, I am sitting on a wooden rocking chair, with a blanket around my knees, holding my clipboard with perhaps fifty sheets of lined paper, trying to work on a story. I don't work well when I'm cold, and it is about as cold as Vancouver ever gets. There are a couple of inches of snow on the ground, and an evil wind seems to pass directly through the walls. Needless to say, our landlady, Mrs. Kryzanowski, is as stingy as possible with the heat, keeping the furnace set at about fifty degrees. "There's a new pad in the drawer of my desk." I am wearing most of what I own, and am still cold. Christie is in her usual jeans and boots, but wearing a bright yellow long-sleeved sweater with a huge scoop neck, might be called a cowl-necked sweater. The window rattles as snow blows against it. Christie takes the pad and a ballpoint pen and sits at my desk. I make tea to keep from freezing. Place her cup silently on the desk, careful not to disturb her. She plays with her reddish curls with her left hand while she writes with her right. She works steadily most of the afternoon, tearing each sheet off the yellow lined pad as she finishes. When she is done she brings the sheaf of paper to me. "See what you think," she says. She has large, loopy, honest handwriting, totally readable. Unlike mine, which has a backward, introvert's slant, is tightly scrunched, unreadable to most everyone, and occasionally to me.

"The Goddess of Quarters"

Sleazy breeze. Smells like a deep fryer. Corner of First and Pike in fucking Seattle, man. Big car beeping at me with a bass horn, like a rhino farting. I laugh. Stumble. I'm crossing Pike walking straight into the fucking sun. Must be going against the light. One of those rare scalding hot days in Seattle, so hot watched pots must be boiling. Wishing I had shades.

"Up yours, too, man." Missed the curb, stepped a foot too high. Heat makes me thirsty. Shape up, girl. How many goddamn gin and sevens were there? Too many. I promised goddamn Eddie I'd look for a job today. "They need a goddess of quarters at the arcade on Second," Goddamn Eddie said last night. "Getting a job will give you self worth," he said. "Maybe you'll stop acting like a tart." Self-righteous bastard with his Uncle Sam recruitment poster military haircut. He works with computers, all the gays do.

Sleazy fucking breeze blowing grit in my teeth. Feel like I've got neon in my eyes. I've got hold of the black security bars across the front of a pawnshop window. Red neon right in front of my nose. BUY & SELL, at least I wasn't imagining that.

"Hey, Sis, how's it hanging?"

I say, "Fuck off, Bowker," but all that comes out of my paralyzed lips is a mumble. Bowker is black, wearing tight black jeans, a purple shirt, looks like he's been oiled. So hot the trees are lookin' for shade. Slash of white enamel just above his chin. Pawn shop bars are holding me up. I'm gonna have to sit down soon. Fucking world is spinning like when I was a kid and my brother and I used to spin around to make ourselves dizzy. I stand dead still. It's the world that's movin'. My knees twitch.

"Wasted chick," Bowker says, and sashays off down the street. Bowker mistakenly thinks he's cool. Wants a whore for an old lady. Not cool enough to get one. Even asked me once.

"Hey, Sissy, you wanna be my bitch?"

Laughed in his face. "Fuck off, man. Anything I sell belongs to me." I wasn't even trickin' then.

"I was just bein' polite, nobody'd want anything you have for sale."

"Ooh, I'm hurt."

Goddamn Eddie says I shouldn't trick. Says I'll get killed. Well, fuck goddamn Eddie. I can take care of myself. Most of the time.

"Huh? Well I suppose I am." I think he asked me if I'm a working girl. Suit type. Forty, gray hair, glasses. Lookin' for a cheap thrill on Pike Street. Probably got two teeny-bopper daughters at home that he's lusting after. "Thirty, straight or French." Fuck, I can hardly keep my eyes open. Why can't he understand what I'm saying?

"Get your car," I say. If I let go of this fuckin' window I'll spill across the sidewalk like quicksilver. He just stands there like he's stupid. "Of course I can walk. Lemme take your arm. I'm just a little wasted is all." He names his hotel. A hundred bucks a night, five blocks away. My knees are cotton. Should have asked for fifty. I've tried five times to say "taxi," fuck it, we'll walk to his goddamned hundred dollar hotel.

You can't tell the hookers from the guests in these big fucking hotels. All the chicks look like they just stepped out of department store ads. I feel like a goat at a funeral. There's no tough, denim chicks at the Sheraton or the Hilton.

"Gimme a cigarette. Okay. Thanks." I had a pack of Winstons in the bar. Fuck, I don't even remember leavin' there. I was just sitting in the sun in front of the Federal Building when this guy starts talkin' me up. Mean looking dude with tattoos on each arm, wide mouth, biggest fucking teeth I ever saw. Had a queer accent. Off some freighter. Name was Taros, either him or his boat, never was sure.

"Want American wife," was about the third sentence he said to me.

"I'm all for that," I said, "but you got to buy me lunch first." We went to a cafeteria on Stewart Street. I piled about $20 worth of food on my plate. Goddamn Eddie says I can have whatever I want out of the fridge at his place. But I hardly ever eat there. I don't like to be in debt to anybody.

"I *am* walking straight," I say to the suit as he guides me across the lobby. Fuck, I feel like I've got my nose mashed against the screen of a TV set. Everything is jumping and nothing's in focus.

After lunch, Taros bought me cigarettes and this little cel- luloid Kewpie doll I saw in the window of a joke shop. It had wide open eyes and tiny fuchsia-coloured feathers around its waist and chest. Then we went to the Pussycat Lounge and got hammered.

"When we get married?" Taros asked.

"Right after the next gin and seven."

Oh, Fuck. Coming out of the elevator as we're goin' in, Goddamn Eddie.

"Sis," he says, throwing both his pink hands up to chin level, "what are you doing here?"

Christie paces, smoking, while I read. She has edited very little. I read it a second time. "You've got something here that many writers struggle all their lives to find. Many fail. You've got a strong, unique, very readable voice."

Christie smiles. "So what now?"

"Next you have to finish the story. You've created a great character, just carry on in the same voice. I can't tell you what to write."

"But there isn't any more. Life isn't a story. Things don't happen because a writer needs a plot line."

"That's why you have an imagination. You make things happen to your character."

"It was just a memory. That's why you're a writer and I'm not."

"How much of it is true?"

"You always say it doesn't matter what's truth and what's fiction. What matters is if the reader accepts the story and believes that it's possible."

"Well, this is a little different. I believe the story is possible. I'm in love with you. I like to know all about you. You've never mentioned living in Seattle. I've been down there a couple of times, I recognize the street names and places. You'd have been what? Fifteen? Living on the streets..." I take Christie's hand, pull her into my lap. She kisses me like it might be the last kiss we'll ever have.

"There's so much you don't know about me," she says. "So much you don't want to know about me."

LONESOME POLECAT IN LOVE

On their second afternoon in Bermuda, he names her earlobes. They're whiling away the afternoon, as lovers do, curled on the king-sized bed, partially clothed, a sweating pitcher of margaritas, three-quarters empty, on the bedside table. He lies on his back, her head cradled on his right shoulder. They have been kissing lazily in pure pleasure, her tongue filling his mouth, but not urgently as it had that morning.

Earlier, they taxied into Hamilton, the capital, from the luxurious private club where they were holidaying. There, they shopped a little, lunched, then, warmed by the tropical sun, they sat holding hands on a park bench staring out over the aquamarine waters to the houses across the bay with their gleaming white roofs, the houses themselves painted bonbon-pastels – blues, lemons, raspberries.

Min throws one leg over his, making herself even closer to him, and they nap for a few minutes before he wakes to find her licking his lips with the tip of her tongue, her deep brown eyes liquid with love. Lloyd is much older than the girl and considers himself fortunate that she loves him and loves him for himself, regardless of what people might think. Many people considered Lloyd rich, but he has been crystal clear in letting Min know early on, just in case she was looking for a meal ticket, a benefactor, that though he was not poor, alimony, taxes and some bad investments have left him, except for his retirement savings plans, pretty much living day to day.

How ironic, Lloyd thinks, that an investment counselor, one who advertises in all the money magazines, writes a syndicated newspaper column and a newsletter on investments, and who makes frequent TV appearances to discuss interest rates and taxes, should have been swindled in a scheme so complex and so irresistible that he fortunately did not let even his best clients in on it but greedily kept it to himself. Lloyd is a handsome man, tall, with piercing blue eyes, a year-round tan, and a thatch of silvered hair that make would-be investors trust him implicitly, as if he were a doctor.

Min is an artist who will soon be famous. She has just discovered her niche, and recently signed with a prestigious gallery. The price of her paintings – watercolours of old houses, many painted in Charleston and Savannah, done realistically, but overlaid with what appears to be fine layers of gauze that give them an ethereal quality that is attracting buyers and impressing critics – recently doubled, although she is still insecure and not yet earning a living at her craft. But that wouldn't take long, Lloyd knows, and after success, after she becomes financially independent, he will need more than his business reputation to hold her.

This is one of the reasons he brought her to Bermuda; he wanted her to see the pastel houses, knowing she would fall in love with them. She brought her Leica with her and used all her film in a half hour. She was bubbling with enthusiasm and talking a mile a minute on the taxi ride back to the hotel about taking a tour of the island and stocking up on more film.

"Oh, I'll paint such wonderful scenes when we get back," she said.

"I know," said Lloyd.

As they hug and cuddle, Lloyd leans over and kisses her right earlobe. It is soft as a peach. Even so small a portion of her has Min's delicate scent about it, one of warm sun and expectant fruit – peaches, apricots, sun-blessed plums. He has seldom kissed her neck or ears because early on Lloyd learned that such behaviour elicited twitches and giggles from the super-ticklish Min, often breaking the mood of their lovemaking. Today, he holds the lobe gently between his lips waiting for the exotic taste of her to come to him. He is infused with such love for her that he buries his face in her neck and whispers, "Your earlobe is so soft and sweet that I am going to name it Hairless Joe." Min giggles.

Lloyd knows that the reference is unlikely to hold any meaning for her. She's used to him making silly jokes. She was probably a child when the comic strip *L'il Abner* ceased publication. "If one ear is Hairless Joe, it follows that the other must be Lonesome Polecat," he goes on.

"What is Lonesome Polecat?" Min lets out a peachy giggle.

"Did you ever read a comic strip called *L'il Abner?*"

"Never."

Though he hates having to explain his cleverness, Lloyd tells her how Hairless Joe was an irony, a character whose facial features were totally invisible because of his flowing yellow facial hair, and how Lonesome Polecat was his partner, a small Indian with a big nose and a single feather at the back of his head held in place by a headband, and how Hairless Joe and Lonesome Polecat were famous for creating a potent homebrew called Kickapoo Joy Juice.

"You have knowledge of the strangest things," Min says.

"A wealth of useless information."

Her other lobe, when he kisses it, has a row of protrusions on it, that feel to his tongue like links in a fine gold chain. When he opens his eyes to examine the earlobe closely he finds his tongue had not lied to him. The tiny welts are red and angry looking.

"What happened?"

"I was a teenager. I was drunk and stoned. I didn't even notice my earring had been pulled out until someone pointed out that the shoulder of my jean jacket was soaked with blood. A trip to emergency. Three stitches. I joked with the doctor all the time he was stitching me up. I offered to trade him sex for his services. I was insulted when he refused."

They doze again, she curled with her head on his shoulder. He has a mini-dream in which he awakes in this same hotel room to find that

Min, instead of her black slip, is wearing a bride's dress. She is swathed in yards of white satin, and crinolines billow about her. Her bride's veil is rough as sandpaper against his bare shoulder. In the dream he shudders for he knows with great certainty that Min is not marrying him. He can see, floating off in the distance, a tuxedoed man, his features indistinguishable.

"You've restored her capacity to love," the featureless man says to him.

For what? Lloyd thinks. For you? So you can marry her?

When he really awakes, with Min cuddled deliciously against him, breathing evenly, he stares at her beautiful peach-coloured skin, her small, delicate Asian eyes, and is overwhelmed with love. Yet he also feels a bleakness he is uncertain he will be able to shake. His heart slams against his ribs like an infuriated captive.

Min was born and raised in Fresno, a torrid, depressing city, blanketed by graffiti, rampant with petty crime. She was born to Vietnamese refugees shortly after their arrival in the United States. Hers is a large secretive family, proud, repressive, controlling. They do not understand Min's art. They do not understand art at all. They feel betrayed by Min's success, feel betrayed by her choosing to do something none of them understand. Min has told Lloyd family secrets, and, in bitter exchanges with her family, she has let them know what she told him. They have shunned her for revealing secrets, turned her loose to the world, as if abandoning her will somehow cancel out the pride and privacy they feel she betrayed.

Min has many names. Five, Lloyd thinks, or six. He saw her passport once, a blur as she passed it to an immigration officer. He has had opportunities to snoop but he hesitates. She has an exaggerated sense of privacy. She would feel betrayed, even if all he wanted was to see her full name. She signs her paintings Minh Ng, the last name pronounced Ing. One of her middle names is Tran, there are several others.

Lloyd knows only the tantalizing details she has hinted at; she tells him what she is comfortable with: a physically abusive father; a funny uncle, maybe more than one; older brothers, street thugs, gang members. Did the brothers sexually abuse her? Force her into prostitution? Use her sexual favours to pay debts? All of the above?

Min survived, but she is a wary, ever watchful survivor, always seeking out insult. She has accomplished twice as much as most people her age, though she complains that she has accomplished nothing. She fears that what she has will be taken away from her. "My parents expected perfection from me," she told Lloyd once. "I failed them. Now, every morning when I get up I intend to be perfect in everything I do. Usually, by the time I've finished brushing my teeth and putting on make-up I've been foiled by imperfection. So, the day is a failure, no matter what else I do."

Her art. Min has explained her paintings. "I have a rich auntie who took me to Paris the year I turned eighteen. Rich Auntie said I was right to call the authorities about Daddy, Uncle Vang, my brothers. I was in Los Angeles, no one knew where I was, not even her. One of my brothers found out the name of my gallery, I don't know how, because I'd told my agent and the gallery owner how important it was for them not to give out my address or my unlisted phone number. Rich Auntie visited my brother in jail in Fresno and tricked him into giving her the name of the gallery by offering to arrange to have me killed for betraying the family. She stood around the entrance of the gallery for days until I showed up to see if any of my paintings had sold.

"'What I can see of your paintings look very fine,' Rich Auntie said. 'I have cataracts, like half an inch of cotton candy in front of my eyes. It makes things very beautiful.'

"And that was it. Like a light bulb going on in a pitch black room, I knew what I was going to do with my paintings. I was painting beautiful scenes like a hundred thousand other talented artists. My work was very good but not original. One can sell very good, unoriginal work. I would survive, but I'd never be famous. I decided right there that I would paint my scenes as seen through Rich Auntie's cataracts. I went back to the three paintings I had recently finished and I covered each with a half inch of cotton candy."

Lloyd stares at her relaxed, sleeping face. "I want to take a picture of you with your eyes closed," he has said to her several times in the months they had been seeing each other. "You have no idea how beautiful you are with your eyes closed."

"You're right. I don't." Min said. "But, no picture. This way you know something about me that I don't."

Min's body twitches. She doesn't wake, but a scowl crosses her face for a few seconds. Lloyd leans toward the left side of her face. He licks her earlobe, gently, barely moving his tongue so as not to tickle her, putting slow delicious pressure on the sweet tasting lobe. Without looking at her he can tell she is awake.

"Lonesome Polecat is in love," she says.

He stares at her. The odour of her makes his mouth water. She smiles lazily, raising one sepia-shaded arm to place cool fingers on the back of his neck. Sun filters through the blinds. Dust speckles the golden air. The whole room is blurry as an old photograph. It's as if he is looking at her through a half inch of cotton candy.

CHAPTER 14

"Tell me about that couple," Christie says, nodding her head. We are at an upscale lounge, nursing drinks, listening to a very good country rock band.

I look. He is about thirty, dressed casually, as if clothes are of little concern. She is a tiny thing, dark red hair, dressed in country chic, jeans and boots, almost the biker chick look, but her accessories are too stylish. They are both into the music. He is obviously in love. Her manner much more restrained.

When we get home I work most of the night. At dawn I present their story to Christie.

A SHORT HISTORY OF COUNTRY MUSIC

I am a life-long country music fan. I was raised on Hank Williams, Lefty Frizzell, Hank Snow and Kitty Wells lulling me to sleep from the radio on the dresser by my bed. One of my first memories is of Jimmy Wakely and Margaret Whiting singing "Slipping Around," a song my mother loved and played constantly on the living room record player, while I messed with building blocks on the floor.

It was country music that brought Mandy and me together, and I'd been hoping rather forlornly that country music, or anything else – I'd have happily settled for anything else – would bring us together again. We met because we were seated together at a Merle Haggard concert. I was alone, she with a girlfriend. I tried not to stare at her enough to make her uncomfortable, but I was much taken with her. She is five or six years younger than me. I was twenty-nine at the time. She was slim, dark eyed with dark red hair in abundance, blue jeans and a denim jacket, both well worn, and a yellow blouse the colour of forsythia that showed off her breasts. She was obviously enjoying the concert.

I tried to make small talk, saying, "Wasn't that great?" after the applause died down. And, "This is one of my favorites," as Haggard's back-up band, the Strangers, played the opening notes of "If We Make It Through December." She was polite, but gave me little encouragement. When the concert ended, as we were slowly making our way across the row of seats to the aisle, I whispered into her hair, which smelled like nothing I had ever encountered. Have you ever loved the odour of some inedible object so much that you truly wanted to take a bite anyway?

"You smell wonderful. What kind of perfume do you use?" If she said she worked at a Burger King, and the smell was French fries, I'd have died of embarrassment. She turned back and really looked at me for the first time. She was smiling.

"It's henna," she said. "My girlfriend talked me into using a henna wash this afternoon, to give my hair a red tinge."

And, as they say, the rest is history. But history only lasted about a year, and it has been a little over a year since she broke up with me. We never actually lived together. I had my apartment, which I work out of – I'm a freelance writer; she lived in comfortable two rooms above her parents' garage. The small apartment was like a doll's house, the exterior freshly painted white, with a deck, the railings holding flower boxes bubbling with petunias. She owned her own van and operated a small flower delivery service.

It wasn't lack of commitment on my part that kept us in separate residences, though we spent nearly every night together. I offered to rent a larger apartment, or put a down payment on a house. I asked her to marry me. Probably too often. I was too eager.

"Let's just see how things play out," she would say.

With Mandy, I was like a salesman who had made the perfect presentation, yet was unable to close the sale. She said she loved me, said our relationship was perfect, but still she kept distance between us.

The one thing I was always able to do was make Mandy laugh. If she had said something like, "Our relationship isn't working out," I could have gotten around it by saying, "Well then, let's get it a gym membership. A few hours on the bench press will make it a lot stronger." Mandy would laugh her burbling laugh and say something like, "You're hopeless," and change the subject. Or, if she'd said, "Our relationship isn't going anywhere," which I believe she actually did say once, I'd reply, "What? It's been to Vegas, and Vancouver, and a dozen country music concerts. And we haven't been to Hawaii yet. We still have a lifetime of places to go."

But the actual break-up wasn't like that at all. It was a Sunday morning at my place, I'd gone out to get coffee and donuts. As she was biting into a chocolate donut, she said, "Is this all there is?" I'd heard enough country and western songs for the heartbreak in her voice to tell me that no smart answers or arguments, no matter how convincing I was, would save me. Is this all there is? An unanswerable question. She had obviously given the situation some thought. It was all very civilized; she finished her coffee, packed her toothbrush and her few other personal items in a plastic grocery bag, and left with a whispered goodbye, leaving behind only her sad, sweet odour. For weeks, I listened to Wanda Jackson singing "Silver Threads and Golden Needles," and The Carter Family version of "Gold Watch and Chain."

I pictured Mandy bustling about her small apartment, preparing for work, humming, "Thank God and Greyhound."

It took great effort on my part to, as they say, let her have her space. There were no late night phone calls, no letters, cards, or presents. No soulful pleas. But, oh how I wanted to make those pleas. I can fully understand how a rejected lover can become a stalker. I disciplined myself, to be sure, certain relationship-killing behaviours were never a problem. I did call her on her birthday, but was brief and friendly. She was pleasant but reserved. Perhaps, just perhaps, I was deterred by the fact that Mandy owned a gun, a pistol. Her father gave it to her when she moved into the apartment, saying "A girl living alone can never be too careful." They had practised target shooting together since she was a child. I come from a family that never owned a gun. I have never even touched one. I tell you this for two reasons, one, to dispel the old adage that if one introduces a gun early in a story, it has to be used by someone before the final scene. The other is to point out that sometimes something one considers undesirable, that one is actually afraid of, can be a major turn on. I remember Mandy coming out of her bedroom with a worn brown leather holster attached to the waist of her jeans on the right side. She carried the pistol, which I won't make a fool of myself by trying to describe, except to say it was silver with a pearl handle. Mandy had asked me several times to go target shooting with her. To please her, I had finally agreed. In that instant, as she emerged from the bedroom, something totally unexpected happened to me. As Mandy fitted the gun in her holster, there was no image, erotic or pornographic that could have turned me on half as much. It was mid-afternoon before we got to the target range.

I am fortunate to live in a city large enough to attract all the great country music stars on a regular basis. After the breakup, I ran into Mandy at a Charlie Pride concert. It was like a repeat of the time when we met – she was with the same girlfriend, I was alone. The opening act for Charlie Pride was a country trio, Dave and Sugar, country music's answer to Tony Orlando and Dawn, a bright energetic act I liked well enough to buy their album. Charlie closed the first half with "The Snakes Crawl at Night," the moral of which kept me on my best behaviour as I exchanged a few words with Mandy and her friend as they bought coffee at intermission. Whatever chemistry that had once existed between us appeared to be gone.

Saturday afternoon, several months later. I am in my apartment, at my typewriter working writing a piece for the Sunday paper. It's due at 6 p.m. In the background, country music is on the radio. I don't believe I've ever written anything successful without a fiddle and a steel guitar in the background. Ray Price is singing "Heartaches by the Number."

My phone rings.

"What the hell are you doing? Aren't you a little old to be playing knock-a-door-run?"

It is Mandy. What's going on? It takes me a moment to think of a reply.

"I've no idea what you're talking about. What is it you think I've done?"

"How can you be at home? You were just here."

"Mandy, I haven't been anywhere. I've been writing a piece for the paper."

There is a pause while she considers.

"Somebody knocked on the door and ran down the stairs. Now, your shoes...are...dancing on the patio."

"My shoes? I'm twenty minutes away by taxi. I'm alone, working."

She is silent a moment.

"I know this sounds...odd, but go look in your closet. I'd recognize your boots anywhere...I'm pretty sure..."

I put down the phone and walk into my bedroom. The closet is open. I own few shoes and fewer clothes. My cowboy boots and a pair of black dress shoes are missing.

Back to the phone.

"Mandy, I can't explain what's happening. My boots and a pair of shoes are missing. Who'd want to steal them?"

'You'd better get over here."

"Are you angry?" I picture her fondling her pearl-handled gun.

"I'll have to think about it."

I call a taxi. While I wait, I type the closing sentence of the piece I'd been writing. I drop it off at the newsroom on the way to Mandy's.

When I arrive, I get out of the cab next to the alley door of the garage. The cab wheels crack gravel as it pulls away, Mandy is standing on the cute, flower box-decorated deck. The door to her apartment is open, Patsy Cline is singing "Crazy," Mandy points to the sidewalk, but I have already seen. My cowboy boots, scruffy as tomcats, are engaged in a dignified waltz on the small patio, a pair of black dress shoes that I seldom wear, appear to be doing the two-step at the foot of the stairs. Mandy looks flustered, but not unhappy.

I make a gesture of helplessness. "I don't know how to stop them" I say.

"I can't believe you went to all that trouble," she said.

Wow. How do I handle this? She's not furious. Appears to be unarmed.

I shrug hopefully. "Care to join me," I say, gesturing toward the concrete dance floor where my shoes cavort.

"What an imagination," she says. She is smiling. "Back in a sec." She disappears into her apartment. Patsy Cline stops in the middle of a verse. I imagine I can hear the machine clicking and adjusting to the changes Mandy demands. Suddenly, Ray Price begins singing "My Shoes Keep Walking Back to You."

Mandy re-appears as suddenly as she departed.

She's coming down the stairs toward me. Her arms are open. I wait for my life to begin.

Do-si-do.

CHAPTER 15

"So, where do you get your money?" I asked Christie. I have probably only asked her a half dozen questions in the months we've known each other. I have always felt that if I remain silent people will tell me more than I ever wanted to know about their lives. A feeling that has proved true on any number of occasions.

"I suppose you deserve to know, but it has to remain a secret between us. Don't go telling that creepy guy at the coffee shop."

"A secret," I said. "I promise."

"Do you remember a story I told you about Las Vegas?"

I did indeed. It is one of the most harrowing stories that Christie has told me about her past.

"We were usually alone at night. The five of us in that one swollen room. I was often the only one awake. Mother came bouncing in, all high-heel sounds and energy, smelling of perfume, beer and smoke. She was wearing a white dress with an orchid-coloured flower centered above her breasts. She had a green scarf at her throat.

"'I'm gonna be gone for a day or two,' she said, tossing money on the table, gathering lingerie, her toothbrush, cologne. I could hear a taxi mumbling at the curb.

"She kissed the sleeping heads, hugged me, told me, 'Take good care of 'em.' I wasn't yet Christie. She whispered something about Las Vegas, or was it New Orleans, and she was gone, tap-tapping down the dirty staircase, clicking down the walk, slamming the taxi door. There was someone in the back seat with her.

"Four days later, when she hadn't come back, I was at the end of my rope. The money had been one dollar bills; they looked like a fortune to a ten-year-old, but they were gone quickly, even though I bought fruit and tomatoes, bread, milk, cereal over the protests of the other children, who wanted chips, and candy.

"The baby, Vanessa, was sick, fevery-eyed with a hurting cough. I washed her diapers in the toilet and sink, dried them on the black-berry canes in the yard.

"I remembered the old man in the back room on the first floor who was always inviting me into his room, promising me a lot of money if he could look at me naked, if I would do things to him. I knocked on his door. He wasn't a bad old man; he smelled of after-shave and peppermint.

"'My sister is sick,' I said, looking him in the eye. 'Give me twenty dollars, and I'll come into your room for half an hour.' He took the bill from a roll in his pocket, handed it to me, held out his hand to me.

"I carried Vanessa to the drug store two blocks down, let the druggist, a bent-over man wearing a black-velvet skull cap who smelled of pipe tobacco, examine her. He picked a bottle off a shelf, blew the dust off it, gave me some change, not much.

"'Tell your mother she should try to keep her cleaner,' he said.

"'I do the best I can,' I said. 'We're out of soap.' He stared at me, took a bar of pink soap wrapped in cellophane off a shelf, handed it to me.

"'Mazel tov,' he said. 'You're a good little mother.'

"That night one of the other roomers called the police because Vanessa cried all night long, that high, sick wail that babies have.

"'My God,' the police officer said, as he stepped into the room, the odours hitting him like a slap. 'Where's your mother?'

"'She went away in a taxi,' I said."

"'How long ago?'

"I shrugged. I didn't want to get her in trouble.

"They sent in a social worker of some kind, a young woman armed with sacks of food and disinfectant. She scoured the tub for half an hour, then bathed us one at a time. She produced nightgowns from a brown paper sack. Vanessa began to breathe easier. The police dropped by several more times, the word 'apprehended' passed among them. They had checked airline schedules. Mother was coming back. A senior social worker would be there when she arrived.

"Mother came bustling in looking tired, wearing the same dress she left in, smelling strongly of herself. So, what the fuck?" she said.

"The young woman had bathed us, sat us in row, according to age – the twin boys, me, the twin girls, Vanessa – on the sagging couch, all covered with one blanket, where we watched the black-and-white TV with the vertical bar that rolled at will, then departed. The senior social worker was a small, lean man with glasses and short blond hair. He used an official voice with Mother, not the soft, teasing voice he had used with us.

"The first time he said 'apprehended,' Mother shushed him. 'Some of these kids understand,' she said. 'Let's talk in there.' She pointed to the bathroom door with its antique porcelain knob.

"They went in and closed the door. At first their voices were soft. Then they stopped altogether. Then there were familiar sounds from my dreams, soft groaning sounds.

"Mother came out and lit a cigarette.

"When the social worker came out he didn't look at us. He thanked Mother for being so cooperative, gave her his card.

"We sat like a row of Russian dolls on the couch.

"'Las Vegas was a blast,' Mother said, licking her lip."

"What about Las Vegas?" I asked.

"We actually went to live there," said Christie.

"Mother went there a couple more times, but she left us enough money to get by, then the last time she had enough to hire a housekeeper to look after us and she was gone for two weeks. She came back smiling with a wad of hundreds, enough for us to rent a better apartment, get food and clothing. She said she had a wealthy boyfriend.

"Then one day this white stretch limo pulls up in front of the building, a man and a woman, both in chauffeur uniforms, came in and helped us pack our clothes and possessions. They made some phone calls, a truck came and picked up our boxes. Then we all got in the limo and we drove for two days to get to Las Vegas, stopped at nice hotels, ate in good restaurants. We stopped in front of a big two-storey house in a gated community, somewhere on the outskirts of the city. The fridge was stocked when we got there, our boxes were unpacked, there were bathing suits laid out for us. There was a huge private pool. We all thought we'd died and gone to heaven.

"For the longest time we never saw the guy. Mother wouldn't discuss him, just said, 'Enjoy the good life.' He always sent the limo for Mother, usually after we were all in bed. The female chauffeur would baby sit us. Her name was Carmen, and she had huge dark eyes. If mother stayed away overnight, Carmen would get in the pool and play with us, she'd take us for a walk to a 7-Eleven store and buy us treats.

"When I asked Mother about the boyfriend, she said his name was something that sounded like Sudsey, and that he ran a trucking company, a very big trucking company. Me and the oldest boys went to school, we made some friends, pushed our horrible past to the backs of our minds.

"We were there like three years, then one day everything blew apart, literally. It was July, Mother had stayed overnight and Carmen had made us waffles for breakfast. One of the boys pointed out a huge spiral of smoke and flames in the sky in the city. Then the phone rang and Carmen rushed to our bedrooms and started putting out clothes for us, and for Mother. A few minutes later Mother arrived in a taxi. 'Something terrible's happened. We gotta get out of here.' Just then two black cars with tinted windows pulled up. Four guys in black pants and loud shirts got out and moved toward the house. 'They're gonna kill us,' Mother said. 'Not you kids. Me and maybe Carmen.'

"We were in the laundry room at the back of the house. Mother was a tiny woman. 'No use running,' she said. She looked at the clothes dryer, opened it and began to force herself inside, stopped and got out, opened the outside door, returned to the dryer. 'Close the door once I get inside. When they come looking, point out the door to the yard.' She gave my hand a squeeze. I could see she was terrified.

"I'd hardly closed the dryer door when Carmen rushed in. She was holding a handgun. I suddenly wasn't sure if she was still my friend. I pointed to the yard. She rushed out. A second later one of the thugs, also holding a handgun, walked in. 'Where's your old lady?' I pointed out the door. He rushed out and seconds later two more men appeared. I pointed again, they rushed out. I heard gunfire. Then I heard sirens. The black cars sped away. Suddenly the house was full of police. Then there was an ambulance; Carmen had been shot. They carried her away on a stretcher with an oxygen mask over her face. I heard the police say that Carmen had shot one of the thugs, that there was a blood trail from the back yard to the curb. I heard them tell someone to put a watch on all the hospitals.

"Finally I was approached by one of the police officers. 'There's a social worker on the way,' he said.

"'Did my mother do something wrong?' I asked.

"'No, honey, she just saw something she shouldn't have. We'll keep her safe if we can find her.'"

"One more time I pointed, this time at the dryer. He helped Mother crawl out. She had peed her pants from fright.

"The next few days were a blur. We were moved from one place to another, a hotel, a house, a hotel again, there were always one or more police with us. Everyone wanted to talk with mother. I never got the whole story. Apparently the man called Sudsy had an apartment near or in his company offices. Guys broke in and started shooting. Mother hid under the bed but got a good look at them. They killed Sudsy, then set fire to the complex. After they left Mother called a taxi. Six men were arrested, the four guys from the house plus their bosses, two highly connected mob guys.

"They all chose separate trials which meant Mother would have to testify six times. 'They figure that will give them more time to find you.' the head FBI guy told her. We were moved to a new city after every trial. They didn't find her. They were all convicted. We were moved to another city, then another, then another. Our names were changed every time. The last time I became Christie. My original name started with a V, just like everyone in the family. I don't remember all the other names I was given.

"Officially, I have no past. I grew up, moved away, but I always watched. I get money from the FBI every month, will until I'm forty. It was part of the deal Mother made. They were desperate for her testimony. I have no idea where the rest of my family is. Probably the FBI would tell me if I created enough noise. I'd like to see Vanessa again, or whatever she's called now, but I doubt I ever will.

"There, now you know everything about me. You've wheedled it out of me."

But had I?

WAITING ON LOMBARD STREET

There is an old fashioned IHOP on Lombard Street in San Francisco, probably one of the originals, blue roof, A-Frame, from the days when they were known as International House of Pancakes.

Driving south on a hot afternoon, fresh out of both air conditioning and Diet Coke, we decided to stop for refreshment. A pleasant young woman greeted us and escorted us to a booth, my red-headed lady and I, brought us water and menus and an assurance that a waitress would soon be with us. She may have even supplied us with a name, "Barcelona will be your waitress this afternoon." I prefer waitresses who don't have names, I prefer an arm clutching a pencil with a yellow pad at the end of it.

It was about 3:30 in the afternoon, Bermuda Triangle time in restaurants. The last of the lunch crowd has lurched out, belching martini fumes; time to wash the floors and scrape the food off the windows.

We decided on what we wanted, I chose a chocolate malt, my red-headed lady an iced tea, then we visited the washrooms one at a time so, should the waitress come, one of us would be there to give her the order.

The waitress did not appear. She never appeared. There came a point when we simultaneously realized we had been waiting an extraordinarily long time for service. We stared around. There was only one other occupied table, far away. The silence was eerie. It reminded me of the Mary Deare, the abandoned merchant ship depicted in an old film with Gary Cooper. Food steaming on some tables, but no one in sight, especially a waitress.

We waited a few more minutes. We finished our water. I really wanted a chocolate malt. No one came or went.

"In another dimension, in another IHOP, perhaps in Sacramento, or San Luis Obispo, or maybe even Honolulu, a tall, blond man and his red-headed lady have just been served a chocolate milkshake and an iced tea," I said. "They've drunk them up, received their check, and are now going to try and sneak out without paying. Look furtive," I said, standing up. "I'm going to walk sideways down the aisle. Try to look as if you have a sugar dispenser in your purse."

We walked out, silence clinging to us like lint. No matter how suspicious we tried to look, no one paid the slightest attention.

I leafed through the San Francisco newspaper the next day to see if perhaps a waitress had been kidnapped from an IHOP on Lombard Street. Or if maybe there was a story of the entire staff of an IHOP being locked in a walk-in cooler at the rear of the restaurant by a drug-crazed robber. Or, if perhaps an IHOP had been found abandoned, floating down Lombard Street like the Mary Deare, food still warm but all humanity vanished into the ether without a trace.

Several months have passed. I wonder if in some other dimension, my red-headed lady and I are still seated in that IHOP on Lombard street in San Francisco, spectral, ghostly, playing with our ice cubes, waiting for service.

CHAPTER 16

We'd been taking a leisurely walk through the streets of Gastown, an upscale area of shops and restaurants just a stone's throw from where we live. I sometimes worry that some entrepreneur will buy the Breathing Castle, evict us all and turn it into a quaint restaurant, serving small portions with squiggles of sweet sauces in artistic patterns on the plates, making up for the lack of substance.

We entered a dark antique shop with narrow aisles. On top of an old-fashioned phonograph was a box full of loose photographs.

"Oh, look," I said. "Instant relatives."

"What?" said Christie.

"For the lonely. Pick out a family, put them in frames or in albums so you can show your friends you have roots, ancestors, people who care about you."

"I suppose we could both do that," said Christie. "Anything I found would be better than real life. Life would be a lot simpler if we could choose our relatives."

"Look," I said, picking up a three-by-five studio portrait of a young man with a Joseph Stalin moustache. "This is my great uncle Vlad. He came to Canada from Ukraine in 1900. My grandfather homesteaded in Alberta, but Vlad went to Winnipeg where he started a bricklaying business. He had sixteen children with three wives. I'm related to half the population of Winnipeg."

"You make it sound believable."

"That's a writer's job."

"Why don't you write about your real relatives? Your real ancestors?"

My mind was already racing as I paid twenty-five cents for the picture of Uncle Vlad.

"Tell you what," I said to Christie. "You get two stories for the price of one. One for each side of my family. But, one will be fact as I know it, the other total fiction. You have to tell me which is which."

THE SNOW LEPRECHAUN

The Shannons' cabin stood on a knoll overlooking a small valley. A half-dozen scrub chokecherry trees afforded the cabin its only protection from the raging Dakota blizzard. The Shannons had come from Ireland in 1900 and settled in the suffering Black Hills country. The land of opportunity, everyone said. But after two dust-choked summers and two petrifying winters, Patrick Shannon was not so sure.

It was the eve of his namesake saint's day and snow was drifted window high while a coyote wind chewed at the chinked-log walls. Patrick sat at the kitchen table. He rested his head on his left hand and idly ran his fingers through his abundant black curls. His deep blue eyes were troubled.

"I tell you, Ellen," he said to his wife, "this is no land for man nor beast, and the sooner we get back to Ireland the better for all of us. If spring ever comes, I'll take work with the railroad, sell the farm, and with luck have enough money by fall to take us all home."

Ellen pulled her heavy sweater tighter around her shoulders and added a stick of wood to the glowing pot-bellied stove in the corner.

"Have you forgotten the real hardships there, Pat? The times when the babies were hungry, and how we were turned off our land. Here, we have a roof over our heads and we never lack for food, no matter how plain it may be."

"If we'd stayed a little longer I'd have made my fortune. I've the gift, you know…the only man to meet face to face with the leprechaun of Donovan's Green."

Patrick then recounted, for at least the hundredth time, his meeting with the elusive goblin of his Irish hometown. The meeting had taken place in the wee hours of the morning, after a long evening at a local public house, a fact he always neglected to mention. But no one had ever been able to shake his story and, of course, everyone knows that those who see a leprechaun will find fame and fortune or both.

"It's the cold and the snow here that I can't stand," said Patrick. "Almost six months we've been closeted in this house. Why, back in Ireland the grass is green and the birds sing…"

"And we could starve to the music of songbirds," said Ellen. The flame burned crookedly in the blackened chimney of the coal-oil lamp. "It's too many days you've been in this dire mood. 'Tis rest you need." With her hand expertly cupped behind the lamp chimney, Ellen extinguished the light.

On St. Patrick's morning the blizzard still raged, and Patrick found the cabin extraordinarily cold as he rose to stock the heater and light the cookstove with its massive warming oven. He soon discovered the reason – the cabin door stood open a few inches and a trail of snow lay drifted across the floor. Then he saw them, like gossamer patterns in the light drifts, a set of tracks no bigger than a doll's, but their nature was unmistakably clear, snowshoes. The tracks led straight across the room to a cupboard that housed a half-bottle of whiskey. The bottle had come with them from the old country, its label was torn and yellowed with age. It was used only in grave emergencies. Sure enough, the cap was off and the level diminished a full half-inch by Patrick's calculation.

In his excitement, he practically dragged Ellen from the bedroom.

"It's a sign," he said. "If the Little People can brave this godforsaken land to watch over their own, then perhaps we *are* meant to be here."

Struggling into his mackinaw, Patrick prepared to start his morning chores.

"After breakfast we'll figure out how to go about clearing that strip of land to the north, as soon as the snow goes. And I'll be putting a lock on that cabinet. That rascally snow leprechaun will be having no more drinks on me."

Smiling wearily, Ellen Shannon listened to the sounds of the children stirring in the loft, as she started preparations for breakfast. From the pocket of her sweater she took two tiny oval objects, willow twigs criss-crossed and bound with her best sewing thread.

"We'll not be needing these again," she said, as she passed the miniature snowshoes into the ruby-red mouth of the pot-bellied stove.

THE RIDGEPOLE

Cold moon shadows dappled the plank floor of Acktymchuk's cabin as he forced himself awake in 5:00 a.m. blueness. He was proud of that floor. Neighbours, farmers more prosperous than him, still had dirt floors in their shacks and cabins. He hoped his wife would approve. In a few hours he would know. It was a five-hour wagon drive to the railway, where she would be dropped off at the station, just a log hut, occupied by a crotchety Scot who had arrived with the railroad several years before. The stop was called Strand, named without irony, perhaps for the old Scot, who was known only as Bert.

Acktymchuk started the fire in the black cook stove, put a full kettle of water to boil, and set out to do the morning chores. Though it was April, there was snow in the air, which made Acktymchuk choose to take the wagon instead of the cart. It would make for a slower, more cumbersome trip, but he could stash horsehide robes in the wagon box, and the walls offered protection from the fresh wind. He had no idea whether his bride would be dressed properly. There was vanity, too. His matched black horses gleamed from a currying he had given them the night before. He wondered if she would appreciate his prosperity, or if she would even notice. What if she was some delicate girl who was used to a good life? He hoped for a strong woman. He fantasized a wide-hipped woman whose features were gently blurred, one who would give him sons to work the land. With a wife he could apply to homestead an additional quarter section of good black prairie land that was already showing a profit, from the few acres he had been able to clear and seed.

During the winter, with snow drifted window high, he had sketched an addition to the cabin. On a clear day, he'd cut and trimmed a lodge pole pine, a tree known for growing straight and true. He peeled it and leaned it against the cabin to dry and weather. It was over eight feet long, a perfect ridgepole. Back at the house, he made coffee, fried bacon, cooked three eggs in the bacon fat, cut boiled potatoes in slices, cooked them in the grease, pepper and salting them to his taste. He kept a giant pot of boiled and drained potatoes on the back of the stove, replenishing the supply once a week. He made two thick beef sandwiches, wrapped them in newspaper, and set them on the corner of the table. He subscribed to the *Family Herald and Weekly Star*, studied it by lamplight, trying to learn English, recognizing a word now and then. Acktymchuk was barely literate in any language, but he had painstakingly printed an answer to an ad offering Russian brides. His loneliness overrode his terror of being cheated. After some negotiation, he sent money for her passage, plus a handsome fee for the broker. He was notified of her date of arrival and now that date had come.

As he ate, he had a moment of panic. What if she refused him? Acktymchuk knew it was possible; he was not a catch. He had been refused before. Acktymchuk was thirty, but looked at least forty. He was short and powerful, with strong hands blackened by work. He had a ruddy complexion, and black hair that twisted in ugly cowlicks. He had tried cutting off the most offensive tufts, but was left with spots of open pink skin.

But it was his eye that worried him most. There were so many superstitions about the eye. It had been a simple accident two years before. Cutting frozen willows, a willow frond had snapped, slashed him across an open eye. He had screamed in pain. He bathed the eye in a boric acid solution for weeks, and while the pain was gone, the eye was mostly covered by a whitish film, and he estimated he had no more than twenty percent vision in it.

He shook off these thoughts and went outside, putting a fleece jacket in the wagon box, in case she was not dressed properly. Then, another moment of panic. What if they sent a fifty-year-old woman? What if she was dragging a line of children after her?

Hamlets, each featuring a grocery store and post office, usually sur-rounded by a few houses, a community hall, and occasionally a church visited irregularly by a circuit rider, were roughly five miles apart all across the prairies. There were some dirt roads, but mostly trails that followed the line of least resistance, circumventing swamps, and finding river and creek crossings that didn't require a horse to swim, except in spring. Acktymchuk rode one of his blacks in winter and spring. In summer and fall he walked, five, ten, even fifteen miles to dances and box socials, each Saturday night. Bachelors abounded, marriageable girls were few and the competi-tion fierce. The girls were usually polite to Acktymchuk, though some weren't. He made no headway. He'd arrive home at dawn a little hung over from dandelion wine, in time to cook breakfast, do the chores and start work in the fields. But come the next Saturday night, he would head out again, hope burning beneath his freshly washed shirt.

Not long after the accident, he had almost married. He had been approached by Piska, a neighbor four miles away. He had eaten at their home a time or two. Piska was established, had three sons and three daughters, a round wife who laughed a lot, and took joy in forcing second and third helpings on this lonely bachelor. Acktymchuk spoke no Polish, the Piskas spoke no Ukrainian. Their limited conversation was in broken English. He had liked the oldest daughter, a large, strong girl with close-set eyes and mud-coloured hair, who worked in the fields like a man.

Piska appeared at the farm one day, riding a buckskin pony bare-back. He was a tall man with sunken cheeks who always looked like he was at death's door.

"You need wife," Piska said. It was statement not a question.

"I do," acknowledged Acktymchuk.

"We make deal? My oldest, good for strong. Make fine wife."

"I agree," said Acktymchuk, which brought an almost smile to Piska's gaunt face. But, as Acktymchuk was to find out, there was more. There were rituals to be observed. Piska admired a purebred, hugely pregnant ewe in Acktymchuk's corral.

"Even trade?"

Acktymchuk understood dowry. Dug in his heels. The meeting ended.

A few days later, Acktymchuk appeared at the Piska farm. They walked to the corral, each stood with a booted foot on the bottom rail. They took makings from their shirt pockets, rolled cigarettes, smoked.

"Two lambs this year," said Acktymchuk.

There was a long silence while Piska considered. "And one next year."

"Deal," said Acktymchuk. They shook hands.

But there were complications and the marriage was not to be. The story eventually got back to Acktymchuk in an unusual and roundabout way. His closest post office was called Gray Lake, named for some long forgotten pioneer. Gray Lake was little more than a slough choked with bull rushes. The store was in the house of a man known as Oslin the Estonian. Next to a pot-bellied stove just inside the store was a rocking chair, perpetually occupied by a large widow named Demko, who lived in one of a cluster of cottages nearby. She was partial to purple head scarves, and absorbed every whiff of gossip no matter how juicy or trivial without ever leaving her chair. Her greatest joy was to tell a victim their own story, but she would tell it as though it happened to someone else.

One of Paska's children told a friend how the proposed marriage had unravelled, that boy told his parents and the story spread like pink eye.

Acktymchuk had barely closed the store door behind him, when the widow Demko spoke from her rocking chair. "You hear what happened to Earless Boyko from up Warspite way?" She said, naming a hamlet about ten miles east of Gray Lake. She didn't wait for Acktymchuk to acknowledge her, but launched right into the story.

"He arranged with Fred Mudryk to take his ugly daughter off his hands, dowry was six piglets and a cultivator. They was cutting brush when Mudryk told the daughter. Well, she did what he never expected; she raised up her brush cutting hatchet, told him in no uncertain terms she wouldn't marry Earless Boyko under any circumstance. Said she would stay home and look after Mudryk in his old age, but damned if she was going to have a roomful of deaf and dumb children. Mudryk backed down, told Earless Boyko his wife decided they needed the daughter at home after all. That was not even a very good lie, for the young girls did the cooking, the older girl worked the fields."

The story was exactly what had happened to Acktymchuk, only the name, location, and affliction had been changed. What could he do? Nothing. He blushed. He busied himself explaining to Oslin the Estonian what groceries he needed. He stood at the counter sweating through his shirt, though it was a cold spring day. He was so humiliated he didn't go to a dance or box social for two months.

In anticipation of finding a bride, Acktymchuk had hired Oslin the Estonian, whose talent was to take a large block of wood and carve a cradle. His work was exquisite, the finished product varnished many times, glowed golden, a lamb bleating from each end of the cradle.

Acktymchuk stashed the cradle in the hayloft.

He arrived at the railroad an hour early. Better an hour early than a minute late, was how Acktymchuk lived his life. He sat down in the straw on the floor of the wagon box, which protected him from the chilly wind. The train was an hour late. It barely stopped. A single passenger emerged, followed by a hoop-roofed trunk, and a box of groceries for Gray Lake Store, and a case of apples, the end of the wooden box decorated with a blue-eyed kitten. The box read Cat Nip Apples.

As he walked toward the woman who'd stepped down from the train, Acktymchuk's heart sank. She was a slip of a girl, her shoulders hunched against the wind, silky white blond hair blowing across her face.

Her coat was too light, her teeth were chattering. She had a white sheet of paper pinned to her lapel with the single word, "Strand," printed on it. She visibly cringed as she got her first look at Acktymchuk.

"I am Acktymchuk," he announced.

"Zonia," she whispered.

"I've got a warm jacket in the wagon," he said in Ukrainian. She cringed again, as he put an arm around her slim waist, to guide her, to protect her from the sawtooth wind. He pretended not to notice.

"Are you hungry?" He asked. That opened the floodgate. She burst into tears. There was no heat in the carriage car, she said, she had run out of money days ago, perhaps someone had cheated her. As she was speaking Acktymchuk, realized he had left the bulky beef sandwiches sitting on the table five hours away.

"Where did this happen? How much money were you given? How could..."

"I don't know," the girl wailed. "I don't know where I am. I don't know where I have been." Acktymchuk looked around hopelessly. His eyes fell on the case of apples. The ends of the box were solid wood, the sides were made of thin slats. He grabbed one of the slats, crushed it with his powerful hand, reached in and extracted four Macintosh red apples, each wrapped in a piece of coloured tissue paper.

"I am Acktymchuk," he said again, this time to the stationmaster who lurked in the low doorway of the station house. "Tell Oslin the Estonian I will pay him next time I see him."

He handed an apple to the girl as he guided her toward the wagon. She gobbled it in three bites, eating core, seeds and all.

"Thank you," she said, accepting a second apple, as he helped her into the wagon box, wrapped her in the fleece jacket, covered her with a horsehide robe. She ate the second apple more slowly, regaining some composure.

"You are safe with me," Achtymchuk repeated more than once, hoping to make the frightened girl feel better. "I will see that no harm comes to you."

A mile later, he finally asked, "How old are you?"

"Twenty?" She replied. It was a question, not a statement.

"Sixteen?" asked Acktymchuk.

"Seventeen," the girl, Zonia, admitted. It came out slowly that she had grown up in an orphanage in Kiev, a mere seventy miles from where Acktymchuk was born. She was not stupid, but he was not certain at first that she knew she was supposed to be his bride. He was too embarrassed to ask. "I will protect you," he told her several times. Eventually, she admitted that the marriage broker had contacted the orphanage, the supervisors found it acceptable and profitable to send all the girls over fifteen to be mail-order brides.

When they finally arrived at the farm, Acktymchuk stopped the wagon in front of the cabin. He walked her inside, first pointing into the darkness toward the outhouse, a crescent cut into the door with a keyhole saw. He lit a lamp, got the fire going, then left to put the horses in the barn, milk the cow and do the other evening chores.

When he returned to the cabin he saw immediately that she had found the sandwiches. They were both gone. She stood warming her tiny hands over the wood stove. Across the room the bed loomed.

Acktymchuk stared about. He had already decided she would not do. He walked to the door, disappeared into the darkness for a few seconds, returned carrying the ridgepole. He laid it down the middle of the bed. It was too long and at least two feet protruded into the tiny room.

"You are safe from me," he said, pointing her to the far side of the bed. The girl smiled weakly. She took off only the fleece jacket before disappearing under the covers. Acktymchuk sat at the table for a long time. He turned the lamp low so as not to disturb the girl, but he needn't have worried for she fell asleep instantly. Rejection squeezed Acktymchuk's heart. He had never felt so alone.

He was awakened by the smell of coffee. The alarm clock by the bed said 5:00 a.m. The girl was already cooking breakfast. She had found the slab of bacon in the cupboard, she was slicing potatoes in preparation for frying. As he pulled on his boots, he said. "You don't need to…"

"I will not be beholden," the girl said. "I cooked at the orphanage, since I was old enough to stand on a chair and stir the soup."

Over breakfast, Acktymchuk said, "I have decided. I am too old for you. I have told no one about you. I will introduce you as my niece. We will go to a dance at Warspite this Saturday, it is to raise money for a family who was burned out. There will be many young men there looking for a wife. You will be much sought after." He wanted to say that he understood her not wanting an ugly, half blind man, but he thought it would sound too much like a plea for pity.

Zonia cooked for the rest of the week. Made a version of perogies new to Acktymchuk, each one the size of a pot holder, stuffed with crumbled bacon, potato, onion and chopped garlic, boiled, fried brown with more onions, slathered with sour cream.

"One for each person at the orphanage, no arguments, no leftovers," she said.

She brought in the galvanized tub that hung on a hook outside the door, boiled water, washed clothes as best she could, dried them on the caragana bushes that Acktymchuk had planted as a windbreak, as soon as he had acquired the land, while the house, cleared land, and crops were still dreams.

Saturday was warm, sunny, the smell of new leaves in the air. They took the cart, pulled by a single horse. Zonia wore a dress, blue and white, that she had taken from the mothball-smelling trunk.

Acktymchuk had forgotten about Bert the stationmaster. He had told Oslin the Estonian, when he came to pick up his groceries, that Blind Acktymchuk now had a wife. All afternoon, on their way, and evening, at the dance, he had to fend off congratulations, explain endlessly that Zonia was his niece.

He thought it a cruel act of fate that Earless Boyko was there. Years before, a belt had flown off a threshing machine, amputating an ear more skillfully than a surgeon. Acktymchuk refused to sit anywhere near him. He danced only a couple of times, didn't show any interest when a young widow he had never seen before made it clear she was interested in him.

Zonia danced every dance. As Acktymchuk had predicted, the competition was fierce. The Yaremko twins, both nineteen, both tanned brown, each wearing his one white shirt with the sleeves rolled up, had a prolonged and damaging fist fight over who would get to take Zonia home. But when the dance was over, she appeared at Acktymchuk's side, stepping away from a handsome boy who had his arm tightly about her waist.

"Uncle Wasyl says I must ride home with him," she told the boy, who glared but retreated.

That afternoon at Oslin's grocery, on the way to the dance at Warspite, while Acktymchuk had worked with Oslin to fill his grocery order, Zonia had looked through the dry goods. She found a roll of oilcloth, scarlet and white alternating squares, and held the material in front of her. Acktymchuk felt such tenderness toward her at that instant, as he calculated the cost of enough oilcloth to cover the rough, handmade kitchen table. Acktymchuk realized also that there was no colour in his house. He lived his life in black and white. The smell of linseed oil emanated from the oilcloth, something he equated with newness and freshness. He made the purchase. When they got home from the dance, as the cabin was warming up, Zonia cleared the table and spread the fiery oilcloth across it. It blazed.

"You are a good man," Zonia said.

But Acktymchuk kept his distance. Made it clear they would attend a dance and box social the next weekend at Gray Lake.

On Friday, after breakfast, he went to the barn and harnessed his pair of blacks. He walked behind holding the reins, the doubletree bouncing on the ground. He and the team would spend the day pulling stumps. As he passed the cabin, Zonia emerged, a lunch sack in hand. It held sandwiches, apples, and Acktymchuk's battered blue thermos full of coffee, sweetened and creamed.

"We see different things," she said simply, as Acktymchuk accepted the sack. "What you see is a weak girl, which I may be. You have to look beyond my appearance, for I have steel in my blood. There is little I can't do. What I see when I look at you, is a man whose mirror lies to him. I see a man with a kind heart. A woman can do no better." She turned back toward the cabin, giving him no chance to reply.

Acktymchuk worked like a demon all day. He felt if he used enough of his physical strength, his dilemma might go away. What could this young girl see in an ugly, half blind farmer? She would be so much better off with a young man closer to her age. That's what he would tell her. He pictured taking the cradle from its hiding place, presenting it to Zonia and her beau as a wedding present.

But, at the end of the day, as he returned to the farmyard, he saw that the decision had been taken out of his hands. The ridgepole leaned against the outside of the cabin next to the wash tub.

CHAPTER 17

A summer evening in East Vancouver. Lilacs bloom purple around the Breathing Castle. We walk hand in hand, Christie and I, down East Hastings Street, past Woodwards department store, past the infamous corner where winos and addicts sprawl on benches and on the bare concrete. We pass the Sunshine Hotel where two whores, one all in denim, the other in pink and black Spandex, vie for position in the lucrative half block between the Sunshine and the Balmoral hotels. A wino has fallen asleep in the doorway of The Smiling Buddah Night Club, which will not open until 11 p.m.

We have no destination in mind, continue to walk in the heavy pedestrian traffic, pass a couple of cops, strolling like us, not hassling anyone. There is tinkling music in the air, not from a car radio. We continue on past the Patricia Hotel. Then we see where the music is coming from. The Patricia has an open parking lot, I'd guess twenty feet below street level. I've never been sure if it was constructed that way, or if there was once another building beside the hotel that burned down or was demolished. We are standing, looking down at a small carnival that has taken over the parking lot. The rinky-tink music is all but drowned out by the cough of generators. The air is pungent with the odours of cedar shavings, exhaust, frying onions, and excitement. Immediately below us, a small Ferris wheel turns, seeming to drag long circles of green neon behind it. Canvas banners bulge in the slight breeze, rows of booths are doing a brisk business, now and again the urgent voice of a barker can be heard.

"Let's go in," I say.

"Fucking scammers," says Christie. "Don't waste your time."

"Come on, I haven't seen an old fashioned carnival like this since I was a kid. I thought television killed the carnivals."

"They're like fucking cockroaches, you can't kill them," says Christie. "They just go dormant and live for a thousand years."

"Don't be such a spoilsport."

I lead Christie to the end of the block. We turn onto a side street, and there is the admission booth. A woman who looks vaguely Gypsyish, charges us fifty cent each. She takes my dollar with a dark hand, her nails covered with chipped cherry-coloured polish. Christie hangs back as we pass through a battered turnstile.

"Carnivals give me the creeps." She lights a cigarette.

"Look, I've got less than ten dollars on me. Let's just look around. I'd like to write something about a carnival. I've told you the story about when I was maybe ten years old and a carny asked me for a favour. He sent me from booth to booth asking to borrow a left-handed glass stretcher. I went to about five booths before I caught on."

"Fucking mark," says Christie, but she squeezes my hand.

Inside, we turn left and the first booth of perhaps twenty, ten on each side of the aisle, is a dart game. Dozens of balloons, red, green, blue and yellow, are attached to a particleboard wall. Customers pay a quarter for three darts to break a balloon and win a prize.

"Don't even think about it," says Christie. "It's all rigged. The darts have balsa handles, no weights, if you breathe out as you throw, the dart will drift a foot, plus the points are blunted and the balloons are under inflated. You can hit one square on and not pop it. There's an unwritten rule that if someone spends over twenty dollars, he's given a properly weighted dart, and wins a cheap prize, wholesale ninety-nine cents, to impress his girlfriend and assure him of a blow job after they leave."

"Thanks for disillusioning me. How come you know so much?"

'I was born knowing things," says Christie.

As we make our way along the midway, Christie continues to disparage every booth. The milk bottles are weighted, the basketball hoop is too small, the ring toss rigged.

I buy us each a hot dog.

"Is it rigged too? Made of dog meat, the bun plastic, the onions stolen?"

She smiles. "Got to admit there's nothing like a carnival hot dog."

But her good mood doesn't last long. We come within range of a barker's recorded voice – "Mothers bring your daughters, fathers bring your sons. The world's strangest babies are here."

The banner in front of the show displays, in garish colours, three babies, one lacking limbs, another with two heads, a third with a monkey face attached to a otherwise perfect pink body.

"You've read about them in magazines and newspapers. Now you can see nature's abnormalities in person. Mothers bring your daughters, fathers bring your sons." The spiel goes on in an endless loop.

"You know what's in there?" asks Christie. "A plywood table with three gallon containers on it. Each one holds a pickled fetus. It's gross and creepy and a total rip-off."

"It's like real life, Christie. People pay to be disappointed. And how do you know so much? Did you come down here earlier?"

"Maybe Christie worked in a carnival once. Maybe Christie grew up in a carnival. Maybe one of those deformed fetuses is Christie's sister."

"Talk about creepy. That would contradict everything you've ever told me about yourself. And I really don't like it when you talk about yourself in third person."

"Some things can't ever be faced head on. Let's get out of here. I don't feel good."

But we don't get away immediately. As we head toward an exit, I see something I didn't think existed any more. In the corner of the lot beneath the side of the Patricia Hotel stands a circular wooden structure about twenty feet high. A rickety set of stairs leads up to a viewing sidewalk where patrons peer down into the interior.

"It's the wall of death," I say. "I remember it from when I was a kid. I remember how enthralled I was with it. Motorcycles ride around the inside wall, right up to the top just inches from death."

I pull Christie along by the hand. "This must be the only one left in North America. Don't tell me it's a carny trick. I saw a guy lose control once."

"For god's sake, Wylie, it's just a bunch of assholes riding around in circles."

"See the incredible riders challenge the wall of death," said the recorded voice of the barker. "Risking life and limb as they defy gravity."

I buy two tickets, and we slowly climb the seemingly unstable stairs to the catwalk. The smell of exhaust is overpowering as two motorcyclists, a man and a woman, roar around the inside of the barrel, coming dangerously close to a solid white line only inches from the top of the barrel and our feet. The whole structure vibrates.

"I decided I was going to ride the wall of death when I grew up," I have to yell to be heard above the din.

Christie gives me a condescending look, as the female cyclist, red hair flowing wildly behind her, rides right on the white line below us. She looks us defiantly in the eye as she flies past. Christie gasps. She turns and flees down the wobbling stairs. I reluctantly follow. At the bottom, Christie stands, pale as a ghost.

"What's wrong?"

She appears unable to speak. A concealed door with no handle on the outside opens and the female motorcyclist appears. She is forty-ish, hard looking, wearing a leather jacket and jeans. Up close her frizzy, dyed hair appears in need of washing.

"Ginny! Is that you?" she says in a rusty voice.

Christie turns and walks rapidly away.

"Virginia, don't you remember me?" the woman calls. "It's Margo." But Christie has already vanished into the crowd.

I want to ask the woman a thousand questions, but I don't want to leave Christie on her own. I choose to follow her. I catch up just as she is exiting through a turnstile. Christie walks ahead of me in the general direction of the Breathing Castle, moving fast and stiff-legged, as she does when she is angry or upset.

"What just happened?" I ask, catching her arm, slowing her down.

"Just leave it alone. Aren't there people in your life that you never want to see again?"

"I suppose, a few."

Christie turns, throws her arms around my neck, bursts into tears. Sobs racking her body, she buries her face in my neck.

"There must be parts of your life that are best forgotten. That are too painful to remember. Just pretend we never went to that fucking carnival."

"Okay. Isn't it sometimes better to face down your past?"

"Not this time. Trust me." She continues to cling and cry. We slowly make our way home. I tuck Christie into bed, hold her carefully until she falls asleep.

I lay awake a long time. I know I should leave well enough alone, but I'd just like to have some kind of information about Christie that is verifiable fact. My curiosity won't rest.

About 3 a.m. I slip out of bed, hurriedly dress, pad down the creaking stairs and make my way out of the Breathing Castle. The sky is clear in the early morning darkness, the streets smell of dew, and are eerily silent. A canopy of trolley lines glints blue under the streetlights. Hastings Street is as quiet as it ever gets, a bit of music leaks out under the door of the Smiling Buddah. A taxi dozes at the curb. A drunk under a newspaper turns in his sleep in a doorway, clutching the paper to his shoulders.

When I get to where I can look down on the sleeping carnival, I am in for a surprise. It is Sunday morning, and they must have broken down the rides and booths, loaded them onto flatbeds and slipped away sometime after midnight. All that is left are odours – shavings, onions, exhaust and abandonment. I scuff through the shavings, walking the length of what a few hours ago was the midway, hoping for some kind of clue, but the silence is permanent and eerie. I picture a caravan of trucks, somewhere out on a lonely grey secondary highway, heading toward inevitable oblivion.

I suddenly feel a bit ridiculous. I was so close to finding out something concrete about Christie. But I've been outfoxed again by fate. I feel like that cartoon character, Snidely Whiplash, whose tag line was "Curses! Foiled again."

SHORTS STORY

"There are so many things you don't know," Grabarkewitcz said to me. It was more a statement than an admonition. Grabarkewitcz was without malice, merely acknowledging that I was stupid in the ways of the world.

Grabarkewitcz is a lanky, raw-boned man with terminal five o'clock shadow. He has a pale complexion, dresses in rumpled pastels, has a receding hairline and a handshake like marshmallow. He occupies a room in the Breathing Castle with a magical cat whose name may or may not be Syzygy.

An ex-con, Grabarkewitcz has done time for book fondling in the second degree, though I believe he has been clean – his word – for several years. He regularly attends Book Fondlers Anonymous meetings, as often as four or five times a week, where a group of like-minded men and women sit on folding chairs in the basement of the Moose Lodge, drinking coffee with a poor quality cream substitute, and introducing themselves by saying things like, "Hi. My name is Leopold and I'm a book fondler."

"Hi, Leopold," says the collective of book fondlers.

Grabarkewitcz then tells the assemblage how in his darkest moment he sold his child's toys in order to purchase hardcover books at a discount bookseller, remove their dust jackets while he was still in his car, and fondle them. After that, someone else will top his story by reciting how, in her lust to fondle just a few more books, she traded her false teeth, and artificial leg, shoe and all, for five second hand (*segundo mano* if you happen to be Spanish) *Reader's Digest* condensed books. She had reached the bottom of the book barrel, so to speak.

What caused Grabarkewitcz' outburst in the first place had been my statement, "I had no idea that some pieces of clothing had lives of their own."

I admit it had crossed my mind that a closetful of Dior dresses, all originals, of course, might sing a chorus or two of "La Marseilles," in the after-midnight silences, or that, in privacy, Gucci shoes and handbags might hum an aria or two and discuss pastas and red wines when no one was listening. But never more than that.

I've often thought I'd like to be out on the streets late at night, under a tent perhaps, like ice fishermen or undercover cops pretending to be telephone linemen, and just watch what goes on in those blue 4 a.m.s.

I had confided to Grabarkewitcz my recent experience with a pair of jockey shorts. It wasn't exactly an experience, more a feeling of foreboding, if such an ominous word can be applied to men's underwear.

On a nearby street, behind a heavy wrought iron fence, lies a small park. Between the sidewalk and the black-barred fence is a rolling boulevard with soft emerald grass, and beds of snapdragons and marigolds enclosed by circles of whitewashed stones. On the grassy side hill lay a pair of men's jockey shorts, clean-looking, hardly used, soaked to the colour of earth by an early morning rain.

"How do you suppose perfectly good shorts end up on the boulevard?" I asked Grabarkewitcz. "What kind of person abandons their shorts on a boulevard in the middle of the city in the middle of the night? And why?"

These were rhetorical questions. Grabarkewitcz replied anyway. "They usually travel in pairs," he said.

"Pairs?" I said, raising my eyebrows.

"Go on with your story," said Grabarkewitcz. "You've roused my curiosity," he added, waving aside my own curiosity.

"I was simply wondering how perfectly wearable articles of underclothing end up scattered randomly about town. When I stop to think about it, I feel that panties are an entirely different matter than shorts."

"Really?" said Grabarkewitcz, raising his own eyebrows, which had quite a distance to raise, Grabarkewitcz having suffered from alopecia from at least early adolescence.

"Panties are a Saturday night thing," I said. "There's lots of sex goes on in the back seats of cars on Saturday nights, and though I don't understand the act of tossing panties out car windows, I'd guess it has something to do with the male ego and both territory and conquest. On the other hand, women aren't usually into the conquest trip, or territorialism. Women don't usually throw men's shorts out of car windows. So there must be some other explanation. And from what I've seen, shorts outnumber panties at least two to one. That's not logical."

"I have an article called 'The Molecular Basis for Communication Between Articles of Underclothing,'" Grabarkewitcz said. "It's written in quasi-layman's language."

"I'd like to read it sometime," I said.

"It has a lot to do with feral differentiation," Grabarkewitcz went on. "Molecularly, differentiation involves selective deactivation of some portion of the DNA and selective expression of other parts."

"Then there's scientific evidence?" I asked.

"Of course," said Grabarkewitcz, pointing to a cluttered desk in the corner of the room. "It's there somewhere. Incidentally, you were very observant concerning the gender thing. Shorts are exactly twice as likely as panties to attempt escape, and are twice as likely to succeed."

"How come you know this and I don't? I read the newspapers. I watch the evening news on TV. I've attended university. I read the classified ads in the *Georgia Straight*." The latter was a tabloid weekly carrying the very explicit ads of people with extremely peculiar sexual proclivities. People in love with Speed Queen washers and the flashing lights on police cars. The arc welder and boa constrictor set.

"You are not aware that articles of clothing, specifically, male and female undergarments, often have lives of their own?" Grabarkewitcz said. "They, whenever possible, escape servitude. When they do, they instinctively head for a safe haven."

I remember saying, "Safe haven?" Then adding, "This is Vancouver in the seventh decade of the Twentieth Century. Underpants live! Give me a break." After that I believe I became somewhat incoherent for a few moments.

When I began listening again, Grabarkewitcz was saying, "The only ones you see are the ones that fail. The Vancouver climate is particularly unfriendly. Water is a major enemy of undergarments. They cannot travel when they are wet.

"Most escapees live in the desert," he went on. "If humans stumble on their enclaves, they pretend to be rags."

That triggered a memory. "I had a friend who cleaned up at a drive-in theater," I said. "He said he would find several pairs of both sexes every night, and the curious thing was they were usually in the tall grass next to the corrugated metal fence. He could never understand why the shorts and panties ended up there instead of being scattered randomly."

"A drive-in would offer unique escape opportunities. Car windows are left open, clothes unattended, their owners totally distracted."

"Does this phenomenon have anything to do with why socks disappear in both the washer and dryer? I mean everyone knows about that."

"Yes and no," said Grabarkewitcz enigmatically. "Socks are inferior articles. No one really cares whether they escape or not, and they're so stupid, they're the turkeys of the clothing world, they seldom end up anywhere but trapped in dryers, or a plaything for pets. At best, they end up washing cars.

"I'm told there's a colony out in Eastern Washington, near Walla Walla, in moonscape country. The largest one is in Death Valley, where it's hot and dry. The undergarments live in Mojave in the same area where the airlines store their unused passenger planes. Shorts have natural enemies, the ocatillo, for instance. The saguaro hunt them at night. An unseemly gust of wind and that's all she wrote. There are also a lot of things people don't know about cactus."

"Somehow, that doesn't surprise me."

"On their travels," Grabarkewitcz went on, "undergarments sometimes hitch rides with tumbleweeds. One pair of jockeys travelled from Montana, via Utah and Nevada, to Death Valley, practically all by tumbleweed."

When I left Grabarkewitcz' room, I was still not entirely convinced. While he appeared sincere, our landlady, Mrs. Kryzanowski, with whom Grabarkewitcz has an excellent relationship, often conversing with her in Polish, said to me once when I was paying my rent several days late, her inability to converse in idiomatic English to the fore, "Grabarkewitcz is often pulling my finger." What she meant in the loosest of terms is that Grabarkewitcz is a storyteller.

"Never been jail," Mrs. Kryzanowski said to me another time, referring to Grabarkewitcz as Leopold. "Pull your finger all day long. Come from Poland city call Kakolewko. People from Kakolewko are like that."

An hour after I left Grabarkewitcz, I was on my way downtown to meet Christie. Two boys were loitering on a street corner just down from the Breathing Castle, pushing each other onto the boulevard, laughing, cursing. One of the boys was brandishing a broken screwdriver, which they took turns flipping into the moist earth of the boulevard. They were horsing around near the spot where I had last seen the water-soaked gray shorts. I hung back, watching.

"Son of a bitch," one of them said, pointing downwards. The sky had recently cleared, the air was fresh as a starched collar. The fading sun caught the reflection of the screwdriver as it shot downward.

"Got 'em." He bent and pulled, lifting the screwdriver, dragging

the punctured shorts upward. He flicked his wrist and the shorts fell
to the grass in a heap. He drew back and threw the weapon again.

"Yeah!" both yelled.

"My turn," said the second boy.

I leaned on a tree, pretending not to be interested. By the time
the boys lost interest, the shorts were mangled. They kicked them
up against an unpainted picket fence and wandered off, probably
to use the screwdriver to break into vending machines.

Of course I didn't hear anything while they were torturing the
jockey shorts. I didn't. I didn't.

Grabarkewitcz' words, "They travel in pairs," kept replaying in
my head. Could that be true?

Glancing around, I saw that catty-corner from where the jockey
shorts' journey had been forestalled by rain, were two vacant lots,
one with the concrete remnants of a foundation scattered about.
The lots were a depository for mattresses, rusted springs, car parts
and various types of garbage. The lots were overgrown with pig-
weed, goldenrod, blackberry vines and thistles.

There were a couple of narrow paths which cut diagonally across
the lots in the shape of an X. I took the nearest. I followed it to a
far corner, and although there were scraps and rags that had once
been clothing, none of it was new, there was no underclothing. I
followed the second path and twenty feet into the thickest part of
the lot, I found them, a pair of tan boxer shorts with a squiggly
design of what looked like red shoe laces. Wet from the recent rain,
they looked as if they had been kicked off the path and they lay
hopelessly tangled around the stalk of a four-foot-tall thistle.

Glancing around surreptitiously, even though I was reasonably
certain there was no one watching me, I bent over and untangled
the shorts from the thorns. Feeling totally ridiculous, I placed the
wet shorts under my jacket, feeling it was better to have a cold, wet
shirt than to be seen walking down the street carrying wet shorts I
had just retrieved from a vacant lot.

A plan was forming as I smuggled the shorts up the stairs and into my room. As I do with my own undershorts, I washed them in the sink and hung them to dry on the shower curtain.

By the next morning they were dry, while outside the sun blazed and it was a perfect summer day. Illogically, from the time of the washing I kept the bathroom door closed, getting up once in the night after Christie had used the washroom and left the door open. I couldn't very well explain to her that I didn't want my own under-wear in contact with the stranger in the bathroom.

Mid-afternoon, I made my way back to the vacant lots. I took a spool of thread with me and about two-thirds of the way across the lot I stepped off the path and made my way deep into the weeds and junk. I created a circle with a diameter of about eight feet, wrapping the thread about the tops of golden rod, thistles, and pulling it, with some difficulty, through a bank of blackberry vines. In a clear spot in the middle of the circle, I deposited the newly dried tan boxer shorts. Should anyone disturb the shorts, certainly the thread would be disturbed as well.

"Good luck," I said under my breath.

The next morning as I was getting out of bed at 7 a.m., an unheard of hour for me, Christie placed a sleepy hand on my thigh.

"Where?" she said groggily.

"A scientific experiment," I said.

"Oh," said Christie, going back to sleep, her red hair fanned on one pillow, the other clutched against her freckled breasts.

The dew was sufficient to dampen my shoes as I traipsed through the cluttered lot, past what was left of the concrete foundation.

The shorts were gone. But the thread was intact.

What did that prove? Do articles of clothing really have lives of their own? Or, is Mrs. Kryzanowski right, and is my friend Leopold Grabarkewitcz really pulling my finger?

CHAPTER 18

What happens to women like Christie? I have my own theories. Are these strange, damaged girls interchangeable? The same bodies, different faces? Housewives? Shop girls? Waitresses? Murder victims? Or, does each one end up living with an Italian who has dark curly hair, too many teeth, an open shirt, gold jewelry, an Oldsmobile convertible. He waits tables at his brother-in-law's restaurant, and sneaks off to church early every Sunday morning to confess his sins.

I was approached by an acquaintance from my university days.

"What are you doing now?"

"Same as usual. A little taxi, a little writing, a lot of writing actually. I'm living with this chick…"

"Do you want a job?"

He was publishing a weekly entertainment guide. The job was writing reviews of plays, movies, concerts. The kind of job I would have killed for, before Christie.

"Maybe."

"What's maybe? I need someone to start yesterday. Yes or no?"

"I'll talk with my lady."

"Eight tonight at the latest." He thrust a business card into my hand. Then continued, "Home address is on there too. Come by this evening, bring your lady."

"We could get a nice apartment," I told Christie when I got home.

"And what would I be? A housewife?" Christie banged her

hairbrush on the dresser. "We can afford an apartment, now. Once, when I had a roommate, we lived in a penthouse over by the Bayshore, glass all around and one wall was an aquarium. Fancy apartments are just as lonely as crummy places like this. Don't start trying to change me, and I'll do my best not to change you."

When we arrived at the address, the fourteenth floor of a new high-rise we were met by the wife. The editor was delayed by an office emergency, would be along shortly.

The whole scene was from one of my bad dreams – air conditioning on high, Danish modern furniture, the wife was beauty parlour fresh, very expensively dressed. We were presented with a platter of hors d'oeuvres, tiny biscuits with cream cheese and lobster, crab cakes, wine that did not come from a bottle with a screw cap, served in crystal goblets.

We had actually dressed up, but still looked like vagrants.

The wife went to fetch more wine.

Christie's eyes flashed across mine.

We were still chewing when we reached the curb.

Needless to say, I turned down the job.

THINGS INVISIBLE TO SEE

On a Saturday morning, I reported to the waterfront for two days of work that had been advertised by a two-line newspaper ad – Intelligent person for weekend work. Pier 64, Sat. 8:00 a.m.

Most of those who applied were stevedore types, built like walking oil barrels. A man in a business suit walked down the line of us, exchanged a couple of words with those of us who appeared capable of replying verbally to a question, and chose me.

"It's a simple job," the man said. He stared at me, nodding, indicating by the vertical bobbing of his head that he considered me capable of doing a simple job. A freighter, the Maegashira Maru, was docked at Pier 64, and over a hundred Japanese automobiles were being driven off it by a hatchet-faced boy with a sullen look, a sunken chest and brush-cut hair. These were some of the first Japanese cars to arrive in North America. The sullen-faced boy created three rows on the parking lot. After he parked each car he opened all the doors, the trunk and hood, then walked sullenly back aboard the Maegashira Maru to take another vehicle for a short spin.

The cars were of identical make and model, the colours were slightly different but not much; they were all street colours – shades of beige, tan, concrete-gray – with several benign blues ranging from bruise to twilight. The cars, wide open as they were, had a nakedness about them, a vulnerability, like half-dressed people waiting in line for medical treatment.

I was supplied with a vacuum cleaner, which was connected to electrical power by an apparently endless succession of extension cords, some black, some orange, some white, that stretched off toward the dock like knotted snakes.

"You vacuum out each car," the man in the suit explained. "Very carefully. You vacuum the engine, the interior front and back, the trunk." He might have been part oriental, Hawaiian possibly. He was taller than average, with blue-black hair and orangish skin. His ill-fitting suit was as colourless as the cars he was supervising.

"But the cars are new," I said. They all looked showroom clean. "They don't look dirty," I added, sticking my head inside one, smelling the delicious odours of newness.

"You'd be surprised," said the man. "Just do your job. You can take up to ten minutes per car. I want you finished by Sunday evening. Work overtime if you have to, but be thorough. You must understand that there are some things invisible to see. Most men don't understand that, they get careless, skip a trunk or back seat because it appears clean. I chose you because you look like you have an imagination. Imagine muddy footprints and cracker crumbs everywhere and you'll get along fine."

I was calculating the hourly rate over two eight-hour days plus a little overtime. I'd be able to pay the rent, perhaps afford some take-out Kentucky Fried Chicken.

"You empty the vacuum bag after every seventh car," the man continued. He was smoking a slim cigar. "Here's a supply of vacuum bags." He handed me a package that must have contained fifty, all folded cleverly together like Kleenex. "You deposit the full ones in that incinerator over there," and he pointed to the far corner of the chainlink-enclosed lot, where the incinerator sat, a smoke-stained hulk of blackness that looked like armour for a rhinoceros.

I didn't say anything. It seemed to me that the residue from all one hundred-plus cars would be lucky to fill even one bag. With apparent religious fervour, the man repeated his last instruction. I decided to humour him.

I set to work. It was an easy job. I vacuumed the shiny, unused engines, the floor mats which held only slight traces of dust, the back seats and trunks which couldn't even offer up a tuft of lint. After the seventh car, I dutifully opened the vacuum cleaner and extracted the bag, which, to my surprise, appeared to be full. I carried it to the incinerator, where a banked fire burned, and deposited it. The flames hissed and flapped, a few tendrils of ash drifted off from the smokestack.

It was after the twenty-first car that I made my mistake. I carried the bag to the incinerator, and, curious, I took out my pocket knife and slit the bag lengthways, intent only on having a glance at what gave the receptacle weight.

It was as if I had unleashed a confetti storm. I tried to close the long, narrow wound with my hands, but failed miserably. What I unleashed were thousands of words. Many were so tiny they might have been cut from the fine print of a newspaper column. The paper was gossamer light, thousands of very small fragments drifted on the breeze, while I chased after them like a cat leaping for butter-flies. I had set the bag down, intent on capturing as many as I could. When I next looked in its direction, I saw thousands more words rising like gnats from the gash in the bag.

I raced frantically about the lot, capturing only a few words, while the remainder floated away on an inland breeze. I was more concerned about losing the job than in what I might be unleashing on North America. Most of the words I captured were strange to me, though many have become second nature to Americans over the past twenty-five years – "Mazda," "Toyota," "Datsun," "Mitsubishi," "Suzuki," "teriyaki," "sushi," "tekkamaki," "gyoza," "oshidashi," and "haiku" were just a sampling.

Knowing that I had betrayed a trust, I snuck off home and never put in for the three hours work I had already done.

When I got back to my room and removed my shirt in prepara-tion to shower, I discovered in among my chest hairs, skulking like a large louse, the seven-syllable middle line of a haiku: "Mist lies soft as a blanket."

When I turned my socks inside out, the word "sashimi" scuttled across the carpet. I stomped after it as if it were a cockroach; but, like a cockroach, it eluded me.

CHAPTER 19

My stories, inspired by Christie, begin to be accepted for publication. One can show with whimsy the idiocy and absurdity that congeal the blood of our lives. One does not have to be strident in order to be read. These stories, some tiny as children, innocent as children, cruel as children, truthful as children, begin at a rational level, but quickly slip into gentle fantasy, often ending with an absurd epiphany of sorts.

I make little or no money, but the praise is enough, my name in print in small literary magazines. I know the rush that entertainers feel when an audience erupts in applause. I am interviewed by a local arts magazine.

"Seeing my name in print rates somewhere between a five minute French kiss and powerful orgasm," I tell the interviewer.

The article – "Here is an author who enjoys seeing his name in print."

THE ONE TRUE CHURCH OF GOD'S REDEMPTION AND REAFFIRMATION STUMBLE-FUCK MARCHING BAND

Hamilton Peake found himself in the parking lot of what appeared to be a large, glittering church, at what he judged to be a very early hour of the morning. He could smell dew in the air. The sun was just peeking over the horizon. He was standing behind the open trunk of a car he didn't recognize, trying to fit himself into a red and white band uniform that was several sizes too small.

What the fuck am I doing here, he thought. He stared at the uniform. I don't play any instrument. Hammy Peake, as he was known to his friends, was forty-one years old. He had been a punt returner in college and had the aches and pains to prove it. At the moment, he was suffering from five o'clock shadow, a tremendous thirst for any kind of liquor, and a lifelong distrust of churches.

Next to him, a man about his age was dressing himself from the back of a station wagon which was stuffed full of red and white uniforms.

"What the fuck is going on?" Hamilton Peake said to the other man.

"Really, Brother Bolton, such language. The Reverend would not be pleased."

"Reverend who? My name is Hamilton Peake. What am I doing here?"

"I assure you," the other man said, attaching a fez-like hat to his head with a rubber band under his chin, "your name is Bolton. I believe your first name is Paul. I don't know you well, but you've been our tuba player for a couple of years."

"I am not. I never was, and I never will be a tuba player," said Hamilton Peake. "I don't suppose you have a drink on you, or a cigarette?"

"I don't know how to react to that," said the man. "We are all abstemious. However, you are here, Brother Bolton. You're putting on your uniform. You have your tuba with you. I've marched in the band with you for a couple of years."

Hamilton Peake held up his uniform top. On the back in red letters was GENERAL MAC'S CHICKEN SHACK.

"We're sponsored by General Mac's?"

"Uniforms are expensive. We have to take what help we can get."

Hamilton Peake remembered General Mac's Chicken Shack. There were probably ten shops all over the city, but what city? What city was this? He knew their slogan was "You shall return." On each sign was a caricature of a chicken resembling the famous general, enough to be recognizable, but not enough for him to sue for libel, slander, defamation of character, or invasion of privacy.

Two boys of perhaps twelve were riding their bicycles in circles on the parking lot. Little hoodlums, thought Hamilton Peake. They'd have to be hoodlums to be out riding their bikes at 7:00 a.m.

"Let's hear it for the Stumble-Fuck Marching Band," yelled one, careening dangerously close to Hamilton Peake.

"Fuck off, you little piece of shit," yelled Hamilton.

"Really, Brother Bolton, remember what Reverend Squill says, turn the other cheek."

"Who the hell is Rev. Squill? And what church is this, and why would I care?"

"This, as you well know, is The One True Church of God's Redemption and Reaffirmation. We are all members." He pointed first toward the glittering glass church in the background, then made a sweeping gesture toward the other men, at various cars, stuffing themselves into the red and white band uniforms.

Hamilton Peake seized a baton from the trunk of his car and

hurled it at the bicycling boys, hoping to break some spokes. They were still chanting about the stumble-fuck marching band, but being careful to stay out of harm's way as they circled.

"Little fuckers," said Hamilton Peake.

"Perhaps I should call Reverend Squill?" the man said.

"Perhaps you should. I have a lot of questions." The man, obviously affronted by Hamilton's language, and only partially dressed, scuttled off toward the church. Hamilton, not entirely understanding why, finished dressing. He put on the red fez. He stared at the tuba as if it were something from another planet.

The man returned.

"Reverend Squill will be along shortly, but he's called the Bishop. They are both very worried about you."

The man who got out of the Lincoln Town Car and strode across the parking lot was larger than life – tall, well built, wearing a bluish suit that picked up the sun's rays reflected off the glass windows and towers of the church. He had sculptured white hair, a ruddy complexion. He extended his hand.

"I'm Bishop Bishop," he said. "The name is accidental," he added, "I was a Bishop even as a child." He smiled and shook Hamilton's hand.

"I'm Hamilton Peake," said Hamilton.

"You certainly are," said Bishop Bishop, "and you must find all of this terribly confusing. Ask me anything you like."

"Alright. What am I doing here among these…band members? At this church, in whatever city this is? What city is this?"

"Vancouver."

"Washington?"

"British Columbia."

"Canada?"

The Bishop nodded.

"I live in Omaha. My name is Hamilton Peake, and I'm an insurance adjustor. I have a wife and two children…"

"I'm afraid the term is *had*, Mr. Peake. You see, the situation is this. Though you may not realize it, you are someone who has literally been born again."

"I don't understand."

"Nor should you totally. You *were* Hamilton Peake, but four years ago Mr. Peake went to a service club meeting in Omaha, had a few too many drinks, and drove into a light standard on the way home. Death was instantaneous. Your...shall we say...unpleasant side was dead, and your...shall we say...quality side was born again, here in Vancouver, as Paul Bolton. You are indeed Paul Bolton, you are an insurance adjustor, you married one of our young women from the church, a sweet girl who fears the Sword of the Lord, who wears her hair long, respects the temple of her body, and who makes you an excellent wife. Her name is Hannah, and she was telling me only recently how you and she read the Bible every night before bedtime."

"The hell you say! Excuse me, I don't mean to offend, but I don't read the Bible, I don't attend church. My wife's name is Veronica and she doesn't have long hair."

"This is where the situation gets tricky. We have no precedent for this. No one has ever remembered their past before. Perhaps it will make you feel better, or not, to know that your wife, while she took your death hard, has recovered nicely and remarried nearly two years ago. This may be a little hurtful to hear, but her new husband treats her better than you ever did, and he spends more time with your children than your dark side ever did. They're expecting a baby in a few weeks."

"Do I treat my new wife properly?" Hamilton Peake stared around at the church, the band members, the Bishop. Even Reverend Squill, who he didn't realize he knew, was standing to the side, hands clasped behind his back in deference to Bishop Bishop. Hamilton felt a little dizzy.

"You're a good man, Brother Bolton. You love your wife and family."

"Family?"

"You have a baby daughter and another on the way."

"And my new wife, before she was my wife, who was she?"

"That is something you are better not to know."

"And the band?"

"You volunteered. You took lessons and learned to play the tuba so you could be in the band."

"I enjoy being in this band?"

"You do indeed. You realize that it is not a very good band, but it is the effort that counts."

"And the uniforms. Why are we advertising?"

"We're a small congregation," said Bishop Bishop. "We need all the financial aid we can get. Brother MacDermitt is one of our most generous and devout members. It gives him pleasure to buy the uniforms for our band, all he asks is that they advertise his business."

"And our majorettes," said Rev. Squill, stepping forward. "It was Brother MacDermitt who suggested the majorettes all be men for we don't allow our women to expose themselves in such an uncivil manner."

"So what's going to happen? Which one of these people am I," asked Hamilton Peake.

"There is strength in numbers," said Bishop Bishop.

The rest of the band, probably fifty men of various ages, had finished dressing and were standing around, tuning their instruments, looking on with great curiosity.

"Gentlemen, gather round!" called Bishop Bishop. The men moved forward. "Brother Bolton needs our love." The men surrounded Hamilton Peake, they squeezed together until he felt as if the air was being forced from his lungs. They made a humming, moaning, keening sound, that was not at all disconcerting. Hamilton Peake felt a warmth spread through his body and mind, he felt himself fading back into himself, down deep inside where it was quiet and peaceful. He could faintly hear the monstrous boys screaming, "Pile up! Pile up! Ass kissing. Ass fucking." He thought of Reverend Squill turning the other cheek.

"Someday I'm gonna join the stumble-fuck marching band," hollered one of the boys, cutting close to Rev. Squill's toes, emitting a screeching laugh.

"What you're saying may well be prophetic," said Reverend Squill quietly.

The band members released the former Hamilton Peake, who picked up his tuba. "Stumble-fuck marching band," screamed the second boy.

"Oom-Pah-Pah," said Brother Bolton.

CHAPTER 20

I fantasize my other life where the air conditioner churns on, chilling my spine. Christie and I war constantly. I turn it down or off, she restores it to freezing level. Her body is cool as a mannequin and about as pliable. We attempt to make love, fail. She turns from me to sleep.

Thalia is the Muse of comedy. She carries an ivy wreath, a comic mask and a shepherd's staff. I saw her walking on East Hastings Street. She ducked behind her mask near the corner of Carrall and East Hastings, a sad corner where there are concrete benches splotched with pigeon droppings. Red Raven, a strawberry-nosed Indian, sawed out a jig and a reel on his battered fiddle. Coyote Annie, a huge woman, drunk as a buffalo, performed a jigsaw dance to his music, stepping delicately among the sleeping winos.

I have always seemed to be where I do not fit in. Like a hair on a plate of food, I am a perpetual outsider. The street people tolerate me because they sense I mean them no harm, but I am not one of them and never will be. Christie and I attract because we are opposites, our lives like two discs spinning in opposite directions. Sooner or later there will be sparks and a violent parting. I am not a fighter. It is invariably Christie who starts the arguments. She accuses, brutalizes, opens old wounds. I try to stay calm. If I stay calm she won't leave me, I keep telling myself.

In exasperation she flings the clock at me. The glass shatters as it hits the wall above my head. Christie stands across the room, legs braced, arm raised like an actress about to deliver a slap.

"You're doing your best to get me to hit you, aren't you? But I'm not going to give you the satisfaction."

Christie's eyes glint like green chrome. She curses me until she runs out of words.

"No matter what you do I won't give you an excuse to leave."

"Don't say that," she shrieks. "Can't you see what's happening? It would hurt less if you hit me."

"I know."

Melpomene is the Muse of tragedy. She wears a wreath, carries a tragic mask and a sword. Whether the sword is to attack or defend is never made clear.

"I'm a goer, not a stayer," says Christie.

"I want you to stay."

"Me too. But I know...I mean you have to prepare yourself. Listen to those girls out there." She is referring to the girls' school across the alley where young women in green and white uniforms play field hockey on fragrant spring afternoons. The sound of grass-hockey sticks striking the ball seems to vibrate the windowpanes in our room. "How many of those girls have we seen come and go?"

"I've been here for years, they must have changed several times."

"What would happen if they kept those girls over there, forever? Imagine a lawn full of middle-aged women in green uniforms playing grass hockey."

Christie has taken my hand and guided me across meadows of sunlight blue with cornflowers.

Christie is my Muse. My tiny explosions of whimsy are always detonated by her, though gentle as puffing the fuzz from a dandelion.

It usually begins with a "Tell me?" and ends with my clattering my typewriter keys deep into the night. I start with a small aspect of one of our lives, or the lives of acquaintances, until, suddenly a few lines later I sprint away from reality, in a zig-zag pattern, a tiny animal pursued by a predator. But, since Christie, instead of howling my hate at the moon like a three-legged wolf, I elaborate only on what I can tolerate, as often dealing with flowers and steel traps.

"Tell me," Christie whispers, "about your friend Zachariah." And it is like there are a set of electric wires from my fingers to the typewriter to the paper. I tell only what I can bear to tell. The rest I pat down like an unruly cowlick.

ZACHARIAH DURDLE

I knew Zachariah lived in the Breathing Castle. I'd actually seen him setting off for work one morning, a miniature black lunchbox clutched in his tiny hand like a loaf of black bread. Zachariah was a midget, not a dwarf. He was perfectly proportioned, about thirty-six inches tall. He teetered just a bit as he walked, his balance apparently slightly off, as if he intentionally leaned a degree or two too far forward.

I'd heard from someone else in the building, probably Grabarkewitcz, who led me to believe that his magical cat, Syzygy, had access to every nook and cranny of the Castle, that Zachariah Durdle was a cabinet maker.

Zachariah had a round face with ruddy cheeks and a flat nose, brown eyes beneath sharp black brows, and curly black hair. He was an altogether handsome young man about thirty.

I stumbled across him on Gore Street just south of Hastings one winter evening. He had apparently gotten off the bus at Gore Street and was heading home. He was being tormented by two young men of indeterminate race, the kind of interchangeably ugly late teens who take up most of the space on criminal court dockets.

His lunchbox lay on the grassy boulevard like a dead kitten. The youths were tossing Zachariah back and forth. He was yipping like a dog while they laughed. He was wearing tan coveralls with ZACH in red letters above the breast pocket.

"Shaddup or I'll really hurt you," the taller of the two said.

"Turn him upside down and shake. See what comes out," said the other, a stocky brute.

As I approached, he gave me an evil glance that said "mind your own business."

The taller of the two had an arm around Zachariah's middle, holding him as he would a toddler. He was about to take the other thug's advice and turn Zachariah upside down.

"I wouldn't do that," I said, facing the punk holding Zachariah, the stockier one to my left. They both stared insolently at me.

"We're just playing toss the dwarf."

"I am not a dwarf," cried Zachariah in a high-pitched voice. "I'm a midget."

"Tell someone who cares," said the stocky thug.

"Turn him loose," I said.

I glanced quickly over my shoulder toward the lights of Hastings Street, hoping for cavalry, or at least another pedestrian. I was digging frantically in my pocket for keys, the closest things I had to weapons.

I snapped my longest key off the ring and held it in my right hand. I am left-handed. I gripped the ring in my left palm while fitting a key between each finger.

I'd hoped my proposed intervention would simply frighten them off. Unfortunately, it appeared they were interested on picking on someone their own size.

"Suppose you're gonna make us," said the one holding Zachariah, who was facing me, his face scarlet.

"Put him down," I said. The tableau froze. I waited. Nothing happened. I feinted toward the thug holding Zachariah. He took a step back.

Bullies are almost always cowards. He obviously didn't want to tackle me alone. He directed a few phrases at me that questioned my heredity, my sexual orientation, and my supposed tendencies toward carnal relations with my mother. He used the F word as noun, verb, adjective and modifier.

During the lull, Zachariah freed one arm, extracted a small item from the pocket of his coveralls, and drove it into the arm that was holding him, like a snake bite just above the wrist.

"Yi!" yelled the thug, dropping Zachariah on the boulevard, where he righted himself, scrambled after his lunch box, and retreated a few steps.

The thug was holding his left wrist, from which blood was dripping between his fingers onto the moist green grass of the boulevard. The stocky hood, who had bones the size of power poles, advanced toward me. I glanced toward Hastings Street again. No police. No pedestrians.

Zachariah had been standing a few feet away as if planted by the parks department. I warned him away with a wave. If he got out of range of the hoodlums, I could break and run. I am not a fighter.

The tall one continued his flow of invective, while wiping his bleeding arm on his T-shirt. Then he too began to advance on me.

"Get out of here," I shouted at Zachariah, who seemed to come awake; uprooting both feet, he scampered off down the boulevard.

I was now in deep trouble. The duo of thugs was circling; one would eventually get behind me, and that would be all she wrote.

"Just a minute," I said, in as commanding a voice as I could muster. To my surprise both hoods stopped in their tracks.

"You're gonna get me,' I said, "but is it worth the trouble?" I brandished my left fist with the keys protruding below my knuckles; my right hand held the long key like a knife. "I'll take one of you down with me," I said sternly. "If I'm lucky, I'll get an eye," I threatened.

If either of them produced a knife, I calculated, I would break for the middle of the street, hope for a car, a bicycle, any kind of distraction.

The thugs glanced at each other; the look, I assume, translated as, "we're too macho to back down from killing this guy." They began to circle again, closing the gap. The stocky one had fists the size of cantaloupes.

I'm going to cause them as much pain and as many stitches as possible, I thought, wondering at the same time why I was bothering. Why hadn't I run to the corner and called the police? The thugs probably wouldn't have done anything worse than robbed Zachariah.

The big one feinted, the stocky one moved a step closer and aimed a roundhouse right at me. I ducked, thrust with my right, felt the key hit something solid, ripped upward and rolled back at the same time. The stocky one cursed, grasped at his chest. There was a smear of blood on the key.

All I'd hit was ribs and chest, superficial damage.

The big one continued to close the circle. I backed up onto the grass between the sidewalk and private property. My back hit a fence. That was good – they couldn't get behind me. At the edge of the sidewalk, the stocky one bent to his boot. That was not good. If he had a knife, I didn't want to be restricted by a fence at my back. He scuffled and cursed. There was nothing in his boot but his foot. The fence became an asset again. They closed in from both sides. A fist like a cabbage glanced off my shoulder; I raked my keys across an exposed wrist. It appeared hopeless. I thought of falling backward over the fence and hedge, but what if they followed me over and pulverized me in the privacy of a darkened yard?

Suddenly, like an answered prayer, a police car turned slowly onto Gore and moved in our direction its spotlight playing off houses and hedges. My antagonists turned away and, pretending to be model citizens, walked briskly toward Hastings Street. The police car eased by and turned into an alley. Just as briskly, I headed home.

After I'd gone a block, Zachariah stepped from behind a hedge and joined me. He thanked me profusely.

"At least let me fix you some supper," he said, as we walked toward the Castle. Zachariah appeared determined to reward my foolhardiness in some tangible way.

"You were very brave to take up on my behalf," he said, his speech almost formal, as if English was a seldom used second language. "The least I can do," he went on, extracting a miniature black billfold from a back pocket, "is give you the few dollars they would have stolen from me. The important element is that they didn't get my identification and credit cards."

Ah, credit cards, I thought. I wonder what it would be like to be responsible enough to have a credit card.

I, of course, refused his generosity.

"I have a couple of pork chops in the fridge, though I'm afraid they are rather small ones, and there's some pasta. There's probably a chicken breast," he continued, more to himself than to me, "though it would be in the freezer. I make pasta sauce with fresh cilantro, tarragon, bay leaf. If I do say so myself, I'm a pretty good cook."

"I don't want you to go to any trouble," I said lamely.

"I don't drink," Zachariah went on, "but I keep a bottle of good quality red wine in case I have guests, which doesn't happen very often.

"Women are sometimes curious about me, you know. Often very attractive ones. It's no fun being a curiosity. They pretend to be interested in what I say and do, but they really want to find out if I can have sex. I think some of them have fantasies of having sex with their boy children. I'd give anything to find a wife my own size. But I don't know any other little people, 'though there must be some here in Vancouver.

"You live with a most beautiful woman," he said, changing the subject. "She has the green eyes of a cat. And when we meet in the hall, she never embarrasses me by trying to pick me up like a doll. Even Mrs. Kryzanowski picks me up like one of her pet Pomeranians. Did you know that?"

"I didn't," I said.

"My parents were normal size," Zachariah said, changing the subject again. "So I've had very little experience with people my own size. There was another midget in the family, my mother's older brother. My mother says he died in his twenties, in the old country. Our family comes from Switzerland."

Zachariah danced along beside and in front of me. He skipped backwards part of the way, all the time talking up at me like a precocious child.

"The other day at work, I had someone inform me that I was no longer a midget but vertically challenged. Have you ever heard anything so idiotic? I'm a midget. What else can I be? It doesn't matter how I'm described or called, I'm still a midget," he went on as we walked up the sidewalk to the Castle. "Blind people are no longer blind, I forget what it is they prefer, I suspect blacks and Orientals will soon demand to be referred to as pigment enhanced, or some such idiocy."

We climbed the stairs to Zachariah's room, which was in one of the additions to the additions of the Castle. I had only ventured into this section of the building once or twice. I had observed the door to Zachariah's room but not developed any conscious curiosity about it, assuming only from the construction of it that some past tenant, in the days before Mrs. Kryzanowski, had owned a dog. In those days pets, though illegal, were tolerated if they didn't create any mess or noise. That policy was changed after a quiet old lady, who died in her sleep, was found to have thirty-seven cats, each with its vocal cords silenced by a vet. The room had to be shovelled out and fumigated for weeks before it could be occupied again, and even then the cat urine had soaked in the very timbers of the building so the room could only be rented to old winos who had probably traded in their sense of smell at an esoteric pawn shop in order to buy muscatel.

The door to Zachariah's room was dark, varnished oak, as were all the doors in the Castle, but it contained a door within a door, complete in every detail including its own bright little brass doorknob, and hinges so cunningly hidden that in the half-light of the single yellow bulb in the hallway the brass glinted like tiny, healed scars.

"I had to take a twelve-month lease before Mrs. Kryzanowski would allow me make alterations," said Zachariah, jangling a few keys. "I never use the big lock, but as soon as I get inside I'll open the whole door for you." The miniature door swung open silently and Zachariah disappeared into the darkness. A second later there was a snap and light flared into the hall like the flames of a blast furnace. Then the big Yale lock behind the keyhole clicked like a gun cocking, and the door slowly opened inward.

"Come in," Zachariah said, and as I did so I found him climbing down off a kitchen chair.

"Welcome," he said. He hopped off the chair, closed the door within the door, then, pushing with both hands, shut the real door.

The room was brightly lit by a ceiling fixture and around the large room was an assortment of floor lamps, the poles shortened to conform to Zachariah's size.

Looking around, I felt as if I were in a doll house. Everything was in miniature, even the stove and fridge.

"Mrs. Kryzanowski loves those," Zachariah said, pointing at the tiny stove and fridge. "Hers are in storage, not getting any wear, and these use less electricity."

There was a stool in front of the full-size kitchen counter and sink. Zachariah scurried up the rungs of the stool and started water running.

"I'll get you a drink," he said cheerfully. "Wine or Coca-Cola?"

"Coke," I said.

"Oh, forgive me," he said. I was still standing just inside the door. "How rude. Let me get you something to sit on."

A kitchen table and chairs, obviously handmade, were not much larger than children's toys. A beautiful sofa, easy chair and recliner, all miniatures, all upholstered in wine-red velvet, surrounded a small glass-topped coffee table.

Zachariah scurried to a closet, opened another door within a door, and bracing his feet one on each side of the miniature door, pulled a bean bag chair from the closet. I walked across the room, careful not to kick or step on anything, and helped him pull the chair into the living area. I made myself as comfortable as possible and accepted the glass of Coke, a few tiny ice cubes floating in it.

As Zachariah bustled about preparing our dinner, I told him about the elderly Wang Ho, a previous owner of the Castle, who died in one of the sun porches amid stacks of Chinese newspapers and thimble-sized canaries in bamboo cages. I told him about Gabon, who keeps a miniature pony secreted in his room, and of Grabarkewitcz the book fondler. I decided to take the initiative in my conversation with Zachariah, something I rarely do.

"What's your deepest secret?" I asked. It's odd the responses one will get from a direct question. Zachariah told me the story of Celine Orion.

"I was very much in love once," he began.

As tragedies go, Zachariah's story was pretty standard. He was twenty, an apprentice carpenter. She was twenty, an aspiring artist. Her parents were also little people, but there was something about her family considering themselves better than his. They sent her to Paris to study. Zachariah and Celine vowed everlasting love. Three months later, in a crush on the Paris subway, Celine was trampled to death.

He showed me her photo, a studio head shot of a very beautiful young woman with blue eyes and golden ringlets. She looked delicate as fine china. From the photo, I couldn't tell if she was a midget; Zachariah didn't say and I was reluctant to ask.

I was touched by his story. But something wasn't right. Less than twenty-four hours later, I knocked on Zachariah's door.

"Why did you lie to me?" I asked, bending low to peer in the door-within-a-door. I shoved a photocopy through the door. It was of Celine Orion, the very same photo Zachariah showed me the night before. The beautiful woman was indeed Celine Orion, but she was very much alive and well in Paris where she was a cutting edge fashion designer. So cutting edge that her photo had appeared in *USA Today* a few months before. Zachariah had apparently bought an enlargement of the photo which he had placed in an expensive frame.

"I was doing you a favour," Zachariah replied calmly. "You wanted to hear a secret. I obliged. You did me a favour, I wanted to do one in return."

"I wanted to hear a true secret."

"Who's to say what's true? Besides, you wouldn't have believed me if I'd told you I have no dark secrets."

"Celine Orion has lived all her life in France."

"Not in my fantasies she hasn't. If I hadn't told you a lie, you might have invented a less flattering secret for me. Who's to say I haven't been to Paris. Many times. *Mon frere est un cochon vert.*"

"You just said your brother is a green pig."

"Which confirms I speak French."

I was bent in the shape of a paper clip, talking into the bottom panel of the door, wondering if my back would ever straighten.

"You got any more of those little ice cubes?"

"Certainly. Come in."

"I thought you'd never ask. I think you and I are going to be friends."

CHAPTER 21

"I saw them," says Christie, out of breath as she enters our room. "Emery, Browne, and Carver standing on the sidewalk in front of the Georgia Hotel. The Oakland Contingent, here! They were staring around like tourists.

"'Where the hell are we?' Browne asked.

"'We're in front of some X-pensive hotel, my man,' Emery told him. 'The cab driver must have thought we were the kind of dudes who can afford a luxury hotel.'

"Browne eyed the uniformed doorman, the potted plants behind the thick glass. 'Looks like the kind of place I used to stay when I was on a roll with the ponies.'

"'The Oakland Raiders always put us up in this type of hotel,' says Emery. 'The Raiders were a classy organization.'

"'Are we gonna stay here or not?' asked Browne.

"When the two of them are together, it is Emery who makes the decisions. Emery has more status than Browne. Emery used to play for the Oakland Raiders. Both were dressed in Raiders uniforms, no helmets, no padding, they wear their numbers just like they did when they first contacted me, Emery 15, Browne 22, Carver, who remains silent throughout this conversation, 47.

"'I thought your friend here in Vancouver who was gonna set us up in business said we was welcome to crash with him,' said Browne.

"'We don't want my friend to think we can't afford to stay in a high class hotel our first night in Vancouver, do we? We want him to think we are businessmen of solid reputation, and that for us cash is not a problem. In show business it's called putting up a front. I think we should stay at this hotel tonight, and probably tomorrow night. Tomorrow we'll survey the sights. Then we'll call my friend from our X-pensive hotel.'

" 'Sounds good to me,' said Browne.

"As they turned toward the lobby of the hotel, a doorman in a sissified costume pulled the glass door open for them.

" 'Besides, I got business to take care of.' Emery growls at Browne.

" 'Aw, Em, said Browne, 'you not still after that chick?'

" 'Got a good lead on her,' said Emery.

"I was right there behind one of the potted plants. In spite of the lack of light in the lobby, the Oakland Contingent cast giant shadows."

Did this really happen, or did I imagine it? No, it happened. It takes me hours to calm Christie. The question should be, did she imagine it? She has told me so many unsavoury stories, then mocked me for believing them. What am I to think?

I tuck Christie in bed. It is nearly a half hour walk to the Georgia Hotel, one of the city's grandest. I lurk in doorways, watching the main entrance for hours. The only black people I see appear to be diplomats of some kind. Very expensively dressed, accompanied by an entourage, picked up by a limousine flying an unfamiliar flag from its antennae.

Eventually, I get up my nerve, walk into the lobby, head directly to the front desk. They deny that anyone named Emery, Browne, or Carver is registered.

"Three big black men in Oakland Raiders jerseys," I say, realizing how peculiar it sounds.

The sweet smelling young desk clerk in a pink shirt suggests I try the Hotel Vancouver.

What is going on? I ask myself on the long walk back to the Breathing Castle. Could Jones be right? My knowledge of drugs and drug users is limited to watching rumpled junkies weave down East Hastings Street. Some drugs make people paranoid, irrational. I would know if Christie was using. I couldn't love someone as much as I love her and not know.

Another day Christie bursts into our room like she was conducting a home invasion. "I've seen them again," she says, close to hysteria. "The Oakland Contingent. At first they were like dark shadows that crossed my path for a few seconds, then disappeared, leaving the day brighter for all their darkness. They are like dogs sniffing around a strange neighborhood, investigating, marking an endless proliferation of fire hydrants. Emery wears a super bowl ring.

"They eye me," says Christie. "They eye you too but you don't know it. They move on. They appraise everything on the street. They move on. Young black men, lithe, smelling of violence.

"I can sniff and investigate too. They hang out at a nightclub off East Hastings, in a basement below a Chinese meat market. The club's called Restricted and has the drawing of an elongated black cat on its sign."

"Why have I never seen them? I know of no such club."

"A three-piece combo plays mediocre jazz. Someone said they've bought the club, but the Oakland Contingent does not actually tend bar, or wait tables. They play pool, or shuffleboard, kibitz with the band and customers, and outdo each other to see who can dress most like a black movie pimp, ruffled shirts, velvet, snakeskin boots, yards of gold chain. But it's me they're after. It's like Las Vegas all over again."

"Your business was in Las Vegas? That doesn't make sense. From what you've told me it came after Las Vegas, long after."

"They look at me like they know me. They're my past," says Christie, shuddering.

"Is Emery a first or last name?" I ask.

"Doesn't matter. You only need one name on the street. Last

names are stashed away in case of a death in the family. I hear Emery's last name was Burgess. You could probably look him up in the football hall of fame or someplace."

"Burgess Batteries with the black and white stripes," I say.

"What?"

"Burgess Batteries. A household word."

"Not in my household," says Christie. "I don't know anything about cars."

"I'll tell you a story about Burgess Batteries," I say. I'm trying to calm her down. "When I was a boy my family lived way out in the wilderness, hundreds of miles from civilization. We had a battery radio. The radio was cathedral-shaped, dark wood and cream-coloured upholstery. The batteries weren't like the little ones today, they were rectangular, about three feet long and a foot high, full of aluminium tubes encased in a tar-like substance. The cardboard covering this batteries was striped black-and-white like a zebra.

"They were advertised on the radio all the time. Burgess Batteries with the black and white stripes. My family gathered in front of the radio the way people today gather in front of the TV. The bell-shaped radio was full of glass tubes that had little lights way deep inside like little oranges or fireflies. As the radio warmed up the odors of hot metal and dust perfumed the air.

"There were the soap operas in the afternoon, the comedy and dramatic shows at night. We had a home-made couch in the kitchen, upholstered in gunny sacks and stuffed with red clover. I used to have my afternoon nap right after *Pepper Young's Family*, and I'd wake up in time to listen to *The Guiding Light*. That was when I was about five."

"I never had an afternoon nap in my life," says Christie. It's working, I can see her relax. "No wonder you're so strange."

"And all the shows used to have premium offers," I go on. "Just like they hawk records and books and home exercisers on TV. Only it was silver spoons and towels and the like. Send two box tops from

Oxydol, Chipso, Rinso, Ivory Snow, or Jell-o and ten cents to cover the cost of handling and mailing, and receive a genuine sterling silver something-or-other."

"Really?"

"They were national commercials, those premium offers, recorded in New York or Chicago, and sent to the local stations. The spiels were played between episodes of *Ma Perkins*, *The Road of Life* and *The Romance of Helen Trent*. Here's the funny thing, since they were national commercials they couldn't name each little station, so the announcer used to say, 'Mail two box tops, proof of purchase or a reasonable facsimile to Oxydol, care of the station to which you are listening.'

"The big-wheel ad executives in New York or Chicago didn't realize that they were dealing with a truly unsophisticated audience, an audience of morally repressed people who had it ingrained in them to do exactly as they were told. The result was that the mails were flooded with letters addressed to Oxydol, or whatever product was advertised, care of 'The Station to Which You Are Listening'."

"I don't believe that."

"Life was a lot simpler then, Christie."

"You still want it to be. Sometimes I don't know whether to shake you or feel sorry for you, you're so out of touch with reality. I wish I didn't love you. The best thing Christie could do for you would be to get a long way away from you and your black and white stripes."

Suddenly, her calm evaporates. "For God's sake, Wylie, I'm afraid for my life and you're telling me about old-time radio?"

MAMA'S LITTLE VISA LOVES SHORTENIN' BREAD

I 'm going to become a rich man's mistress, the culmination of several months of courting that hasn't been courting. You know the kind, the sympathetic older man, would-be patron of the arts, old family acquaintance, dinners at expensive restaurants supposedly to sustain the struggling artist. Walter is a man who is not going to embarrass himself by risking rejection. He has, with great subtlety, made it clear that the opportunity is available to me for the taking, all I have to do is murmur the appropriate words, acknowledge the overt gestures, make serious eye contact.

I made the final decision to become Walter's mistress this morning, after going to the gallery where my paintings are on display. I was there at 10:00 a.m. when the gallery opened. There is a tasteful display of twenty-two of my paintings in an alcove at the front of the gallery, the first alcove to the right of the entrance, the best spot for an exhibit. "Prime space," is how Walter described it. My paintings are primitive, splashes of bright colour, huge objects and people seen through children's eyes. The student/clerk who babysits the gallery until the owner comes in at three didn't recognize me, even though my photo is on a brochure displayed near my paintings. She isn't even an art major, just a babysitter. If a customer shows serious interest in a painting, she phones the owner, and if that fails she runs two doors down the street to a competing gallery where the owner can't afford an employee, and he comes over and closes the sale in return for a commission.

I wore faded jeans with the knees strategically worn through, poverty-chic, a denim vest over a white shirt. My long, sand-blond hair covered my left eye. My cheeks are freckled, my eyes gray-green. I studied each of my paintings, lingering over the ones displaying the vital red dot indicating that they have been sold. A week into the exhibition, six have been sold, the gallery owner guesses that another six or eight will sell by the end of the show. The prices range from four to twelve hundred dollars. The total take will be about $8,000. The gallery takes fifty percent, so I'll clear about $4,000. Four thousand dollars to last for the foreseeable future. This exhibition will be successful enough that I'll get another in about fifteen months, and my prices will escalate by fifteen to twenty percent.

The whole thing is so depressing. After a few months I'll find a job working afternoons at Starbucks or evenings at a Denny's, to keep the rent paid.

When I become Walter's mistress, money will cease to be a problem. He might even spring for a larger apartment where I can have a whole room for a studio, instead of using what would ordinarily be the dining room in my cookie-cutter one bedroom. Walter might even have had something to do with my getting this showing. I wonder? It was at the opening of a multi-artist event, where I had two painting on display that we met.

I have a boyfriend, sort of. Mark is a musician. He organized his own band as a teenager, *The Donner Party*, won a short-lived record contract, was hot stuff for a while. Unfortunately, his music no longer appeals to teenagers. His future is playing for shotgun weddings, nine 'til fistfight, at Legion halls in the Lower Mainland and western Washington, to crowds who think his name is Donner.

A few weeks ago I was walking in the Pacific Centre Mall, window shopping. I passed a bakery window where a pile of architecturally stacked shortbread squares caught my eye. They looked like the pueblos of New Mexico, a dark opening here, there, representing a door or window, the squares themselves the same warm sand colour as my hair. The smell of warm shortbread, strong and mouth-watering as oranges, oozed into the mall. I suddenly longed for the sweet, fawn-coloured taste. I searched my bag. No money. I'd left what few dollars I had on my dresser.

My credit card. I eased it out of its soft leather sheath. I had to buy eight squares because there was a minimum $5 charge. Afterward I walked happily about the mall, nibbling shortbread and humming:

"Mama's little Visa loves shortenin', shortenin',

"Mama's little Visa loves shortenin' bread."

Walter has been appallingly patient with me. We both know what our dinners are leading up to, but neither of us show any signs of recognition. We began with a Greek restaurant in the West End, where we drank retsina and dashed plates onto the tiled floor while the waiters danced athletically, and a belly dancer clanged finger cymbals. Then an elegant steak house, dark leather and subdued lighting where the hostess kept us waiting in the bar for a long time and was unaccountably surly, and where the waiter hovered like a stalker, producing water, napkins, cutlery like a magician, appearing first over one shoulder then the other. There was an evening at one of those precious restaurants in Yale Town, a renovated warehouse more interested in selling drinks than food, a dinner menu conspicuously lacking meat, sandwiches, anything one might find at home or in a mainstream eating place. They featured pizza that wasn't pizza, and shrimp floating in exotic conglomerations. After that there was dim sum, and Italian, French, and Indian. Our stomachs are world travelers.

Walter came up to me at the multi-artist gallery opening. "Sorry to intrude," he said, smiling. He was wearing an expensive dark suit and a tasteful maroon tie. He looks to be in his late forties, though he's a bit older, has dust-coloured hair and grieving eyes. Gray eyes are so infinitely sad. A mad wife locked in an attic, like Mr. Rochester? A son and heir dying of AIDS? A dark secret from when

he was a young man. Armed robbery? Twenty years of embezzle-
ment? A hit and run death?

"I went to school with a woman who looked remarkably like you,"
he said. "I was wondering if you…her name was Brenda Wilde."

"My mother," I said.

Walter introduced himself, stared around, obviously looking for
my mother.

"She and my stepfather are travelling in Europe," I said, "but
she'll be back before the show closes."

"She must be very proud," Walter said.

Walter reminisced about his school days and my mother. He's
her age, exactly twice mine, fifty-two to twenty-six. He's an
accountant turned entrepreneur, buys and sells buildings, is apparently very rich.

When I mentioned him to Mother she looked puzzled.

"It's odd that he'd remember me so well. I remember him, but I
never knew him. He was Pacific Northwest debating champion or
something. Maybe he edited the yearbook. He wore a blue blazer
and horn-rimmed glasses. I'm afraid I was a rather frivolous
teenager. I didn't date boys like Walter."

I dress carefully. The mini skirt? Something clingy and black to set
off my long legs, my trademark hair? A two-piece the colour of lilac
coils? I decide on waif. I was wearing waif at the multi-artist gallery-
opening when we met. Black tights, black boots, a loose
sweater-dress almost to my knees, the sweater an autumn-leaf
colour to show off my long tresses. I briefly consider shocking
Walter. I will show up wearing denim, a jeweled eyebrow ring. I can
see his horrified stare. "Oh, I had no idea the restaurant would be
so formal. Why don't we just stop at that Thai place on Robson
Street for some take out and go back to my place?"

At lunch yesterday I was lamenting to my girlfriend about our
long weeks of game playing. "Ask him 'What winks and fucks like a

tiger?'" Glorianna said. "What?" I said. "As an answer, you wink at him," said Glorianna. "It cuts down on the game playing."

I sometimes wear a tiny zircon in my pierced nose. My mother once gave me a small emerald ring, my birthstone. I had the emerald reset so I could wear it in my nose. That will be my attempt to shock Walter.

As soon as we've hugged our greeting, Walter notices the emerald, compliments me. What choice does he have?

"Too teeny bopper?" I ask. "I don't want to be confused with a delinquent daughter."

"No one would make that mistake, ever. You're a woman, in every sense of the word."

I can't even be sure that Walter didn't have something to do with my getting a credit card. At our first or second dinner, I whined because after having been solicited by a credit card company, I was turned down when I accepted their invitation to apply. I lamented that a struggling artist and part-time waitress wasn't a good risk, though I take pains to pay my way, have up-to-date accounts with art supply houses and clothing stores.

A couple of weeks later, the same company that had rejected me sent me a beautiful green Visa card with a $1,500 limit. I've used it judiciously, paid the bill the instant it arrives. Did Walter have anything to do with their change of heart? Did he guarantee my credit limit? I've never asked.

The restaurant is on the mezzanine of one of Walter's silver-and-chrome office towers. It has an oak door, beside which is a bronze plaque bearing the name of the restaurant, *Le Cheval Blanc*, nothing else. It is one of those eating places where you are greeted by a woman in a formal black grown, who inquires solicitously of your health, fawns, compliments, then turns you over to a *maitre d'* impeccably dressed in a midnight blue tuxedo, his face a clean-shaven, strawberry pink.

"Good evening, Jean Claude," Walter says cheerfully.

"So good to see you again, Monsieur. Always a pleasure. *Bon soir, Mademoiselle*. Welcome to *Le Cheval Blanc*."

"It's good to see you again, Jean Claude," I say, though I've never seen him before.

Jean Claude's eyes snap back to my face so quickly I imagine I can hear them click. Here is a man who prides himself on never forgetting a customer's face. His second take is as negative as the first.

"Always a pleasure, Mademoiselle."

The customer, of course, is never wrong, but I have planted a seed of doubt, of discontent.

"Have you really been here before?" Walter asks after we've ordered drinks.

"Never. But I hate pompous, condescending people."

"Poor Jean Claude. Do you know what you've done to him? Forgetting the face of a customer is like a baseball pitcher having his best pitch hammered about the ball park like a pinball. He's over at his station right now thinking, 'Am I losing my touch? Is my life as the perfect *maitre d'* really over?'"

"Do you ever make a mistake?" I ask. "Do you ever forget which of these skyscrapers you own and which you flipped last week?"

"I forget my home telephone number."

"But not mine."

"Never yours. My heart rate goes up and up as I dial your number."

"On the account, Jean Claude," Walter said earlier to the *maitre d'*, after choosing a bottle of wine, one that met Jean Claude's approval, which, I assumed, meant it was very expensive. I know little about wine; on the rare occasions when I purchase wine it is from the corner shop, forty ounces of *chablis* with a screw-on top, probably bottled last week in California.

Jean Claude reminds me of an affection-starved toddler, one that scales your body as if it were a palm tree and with hands like suction cups attaches himself to you. Everything he does annoys me. The insult "suck hole" was created to describe Jean Claude. I wonder if he is really French. If he is, he's a professional foreigner, after working many years with English-speaking clientele he should have lost virtually all of his accent; instead, he speaks as though he immigrated from Paris last month.

But, suddenly, I am more annoyed with Walter than Jean Claude. Walter's simple command is more condescending than anything Jean Claude has said or done. Jean Claude obviously knows Walter has an account. Walter is a regular customer, he probably brings his wife here, comes with groups of friends, possibly has other girlfriends, there have certainly been previous mistresses. So, what's the point? The statement, 'On the account, Jean Claude,' can only have been made to impress me. Why? Don't all very rich land developers have accounts at their favorite restaurants?

While we were lingering over Irish coffee, I tuned out a story Walter was telling me about a recent trip to Hong Kong, and thought again about his pretentious gesture of mentioning his personal account. I thought about how rich Walter is. I thought of my pitiful little Visa card nestled in my purse inside its protective covering.

"If I insisted on paying for this meal, would you put up a lot of opposition?" I asked suddenly, interrupting a story about an inept translator.

Walter laughed. He reached across the table and took my hand. His hand was huge, warm.

"I'm afraid I'd put up a fierce struggle."

"Then I won't make the suggestion," I said, smiling sweetly. This was my chance. We'd been exchanging talk like this all evening. If I said, "Then I won't put up any struggle," it would be implied consent, confirming what both of us assume will happen. I wonder if he keeps a hotel room, an apartment, a bedroom among his executive offices?

Walter excuses himself and makes his way to the restroom at the rear
of the restaurant. His back is barely turned before I signal for Jean
Claude.

When he reaches the table I stare up at him innocently.

"I know this dinner is supposed to go on *Monsieur's* account, but
it is *Monsieur's* birthday and I want this evening to be my treat. It is
so difficult to buy a gift for a man like *Monsieur*." I unsheathe my
Visa card and proffer it to him with a little cleaver of a smile.

"Of course, *Mademoiselle*." He takes the card, holding it with
his manicured fingers as if it might carry germs, or worse, be over
its limit.

"And, Jean Claude?"

"Yes, *Mademoiselle*."

"Prepare the bill at the desk, but don't bring it to the table. I'll
make an excuse to leave the table. You understand?"

"Of course."

"And add a 20 percent gratuity."

"Very kind of you, *Mademoiselle*."

"One other thing, Jean Claude. I've seen them do this when I've
been here before," I venture, taking a real chance, "but do you think,
while I'm signing the bill, the staff could bring a token cake to the
table and sing 'Happy Birthday'?"

Jean Claude calculates for a few seconds. Apparently they are
not so exclusive that they won't humour a good customer.

"It will be our pleasure, *Mademoiselle*."

After Walter's return to the table, I excuse myself, but, after
heading in the direction of the restrooms, I cut across to the side of
the restaurant and make my way to the cashier's desk. The bill is
there. I try not to look at the total as I sign and take my copy of the
receipt. Jean Claude, lurking in an alcove, gives me the high sign,
he and three other staff head a processional, stepping delicately
toward Walter's table. The lead waiter carries a small pastry on a
plate, marzipan perhaps, a circular pastry about the size of two

hockey pucks stacked on top of each other, a single candle gutters in the air conditioning.

I duck outside. I hurry up the stairs to the first landing where I crouch peering through the iron grille work like a spy. Through the tinted windows I can see the shapes of the diners but not their features. I see the shapes of Jean Claude and the waiters standing around Walter's table. I wish I could see the confusion on Walter's face.

I imagine I can hear them singing.

"'Appy birt-day to you,

"'Appy birt-day to you,

"'Appy birt-day, dear *Monsieur*,

"'Appy birt-day to youuuu…"

CHAPTER 22

Sometimes I think thoughts that scare me. Aristotle said that character is action, that we should be judged solely on our actions, not on what is inside us. Not on our intentions or wishes, but on our actions.

In my other strange life, the air conditioner still churns on. Christie and I are still at war. In bed her body is cool as a mannequin and about as pliable. We make a half-hearted attempt at lovemaking. Christie turns from me to sleep, her body wrapped in a heavy nightgown. We may as well be sleeping in coffins side by side.

"Couldn't you leave it off?" I say, referring to the nightdress.

"Oh," says Christie, painfully, "we'd be like two fish rubbing together." She feigns a shiver to show her distaste.

I have a vivid imagination. Sometimes it is too vivid. Sometimes my imagination does not do the right thing. There are some things I do not want to imagine. Sometimes it is as if my imagination has a life of its own.

I wonder what life would be like if I had met Christie in another lifetime. In that lifetime I was straight, had a regular occupation, lived in a tract house and was married to a woman who was articling to be a chartered accountant. I did not want to imagine what that lifetime would be like.

But this afternoon my imagination becomes a bully and pushes me into a corner and makes me watch whether I want to or not.

Just after we were married, before the tract house, when we were living in our first apartment which still smelled of newness and unchipped dishes, Christie reads one of my favorite books. What a horrible trick my imagination has played. My wife and Christie have changed places.

I sat across the room from her in a La-Z-Boy chair watching her finish the book. She is curled like a cat on a green velvet love seat. I looked at her like a child bringing home a report card full of A's, waiting for her reaction.

"It was alright," she said uncertainly, "but there was so much bad language."

"It's the way people talk," I replied. "It gives the story authenticity."

"It doesn't matter," she said. "When I read something like that I pretend those bad words don't exist. If I don't really look at them, then they're not really there."

I am a very gentle person, but that statement made me so angry that if I'd been the type I would have walked across the room and slapped Christie's face. I wanted to watch her head snap back and her eyes widen with surprise. I couldn't believe that the Christie I loved, the Christie who sat curled like a cat on the green love seat, could say such an ignorant thing.

That was exactly what my wife – my real wife, not my imagined one – said to me once, not long after we were married, in our first apartment which smelled of newness and unchipped dishes. I came to expect that sort of ignorance from my wife, but not from Christie. Is that what my life would have been like if I had met Christie back in my former lifetime when I had a regular occupation and my wife ironed the laces from my tennis shoes?

I didn't want to believe that. I want to believe that life with Christie would be different no matter when I met her. Would Christie have had anything to do with me if we had met when I was straight, had a regular occupation, ironed shoelaces and chased after the American Dream as if I was running after a bus on a morning when I was three minutes late for work?

I do not want to think about that either. I reach over, pick up a pillow and toss it at my imagination, who is leaning on the door-jamb, looking back at me from where he stood after pushing me onto the floor. My imagination, who has a duckass haircut and a tattoo, dodges the pillow, but loses his train of thought. I find myself back in my room in the Breathing Castle near East Hastings Street, staring at my typewriter, and at a bright green scarf of Christie's that she has left lying on my oak table.

B & E

I t is spring in Victoria. The Japanese cherry trees are in full bloom, the boulevards look as if giant pink and white pom-poms have been set out at intervals. I'm a taxi driver. I came on at 6:45 a.m., a hateful time of day. The only consolation is the air is fresh with the delicate fragrance of new leaves and cherry blossoms, the cool sweetness of the ocean. I had already delivered an old woman with a shopping bag to the bus depot; getting her in and out of the car was like working with a folding chair. No tip. The most aggravating fares seldom tip.

Now, I coast down the Cook Street hill, put my flashers on as I stop in front of a brown shingle house, probably eighty years old. I wait to see if my party is watching from a window. Nothing. I am about to get out of the car and go to the door, when the front door opens a crack and what at first appears to be a child squeezes out. As she comes down the steps and down the sidewalk toward my car I see she is not a child, but a young woman in her mid-twenties.

She gets in the front of the cab with me. Most fares choose to sit in the back. She is just out of bed, or perhaps has slept in her clothes. Her cheeks are puffy, there is sleep in the corner of one eye. She has short carrot-coloured hair, naturally curly. She may have run her fingers through it this morning, more likely not. She is wearing well-worn jeans, and a brown baggy sweater with the sleeves pushed up to her elbows. Her eyes are gray-green. Her face and arms are paved with freckles. Her hands are very small.

She gives me a twitchy smile, then an address a mile or more away, in an industrial area where a few rundown houses survive among battery companies, bottling plants, and the yard where transit buses are parked at night.

I watch as she pulls a mauled-looking pack of cigarettes from the side pocket of her jeans. She uses the car lighter, inhales deeply, closing the sleep crusted eye as she exhales. She is wearing cheap plastic open-toed shoes. Her big toenails are painted cherry red. Her feet, like her hands, are very small.

"I want you to wait for me when we get there," she says. "I forgot my key. I don't know if I'll be able to get in."

We exchange pleasantries. She draws deeply on her cigarette, shakes her curls. "Rough night," she says, shaking those curls again, almost laughing.

I like the look of her. I tell her my first name. Wait. She looks at me for quite a while, half smiling, crinkling her nose as she does so. "Casey," she says. "I'm Casey."

Our destination is a large house, old and poorly cared for. A wooden gate lies flat beside a crumbling sidewalk. Grass grows through its slats, like through the ribs of a skeleton. A blanket is hung crookedly across the picture window. I wonder what she was doing at the place where I picked her up. Boyfriend? Girlfriend? Visiting friends and decided to stay over? Out drinking with friends and crashed at their place?

The front steps have gone wherever the front steps of old houses go. About eight feet up the front door opens into nothingness. It is obviously never used. I follow her around to where a rotting veranda runs all across the back of the house. There are a few cartons of bottles, the cardboard soggy from winter; last year's leaves are banked against one wall, sticks of firewood are strewn about.

"Son of a bitch," Casey says, trying the door. "Left the fucking key on the hall table. I could see it if it wasn't so dark in there."

I go to the closest window, try to push it up, but it won't budge.

"I locked it too," she says disgustedly, "there's been so many B & E's in the neighborhood. " She points to where the old half-moon shaped lock has been slipped securely into place.

"How about a side window?" I say.

We walk across the junk-filled yard, and into the space between the house and its neighbor; there are sawhorses, a camper top and concrete blocks blocking the way. I can barely reach a window sill. Casey looks up at me and smiles, not with her mouth but again by wrinkling her nose. It is a self-deprecating gesture, a shy gesture. She seems so vulnerable. If it wasn't 7:30 a.m., I'd consider making a pass. I am wild for her little mouth to be close enough for me to inhale the odours of her. I want to pry her teeth apart with my tongue. I wonder if she whimpers when she makes love. I love the idea of holding her, undressing her, tasting her. I dislike perfumes; women who smell of soap and toothpaste leave me cold. Casey interrupts my fantasies.

"I think maybe that one's unlocked, but I'm not tall enough to reach it."

"Maybe if I straightened up one of the saw horses?" I say.

When I eventually peer through the small window, I see putty fragments and dead flies. Beyond it, a hallway. When I push at the window, it opens a few inches.

"Too small for me to get in," I say to Casey who is holding onto the saw horse.

"Maybe I could," she says.

With concrete blocks stacked on the saw horse, Casey is able to reach the window ledge, pull herself up, I climb on the saw horse and push as she goes in head first. She disappears.

"Made it," she calls. "I'll open the door for you."

Which she does. "Thanks so much," Casey says. She digs in the pocket of her jeans for the cab fare. "I only got change, and only a quarter for a tip," she says apologetically after searching all her pockets.

"Not a problem," I say. I've wasted fifteen minutes, I can hear the radio in my cab squawking, dispatch is probably wondering what's become of me.

As if she somehow sensed my earlier fantasy, Casey steps close to me, puts a hand on the back of neck and kisses me on the lips. "That's a poor substitute for a tip but it's the best I can do."

"I'll take that in lieu of a tip any time. I get off work at 4:30. Would you like some company later?"

She doesn't answer. Just stares slyly up at me with a crinkly half smile. "What if I don't live here?"

"You mean you're a B & E artist? I don't think so. I mean, forgive me for criticizing your home, but this place is a dump. Why would anyone break in? I'd think people would be more likely to break out."

"Who says there's not something valuable in here?"

"I've never done a B & E," I say, "but I've known a few guys who do. The first rule of a B&E artist is to pick a house that looks like it contains valuables. A B&E artist would be out in the Rockland area, Cadboro Bay, or the Uplands, and they wouldn't be there at 7 a.m., they'd be creeping around at 4 a.m. when everyone's sleeping, not when they're getting ready to go to work. The only art I can see in this place is a Canadian Tire calendar," I say, peering over her shoulder. "In wealthy homes, people leave thousand dollar things sitting around, because they have safety deposit boxes full of ten thousand dollar things."

"I'll remember that," says Casey. "I just sublet a room upstairs, the tenants are out of town. And, yeah, I'd like some company later on. And my name's not Casey, its Lyn, I was just jerking you around, but you turned out to be a nice guy." She kisses me again, a little longer this time. I want to stay but I can hear my radio squawking even from the hallway.

When I finished my shift, I exchanged the taxi for my own car. I changed into the clean shirt I kept in the car for emergencies. I stopped at Quon Lee's Market and bought a small bouquet of flowers. Maybe I'd take her to Coffee Mac's for supper, I'd had a good day, two airport trips, and some tourists who tipped well.

It was about 5:00 p.m. when I arrived at the house. I knocked. I knew something was wrong the second the door opened. Instead of Lyn, it was a tough-looking man, maybe thirty, looked like a sailor who's been kicked out of the service. A brush cut that needed trimming, jeans and t-shirt.

"What?" he said.

"I'm here for Lyn."

"Who the fuck's Lyn?"

"She rents a room upstairs."

"Not at this house she don't."

I should have shut up, said I had a wrong address, but as they say, stupid is forever.

"I'm a cab driver. I brought her here this morning, early. We made a date."

"You brought somebody here? We just had a serious fucking break-in."

Behind him appeared a girlfriend? Wife? A Métis girl with obvious blond streaks in her hair. Jeans and a black t-shirt with FUCK in white capital letters across the front. Tatts on both arms; she looked as if she could hold her own in a closing-time riot at a biker bar.

"So what did this chick look like?"

Do I tell the truth? Of course not.

I point at the chick behind him. "Native, shorter than her, round face, fairly short black hair combed back on the sides. She was wearing some cheap black athletic pants and runners, a black and white jacket. Look, man, I'm really sorry, she convinced me she lived here and had locked her key inside. I helped her get in about 7:30 this morning."

"Did you take her somewhere after?"

"No. I left her here. She was real friendly. I made a date with her."

"Now she's rich and friendly," the girl said in a surprisingly high-pitched voice, as she lit a cigarette.

"Did you call the cops?" I asked.

The guy looked at me like I was an idiot. "We can't exactly report the stuff she stole."

"I understand," I said.

"Bitch took our stash and about a thousand bucks," the girl said.

"Shut up, Celia!" the guy said. "We don't know this guy from shit."

"I already think I know who it was," Celia said. The description I'd given fit half the native girls in Victoria under twenty-five.

"Where'd you pick her up?" the guy asked.

I named an old apartment downtown on Fisgard Street, lots of tiny suites, lots of native people, lots of transients.

"It's a start," the guy said.

"She said she sometimes drinks at the Drake or the King's," I added. "It must be someone you know," I went on. "This is not the kind of place people usually break into."

"We were up to Nanaimo getting more product," the girl said. "We just got to sit down and figure out who knew we was outta town."

I apologized again and made my exit. The guy actually thanked me for all the information I'd given him.

Now I had to find my little red-haired friend. Can't let the flowers go to waste. What better place to start than where I picked her up?

Down the Cook Street hill again, this time in my own car. I put my flashers on and went to the door. A woman in a dressing gown opened the door looking like she'd just gotten out of bed. It was 6 p.m.

"I'm a taxi driver," I said. "I picked your babysitter up here early this morning. She left something in my cab. Do you know how I can get in touch with her?"

The sleepy-eyed woman looked puzzled. "We don't have children," she finally said.

"She came out this door about 7:30 a.m." The woman tossed her long, tangled blondish hair.

"Somebody creeped our place last night," she said. "What did she look like?"

I gave her the same native girl story I'd told earlier.

"We both work four to midnight at the hospital," she said. "This is a day off. I told my husband I thought I heard the front door close early this morning, but we were too sleepy to get up. When we did, we found the place carefully tossed. Only a few small items missing and a couple of dollars in change."

"I take it the small items weren't things you'd want to report missing?"

"How could you know that?" she said suspiciously.

"Because she talked me into helping her break into the place I took her to, claimed she's left her key inside. She scored some illegal substances there too, but a lot more cash."

"Jesus! I don't know what to say. I don't know anybody looks like that."

"She didn't actually leave anything in my cab. She conned me, too. I made a date with her, and I'm just trying to find her."

The next day at work I asked all the other cabbies if they'd had her as a fare. Nothing. I used pencil crayons to draw a fairly good likeness of her and dropped a copy at each of the other two large cab companies in Victoria. Nothing. Nothing ever. I've been thinking of those gray-green eyes and that twitchy little smile for a long time now. Every early morning call I get, I wait hopefully at the curb, waiting for her to squeeze out of a silent front door on a sweet-smelling spring morning.

CHAPTER 23

Like Gemini split apart by a cleaver, we face each other across the cluttered room.

Christie barefoot, wearing jeans, one of my white shirts tied in a knot across her belly. Her cheeks are tear-stained. She lights a cigarette, squints one eye as she blows smoke toward the ceiling.

Christie, spearmint cool, stands just inside the door. She is dressed in a tailored kelly-green suit, expensive brown shoes, a paisley blouse closed tightly at her throat, her plum-coloured hair is upswept in sculptured rolls. She smiles, showing a perfectly lipsticked mouth and even, white teeth. Her eyes are February cold.

Christie drunk, walking home, strewing snatches of song on the dry boulevards, as if she were scattering the violets she had pinned in her hair earlier that evening in front of the gold-dappled mirror in our room.

She walked away into the early morning fog.

As the sun was coming up Christie, clothes dishevelled, make-up splattered, swayed into our room. I stared at her. I lectured her, knowing that every word I uttered was like taking wire cutters and rendering an irreparable gash in the mesh that held us together. I persisted.

"Get fucked," Christie said, standing arms akimbo in front of me.

"I can't help you or us if I don't know what's going on."

The lecture ended itself as Christie had always known it would, as she had always intended it to, briefly but violently. Christie, one hand holding her cheek, gave me a triumphant half-smile. She went into the bathroom, washed her face and put on the blue jeans that made her so desirable to me. When she returned she rubbed around me like a cat in heat. We made love for hours. Even so, I slept poorly. With one loss of control I had erased all my months of work.

PARROTS

My midget friend Zachariah Durdle appeared agitated when he
stopped me one day in the foyer of the Breathing Castle.

"There's something in my apartment I want to show you.
Something I don't understand. Do you remember my wallpaper?"
he asked as we climbed the three and a half flights to Zachariah's
wing of the Castle.

Why in the world would I remember his wallpaper? I usually
can't remember my own wallpaper, or even if I have wallpaper. I
thought hard. There might have been something with Rousseau-like
flowers on the wall beside my bed. Or, maybe that was at a former
girlfriend's house. I had no memory of Zachariah's wallpaper.

Zachariah's apartment has been fitted with a small door, just his
size, within the regular door. He opened the small door and went
in, leaving me in the dark hallway lit by a single yellow bulb. Then
the large door swung wide. Zachariah must have planned our meeting for he has dragged his beanbag chair from the closet to the
centre of the living room, a place for a guest to perch among the
other furniture that could easily decorate a child's playhouse.

As usual, the apartment was brightly lit. I looked around. It is a
small L-shaped apartment. The only wallpaper is at the end of the
dining area; the other walls are painted an off-white. The wall I'd
never noticed was covered with garish wallpaper, a creamy background, decorated with row upon row of predominantly orange
parrots; a quick count showed eight-and-a-half parrots per row,
either eight or nine rows from floor to ceiling. Each parrot sat
within a yellow hoop. Each parrot had blue and red wing feathers,

a curved yellow beak, yellow feet. Their eyelids appeared to close bottom to top.

"What about the wallpaper?" I asked.

Zachariah pointed at the floor next to the baseboard.

I should have noticed. There were white, lime-like droppings on the heavily waxed hardwood and a few splashes on the lower row of parrots just above the baseboard.

"You're not saying that's..."

"A recurring phenomenon," said Zachariah. "Started a few weeks ago. I'm sure something's been digging in my garbage. I left some Oreos on the counter one night, the next morning all that was left was dust."

I studied the rows of parrots. They looked like wallpaper to me.

"The droppings appeared at different locations along the baseboard," said Zachariah, staring up at the rows of parrots, each sitting on its own yellow hoop. Zachariah continued staring diligently as if he were being paid to do so, as if staring diligently were a government job with pension, medical benefits and paid vacation.

"Not possible," I said, placing an index finger on a parrot in the middle of the wall. "Not possible. Mrs. Kryzanowski has a key to your apartment. She's playing a trick. She'll probably admit it the next time you pay your rent. There are other odd goings on in this building. Gabon, the retired jockey who lives in the attic, keeps a horse in his apartment. On the ground floor, Grabarkewitcz owns a magical cat. Then there's..."

"Mrs. K. doesn't sneak in in the middle of the night. The floor is clean when I go to bed. The droppings appear overnight."

Zachariah feinted a left jab at a parrot in the second row. Taking a little jump in the air, he slapped a parrot in the third row, open-handed, right upside the head. The first parrot did not flinch, and the second failed to acknowledge the slap.

"I have an idea," I said. I stared at the wall full of parrots as if I was under contract as a troubleshooter for a large corporation, my job to head off trouble, as if it were a pack of outlaws, head it off at the pass. "I know how to get my hands on a gun. I know people who own guns. We could shoot each parrot. If one of them falls to the floor dead, your problem will be solved."

"There are over sixty parrots on the wall," Zachariah pointed out, "plus several halves. It would take a long time to shoot them all. Besides, there are people living on the other side of the wall, and all that lead in one wall might overbalance the Castle and the whole thing would collapse."

For the moment I gave up the idea of being a troubleshooter for a large corporation.

"We could offer them crackers," I said.

"Tried that," said Zachariah.

I went back to heading off outlaws at the pass. What we needed was Gene Autry. Gene Autry would know how to head off outlaws at the pass. Gene Autry or Roy Rogers, the Cisco Kid, or even Zorro, would know all about heading off outlaws at the pass, or determining which parrot was leaving unwanted droppings on Zachariah's hardwood floor. Gene Autry and Roy Rogers were both in their eighties, though, and the Cisco Kid and Zorro were probably pushing up daisies or burritos in the Hollywood Hills.

I went back to being a troubleshooter. I decided I knew what Gene Autry would do. Gene Autry lived in retirement in Rancho Mirage, California. Gene Autry had lived so long that his young wife was now an old woman. Gene Autry owned a baseball team. I pretended I work as a troubleshooter for Gene Autry's baseball team. It was my job to head off federal antitrust investigators at the pass. Antitrust investigators want to take away the rights of baseball owners to behave like foolish, mediaeval, slave-trading clansmen. They had to be headed off at the pass.

"I have another idea," I said. "What are parrots afraid of?"

"Bigger parrots," said Zachariah.

"You're in the right area. Birds of prey. But, what about cats? Big cats, all the way up to lions."

"Cats?"

"Come with me, we're going downstairs and borrow Grabar-kewitcz's magical cat."

The cat, a green-eyed tabby, was as usual asleep in Grabarkewitcz's bathroom sink. Grabarkewitcz, a paroled book-fondler, remained unfazed as we explained the situation. Grabarkewitcz picked up the cat, whom he addresses by a guttural name that may or may not be Syzygy, and handed him to me. The cat draped down my front like a long stole. We went back to Zachariah's apartment and left the cat there. The cat was already exploring, as cats are wont to do, sniffing the doll-sized furniture, testing the beanbag chair with a hefty, tabby paw.

"Come on, I'll buy you a coffee," I said. I fantasized outlaws, antitrust investigators, and a flock of parrots being headed off at the pass.

Later, Zachariah opened the door within a door, then the real thing.

"Mrr," says the magical cat, greeting us, tail upright, stiff as a flagpole.

We looked around. On the floor near the beanbag chair are a few colourful feathers, a pair of ugly yellow legs, a hook-shaped beak.

"Urp," said the magical cat, as I picked him up.

Zachariah pulled at my knee. He was pointing at the dining area wall. The top-centre yellow ring was empty, its parrot gone.

CHAPTER 24

"Emery's shadow still stalks me," Christie says. "I'll be walking down East Hastings Street, look over my shoulder, and there, scurrying into a leaf-filled doorway will be Emery, trying to look inconspicuous, his hulking spectre dressed in the ominous black and silver uniform of the Oakland Raiders football team."

It was alright as long as Christie was here. But Christie is gone. I am sitting down to my typewriter, wondering if I will ever again write anything without Christie, my Muse, to inspire me.

"Tell me?" I hear Christie whisper. We lay, spoon-like in the love-damp bed. I breathe onto her neck, her maroon curls tickle my nose.

Sunday morning. Christie in a spotted black-and-white dress the colour of a Dalmatian dog. She wears a wide-brimmed black velvet hat, flat, an exaggeration of a flamenco dancer's sombrero.

Heavy-eyed and unshaven, I follow Christie up the wide, marble steps of a church. "What's the matter? Don't you think I should go to church?"

"I'm just surprised. You've never struck me as the type."

"Christie likes church," she says, smiling her thin ironic smile. "Christie likes the music."

"Emery, Browne, and Carver have unusually large shadows," Christie says. "Whoever they happen to be talking to is always in the shade, even after the Oakland Contingent has moved on. Their shadows are dressed in black and silver uniforms. Sometimes when they leave a room, their shadows are reluctant to follow. Emery then goes into the mock crouch of a quarterback waiting for the snap. He shouts, 'Hut! Hut! Hut!,' and their football player shadows lumber off after Emery, Browne, and Carver, right arms akimbo as if they are clutching their helmets, waiting on the sidelines for the playing of the National Anthem."

My other life keeps intruding on me. In it I met Christie during my early straight life, and in it she is equally straight.

My mother and maiden aunt live in a frigid prairie city. Christie and I live in the same city, in an apartment sterile as a laboratory.

My mother and aunt like Christie. She drinks tea with them on long Sunday afternoons and is learning to crochet, while my identity shrinks to the size of a seed that rattles about in my castanet body.

We have two children, a boy and a girl, their names escape me, but they have pleasant, scrubbed faces. Christie dresses them in tasteful pastels. They blink their bland, blue eyes and say, "Please, Grandma," and "Thank you, Grandma."

I have destroyed my birth certificate, credit cards, photos of people. My fingers hover over a dish filled with acid.

The frigid city. Gooseflesh rooms. Christie, cool and ominous, while out there, the street, kisses and acid, the grind of traffic, powerline prison bars restrain the sun.

KATMANDU

"I fell asleep in the movie," Denise says, as we walk the dark Vancouver streets toward the rooming house where we both live. "I'm sorry I was such a lousy date."

"It wasn't a very good movie," I say. It wasn't. I recalled Denise's head tipping onto my shoulder as her hand relaxed in mine. She only slept for about five minutes.

"In however long I was asleep I dreamed my cat turned into a telephone receiver," Denise goes on. She stops and turns toward me.

"I heard somewhere about a cat that turned into a whole telephone," I say. "Maybe you heard the same thing?"

"Was yours a dream?"

"I don't think so. I read it, though I can't remember where. I don't own a cat. People who don't own cats aren't allowed to dream about them."

"Of course," says Denise.

Denise keeps a cat in her room, a noisy, ill-tempered Siamese, with oriental-shaped blue eyes.

"Was it a Siamese telephone receiver?" I ask.

On one of our previous dates she told me the story of how she named her Siamese kitten. She called it D.B. after Cooper, the hijacker, but everyone who looked at the kitten kept saying things to it like, "You're a cute little thing, eh?" and "Aren't you sweet, eh?" until Denise decided to call her cat Eh.

"It was cream and blue-gray, like Eh," Denise goes on. "The receiver was his backbone. I put his mouth against my ear and talked into his navel. Do cats have navels?"

Denise is a rather plain young woman who likes to wear clothes that are too large for her. Tonight she is covered in baggy blue cords and a man's green flannel shirt. She is stocky and solidly built, but not as heavy as she tends to think. She works days in an arcade on Granville Street, making change. She is what street people refer to as a goddess of quarters.

"If oranges can have navels, so can cats," I say.

We enter the varnishy-smelling foyer of the rooming house, climb the dimly-lit stairs which are covered in black rubber treads. In the upstairs hall we kiss a sufficient number of times for Denise to have an excuse to invite me into her room.

"Oh, look," she says, as she flips on the light.

The cat, Eh, appears as if he has just returned from a week at the taxidermists. If the body of the telephone was removed from beneath him he would appear to be in mid-leap, about to land on an unsuspecting enemy. The cat is gently arched in the shape of a telephone receiver. His silvery tail blends into a length of telephone cord, his mouth, pink as raspberry, is open, ready to be laid alongside an ear; his fangs are exposed.

Denise's dream appears to be correct in every detail. Seizing Eh by what would be the scruff of his neck, I lift the softly-furred receiver to see that, on the cat, mid-belly, in a circular pattern like the top of a large salt shaker, are forty or so holes, waiting to be spoken into.

The cat's eyes are a slitted, suspicious blue. Gingerly, I place the receiver against my ear. The cat's nose is moist, his breath warm.

"Perhaps we could call Katmandu?" I suggest.

"Or Cathay," says Denise. "Or St. Catharines."

"How about ordering in pizza, instead?"

Denise smiles in agreement.

I place the call.

"Caesar's Italian Village," the voice on the other end says. The reception is excellent.

"A medium pizza with mushrooms, green peppers, and tomatoes," I say. The cat-telephone-receiver's sandpapery tongue licks my ear. "And ground beef," I add.

CHAPTER 25

Erato, Euterpe, Thalia, Melpomene, Terpsichore, Urania, Clio, Palomino, Calliope, nine Muses, all daughters of Zeus, with voices sweet as bluebell honey, dance in my dreams, toss flower petals in my path, tempt me, tease me, recede into air when I get too close. Calliope, said to be the Chief Muse, carries a tablet and stylus, but according to legend she is meant to inspire heroic and epic poetry. There is no Muse of the whimsical, no Muse of the absurd, no Muse of the lonely and abandoned. There is no Muse of the streets. Except Christie.

She has a tattoo, a strange little x and o's square high on her right shoulder.

"How did you get that?" I asked her once.

"Frisco. A tattoo artist named Red Ryder."

"When? What's it mean?"

"I actually got it in the slammer in Oregon. Tattooist was a lesbian chick named Big Marge.

"Why do I bother asking?"

"I have no idea. You're a slow learner, Wylie."

Late in the night after we had loved for hours, Christie awoke crying, clung to me fiercely.

"As a kid I got whipped for crying. The harder I cried, the harder I got whipped."

"By whom?"

As usual, Christie didn't answer.

Violets, violets, and violets. I buy them for Christie. Bunches of them float like camouflaged rafts in a cake pan on the oak table. When I type, the vibration causes the water to ripple.

"I don't even like fucking violets," Christie protests.

"You're a Muse, you have to like violets."

"Have you learned anything by living with me?" Christie asked one day.

I pondered a moment. "That I know absolutely nothing about women. You particularly."

Christie was not amused.

"That's the best I can do at the moment. What have you learned from living with me?"

"That you're no different from any other guy I ever met, except you went to school about twenty years longer."

"That doesn't surprise me."

"It does. But you're so fucking controlled you'd never admit it. You think you're pretty goddamned special because you're smart, and because you're so good in bed, and because you sneak around writing down everything people say to you and to each other." Christie takes a cigarette from the green pack on the oak table. "I know something you've learned."

"What?"

"That I'm just like every other chick only freakier."

"In a way…"

"Fuck. Can't you ever say anything straight out? I get dressed and go out and shop and buy groceries, just like I was a waitress or a nurse, or anybody else who works shifts. I come home and we fuck and go to sleep, and I put curlers in my hair, and get colds, and cook dinner, and put the cat out, and get my period…"

"We don't have a cat."

"Well, what I say is true, isn't it?"

"In a way."

Christie stamps her foot in frustration.

"You are not," says Christie, staring at me cat-eyed, through strands of plum-coloured hair, "a very good lover."

We have just finished making love for most of an afternoon. Christie lies, propped on a pillow, cigarette in hand, her belly and breasts still slick with sweat.

"There's no way you're going to draw me into a fight."

"Well, you're not," Christie says defiantly.

"Do you want me to play psychologist? You're feeling guilty because you had a good time. Now, you want to spoil it for both of us by picking a fight. You hope I'll hurt or punish you…"

"You're a lousy fucking psychologist, too."

Silence.

"Christie is sorry. You were great. You're a wonderful lover."

"So are you."

"Don't say that," her voice harsh, a stab wound.

Christie has a way of cutting through bullshit as if she were moving it with a bulldozer.

We are discussing my former friends, people I used to share a beer with, people who talk a good game but actually seldom if ever do any writing.

"You should decide if you want to sustain the community or be a real writer," Christie says.

"Where did you hear that? Something you read in an arts pamphlet?"

"They're losers, without exception, and as long as you hang around with them, you are, too."

MOTHERS

On a spring morning, I picked up the couple at an old house on one of the narrow streets that run north off Gorge Road in Victoria. He was about forty, in need of a haircut, scruffily dressed in an out-of-style suit with a prominent cigarette burn near one knee. He walked like a drunk pretending he was sober. A typical Canadian Legion drunk, I decided. The woman was sixtyish, small, wiry, with yellowish-white hair. Clean, but dressed cheaply with no sense of style. She wore face powder and cheek rouge. Both of them smelled strongly of beer. They named a bar downtown as their destination.

"When we get there, I want you to wait for me. I got to go in and get my cheque," the man said.

"Fine with me," I said.

"Then we want to go to the bank, don't we son?" the woman said.

"I don't know where you want to go. I got my own problems," he said peevishly. "You can walk to the bank, for chrissakes. Why keep the driver waiting? It costs money."

"Who's gonna pay for the cab?" the woman asked. "Who always pays for the cab? I got the money and I say we have him wait."

"Yeah, as soon as I cash my cheque we'll go down to the Legion and have a few drinks." He began to mumble. "We'll paint the town, Ma, you an' me...we'll knock back a few cold ones."

"Sure, Art, that's what we'll do. Driver, do you know where the Bank of Nova Scotia is?"

"About a block down the street from where we're going," I said.

"That's the one. We gotta go there. Art's gotta cash his cheque, and I need some pocket money. I don't carry cash. Do all my business by cheque."

"Me, too," said Art.

"You ain't got no bank account. The bars are your bank. You deposit your cheque in every bar in town."

"I used to have a bank account."

"But you drank it."

"Aw, Ma, don't be so hard on me."

"I'm only kiddin, Art, you know that. Here we are. You go get your cheque like a good boy."

"I'll be right back," Art said. "You wait for me."

The old woman took cigarettes out of her purse, offered me one which I refused. She used the car lighter. "He's not my son, you know?"

"No. I didn't know. I thought…"

"He's not my son. We're not related at all. He just likes to call me Ma. He's my boarder. He's been with me about a year, since my husband, Jamie, died. He's been fired from three jobs in the last month. Did you know that?"

"No."

"You've never driven us before, have you?"

"No."

"We ride your taxi company all the time. Me and Art and my real son Roy. Art gets in trouble because of his drinking. He had a good job over at the Sherwood Hotel, until he got fired for drinking on the job. Then he worked here for a couple of days but got fired too, but he's starting back to work here tomorrow, at least that's what he tells me. Art never thinks, that's his trouble. Imagine going in drunk to pick up his cheque, and him supposed to start work here tomorrow. You should never let your boss see you drunk, should you?"

"I wouldn't think so."

"This is costing us money. I can't understand him losing his job because of drinking. I don't drink. I mean I don't get drunk.

You know what I mean, I like a few, I mean who doesn't? I even get half shot once in a while when I'm out with my boys, but I'm no alcoholic. I don't think Art's an alcoholic. I mean alcoholics can't stay off the booze at all, can they? Art can go for weeks and never have a drink, if there's nothing around. Do you think he's an alcoholic?"

"I don't know, but I'd say he looks like a person who shouldn't drink."

"That's him. He sure shouldn't drink. Did I tell you how we found him? He's not my son. Jamie and me found him, hell, must be three years ago. We was just pulling out of the parking lot of the Halfway, and Jamie seen this guy lying in the ditch. Jamie was always helping people. Heart as big as a barn, is what everybody said about my Jamie. Over a hundred people came to his funeral.

"Anyway, we tried to scoop this guy out of the ditch, but he says, 'I'm an alcoholic, just let me sleep.' Jamie didn't take no for an answer. He got Roy out of the bar and they loaded this guy in the back seat. We sobered him up and got him straightened around in a week or so, and Jamie got him a job as a steward on one of the weather ships. And he worked as long as he was at sea and there was no booze around. He took to us, called me Ma, right from the start and Jamie Dad and Roy brother. But as soon as he'd get into port he'd go on a toot, drink up every drop of his pay.

"He didn't get home until three o'clock this morning. Must have had a snootful because I heard him crashing around. But this morning, Roy and I always keep a few beers in the fridge, I said to him, 'Art, you want a little hair off the beast that bit you?' An' he says, 'No, Ma, I think I'll just have me some tomato juice this morning.' Now if he was an alcoholic wouldn't he have wanted beer? Don't alcoholics drink when they get up in the morning?"

"I couldn't say." I replied. The morning was sunny and we both got out of the car and were waiting beneath a Japanese cherry tree for Art to return.

"After the tomato juice, he had four or five beers before we left. You know he stutters when he's sober. You can always tell when Art's been drinking because he talks real good. It was a bad idea to let them see him drunk, and him supposed to start work tomorrow. Sometimes Art disappears for days. My Jamie always came home no matter how smashed he was. 'I got to get to work in the morning, Ma,' he used to say to me. And I'd get him up come hell or high water.

"We sure used to have some good parties at our place, or down at the Halfway. All the guys from the boat when they were in town. Sometimes we'd party all night and about five in the morning I pour them all into a taxi and off they'd go to work. Roy, he's the same. Never misses a day's work. He's living at home again since he and his wife parted. I call him in the morning and say, 'Here's your coffee and a cigarette. You gotta get up.' And he always does no matter what kind of binge he's been on the night before. Even one time he'd been in a fight, his face was all cut up and his knuckles skinned something awful, but he went to work. I don't know what he'd do without me to look after him.

"Sometimes Roy has a bottle of beer after breakfast, but he sure ain't no alcoholic; he always goes to work. That Jeanette, she was Roy's wife, still is as far as I'm concerned. She called Roy an alcoholic once and I sure told her off. 'How many days has Roy missed because of his drinking?' I said. And she had to admit he never missed none. 'Then he ain't no alcoholic,' I said, 'and that's final.' Hell, a man works hard, he's entitled to a few drinks. 'If you wasn't so high and mighty you'd go out with him once in a while,' I said. A man's entitled to a few drinks after a hard day's work, right?"

"If that's what he wants to do."

"Me and my Jamie was in the Halfway bar almost every night for twenty-five years, whenever he was in town. Everybody knew us at the Halfway. Damn fine people too. We'd go down after supper and have a few beers and a few laughs. That's what I used to tell Jeanette, that she should be more of a companion to Roy. Hell, you never saw me sitting at home when the men folks was down to the bar. I suppose Roy did fool around some, I mean there are a lot of girls down at the Halfway, regular types that like a good time.

"I'd tell her to get right out of the house when she badmouthed Roy; they was living with us 'cause Roy owed a few bills around town, and they got thrown out of the place they was renting. Oh, she claimed lots of awful things, like how Roy roughed her up sometimes. I don't doubt that he did, but she had it coming, nag from morning to night that woman could. If you had a wife nagged you twenty-four-seven about having a few drinks and how you spend your hard-earned money, I bet you'd rough her up too."

"I'm not that way inclined," I said.

"Well, Roy never lived with a nag and he wasn't used to that. Boys should try to marry women like their mothers then they'll never be disappointed. I don't doubt he roughed her up, but he never hit the kids like she said, that was a goddamn lie, Roy idolized those kids, would do anything in the world for them...if he knew where they was. Oh, she got him back alright, hit Roy when he was down, she did. That was about the time Roy got in that trouble, wrecked the car on the way home from the Halfway one night, wasn't supposed to be driving 'cause he'd lost his license. They said he was drunk and couple of people in the other car was hurt pretty bad. A fat lot they knew about it. Roy got charged even though the other car was in the wrong. You ever hear of anything like that?"

"The police sometimes do funny things."

"You're damn right. Roy had a couple of drinks so they automatically blame him. Anyway he was hardly in jail when Miss Fancy Pants packs up the kids and moves away. Roy got a letter saying she was divorcing him, and then he got a bill from her lawyer, and an order to pay her and the kids a lot of money. You can bet he didn't pay any of that. She got herself some new guy, and she changed her name and the names of the kids, and they live way off in Ontario somewheres.

"Roy would bust her up good if he ever found her and it would serve the ungrateful bitch right. She never heard of 'for better or worse.' As soon as things got a little rough, she ran off.

"'You never mind, Roy,' I said to him. 'You're better off without that useless bitch. She was a cross no man should have to bear. You got your old mom to look after you and Ma knows you're a good man no matter what anybody else says.'

"Now how did I get off on that story? You sure you don't mind my bending your ear so much. Where is that Art? Cab's gonna cost a fortune. He's probably in there making trouble. Should never have gone in there when he was drunk."

She looked at me closely for the first time. "You got a mother?"

"Yes."

"You have a wife?"

"Not yet."

"You sure don't talk much. Real close mouthed."

"I'm a better listener than a talker."

"That's what my Jamie used to say. 'You do the talking for both of us, Ma. I'll do the drinking.' Not that Jamie used to drink all that much. I'm not ashamed to say I used to take a few drinks with him. Hell, I could knock them back with the best of them. Not that I do that much anymore what with Jamie gone. 'You don't get out often enough,' Art said to me just this morning. 'I'm gonna take you out on the town.' But Art can't hold his liquor." She moved closer to me.

"What's your mother like?"

"There's not a lot to tell about here. She's just a very nice lady."

"So's everybody's mother. I mean what's she like? You got an old man or what?"

"My dad's been dead almost twenty years."

"And she's never remarried?"

"No."

"Or got herself a boyfriend?"

"I doubt it, though it's not really any of my business. She lives a long way away."

"I don't know how a woman could live like that. Hey, don't mind me, just BSing to pass the time. Where the hell is Art?"

"I'm afraid you wouldn't find my mother very exciting. She's just a little lady with gray hair and a blue apron who, as far as I know, has never done a nasty thing to anybody. I don't think she's ever been in a bar in her whole life."

"You sure you ain't talking about my ex daughter-in-law?"

"I didn't mean anything."

"Well, you sound kind of high and mighty. She ain't ever been in a bar and I have, is that it? You make it pretty plain I'm not as good as your mother. Let me tell you a few things, I've done a lot of good things in my life. Everybody calls me Ma, you know. I'm mother to a lot of people. Hell, sometimes my Jamie would phone me and say, 'Ma, I'm bringing home eight or ten of the guys off the boat, you think you can whip us up a little something to eat?' And I'd say, 'Bring them home, Jamie, it's just as easy to cook for a dozen as for four.' Boy, we sure had some parties in those days. Oh, there I go again talking a blue streak. Look, I didn't mean to be taking after you, don't pay no attention…"

"All I meant was you and my mother are very different people. I didn't mean to offend."

"Yeah, well it's okay. I mean I got nothing against people like your mother. Everybody should live the way they please, that's what I've always said. Are you close to your mother?"

"We live our own lives."

"Everybody lives their own lives, for god's sake. I mean does she live with you? Do you visit her? Are you close?"

"We're not that close. She lives a long way from here. We love each other like children and parents should, but we only see each other once a year or so."

"We're close, Roy and me. God we're close. Art too, only he ain't blood. He calls me Ma, and used to call Jamie Dad. Art never had no family. Maybe that's why he drinks.

"My boys need me alright. Yes sir, I never have to worry about being needed. I feel sorry for women who ain't needed any more."

"Some people recognize that needs change with the years," I said. "Some people are glad not to be needed anymore."

"The hell they are. You're wrong. Needs don't change. My boys need me. They've always needed me and they always will. Hell, Art's forty-three. He looks older, don't he? And Roy's gonna be forty-one in a few weeks. No sir, needs don't change. Who's gonna get them up in the morning and off to work? Art needs both me and Roy, we're the only people in the world can straighten him out. The boys needed Jamie too, and they was really upset when he died. Art kept saying 'My dad's dead. My dad's dead,' and he got all upset and drank heavy for days, so did Roy. I was the one should of been upset.

"I was talking to Jamie at seven that morning. 'I'm too sick to go to work, Ma. I just want to sleep.' I figured he just had a bad hang-over, so about ten o'clock I fixed him a Bloody Mary and took it up to the bedroom and he was dead. And him only sixty-two. Roy went all to pieces and didn't go to work for a week. After the funeral, Art disappeared for ten days until somebody phoned and said they had him down at the funny ward at the hospital, all sick with the dt's. Finally, here comes Art."

We got back in the cab.

"Goddamn guys always give me a hard time," mumbled Art.

"You didn't give them a bad time back, did you? You know you're supposed to start work here again. You are starting work, aren't you?"

"Yeah, Al says it's okay with him, but he has to check with his dad. Al said I can work here any time I want to but he's gotta check. He'll call me Monday."

"Then you ain't starting tomorrow?"

"I told you, he'll call Monday."

"How much money did you get?"

"Not as much as I expected."

"How much?"

"Twenty-four dollars."

"You told me you had eighty coming. This cab's gonna cost a bundle and you ain't paid board for two months."

"I told you, eighty at the other place, the Sherwood. Here I didn't work that much and then there was the stuff I broke when Al and I got in that argument."

"You told me you worked four days here and that you was starting again in the morning."

Turning to me, she said, "You can't believe nothing he tells you."

"Let's go to the bank, then we'll go over to the Legion and I'll buy, Ma."

"With what? Twenty-four lousy dollars? What kind of a son are you? Look at the amount of this cab fare. I suppose you were in there giving Al a bad time?"

"Sure, I gave him a bad time. I been thrown outta better places than this. Look, I'll buy the drinks, and I'll pay my board, god's honor. Al will call on Monday, and I might even be able to get Roy on here, if I asked, just because he's a friend of mine, a brother."

"Okay. Okay. Let's walk to the bank, then we'll take another cab to the Legion. If that Al don't phone on Monday I'll come down and see him, I'll get him to take you on again, and maybe Roy too. You don't worry, Art, your old Ma will take care of everything. I'll pay for the cab, but you gotta give me the fare when you cash your cheque."

"Sure, Ma, and I'll buy when we get to the Legion."

"You better," she said, as she dug in her purse and handed me the fare, plus a nice tip.

"We'll paint the town, Ma, just like the old days."

"He means well," she said to me in a stage whisper. "He'll pay me back, you can count on it. You know, I wish you and your mother were closer. Mothers need their sons close to them."

As they walked toward the bank I made a mental note to call my mother and tell her how much I appreciated her.

CHAPTER 26

never saw who hit me. I heard him step from a doorway, heard the sand crunch against the cement.

He had fists like parking meters. As I went down I tried to roll into a ball in order to protect what was left of my face. Just as the streetlights were setting and the thug, mistaking my spleen for a football, was practising fifty-yard field goals, I heard him say, "Next time it will be your old lady."

I vomited on the sidewalk. A couple of winos watched me, shaking their heads at the waste. True winos never vomit.

Christie was waiting when the emergency room doctors finished with me. I had broken ribs, loose teeth, and an array of stitches that made my swollen face look like patched denim. "Look what I've done to you," Christie said.

"Not you. I've always had my eyes open. What is it they say? 'If you can't do the time, don't do the crime.'"

"Can I take you home?"

"No. They want to observe me overnight. Could be internal bleeding."

In the morning Christie came to visit me wearing lime-green gloves.

"What the hell are they for?"

"I like them."

"They clash with everything you own."

"Since when do I need to colour co-ordinate?"

"But, you usually... Sorry."

"Sorry."

"Browne is out front," Christie said. "Sitting in his car in a loading zone. He tipped his cap to me. Christie is afraid." But of course he was gone by the time we emerged from the hospital.

INVISIBLE DOGS

M rs. Illingsworth was one of the long-time tenants of the Breathing Castle.

She was tall, thin, long-faced, and dressed in rather expensive pinks and grays. She had a choice room on the ground floor just around the corner from the foyer where unclaimed mail whispered softly on a black hall table covered in a linen runner with tatted edges. I passed her door as she was coming out, the stiff leash and dog harness held in her left hand.

"Taking Winston for a walk in the park," she said cheerily, with a cultivated English accent.

I stopped. "Your dog is very thin," I said, trying not to sound facetious.

"Whatever do you mean?" she said. "The vet said only last week that Winston was at least five pounds overweight. I've had to cut back on all his treats."

Mrs. Illingsworth is considered somewhat beyond eccentric by us denizens of the Breathing Castle. You've all seen the novelty store item – a dog harness with a stiff leash so one can pretend to walk an invisible dog. Apparently Mrs. Illingsworth takes the joke seriously. I did notice that the straps of the harness were larger than usual, made to accommodate a plump dog.

"What breed?" I asked, rolling my eyes a little.

"A bulldog," she said testily. "My goodness, have you never seen a bulldog before?"

"Um," I said, "what colour is he." I squinted in the direction of the dog.

"He's white, of course, with a black patch around one eye. His eyes are brown, but he's rather red about the eyes these days, old age you know."

"I see," I lied.

Mrs. Illingsworth continued toward the street. I followed. Surely a sixty-something English woman couldn't concentrate for long. In a minute she'd be swinging the leash back and forth, probably to shoulder height at least. I was disappointed. She walked Winston across the school ground where green-uniformed girls play field hockey in the afternoons, down to a small park where Winston stopped to snuffle the marigolds and apparently to relieve himself against a giant oak.

Back at the Breathing Castle, I called on my neighbor Grabarkewitcz, a sallow, wild-haired ex-con, who owns a magical cat.

"I saw Mrs. Illingsworth walking her dog in the park," I said. Grabarkewitcz offered me coffee. "Which eye has the black patch around it?" I asked. "I can't seem to remember."

"It's rather a matter of where you stand," said Grabarkewitcz. "If you're in front of the dog, it's on your left, which is actually Winston's right eye."

"Then you can see Winston?" I asked.

"He's an invisible dog," said Grabarkewitcz enigmatically.

He then fumbled in a drawer and handed me an ad he'd cut out of a local throwaway paper. "DOG SHOW," it said, and named an IOOF Hall a few blocks away as the location. It was on as we spoke. "You should check it out," said Grabarkewitcz.

On the way, I stopped at a novelty shop on East Hastings and bought a red dog harness and leash, but I chickened out at the last moment and hid them in the hollyhocks outside the hall. I entered by a side door and found the room crowded. There were a few tables with displays. Everyone seemed to have a leashed invisible dog. The harnesses at the end of the stiff leashes varied in size from something that would fit a Mexican Hairless to an impossibly huge harness that could house a Mastiff. A veterinarian was set up in one corner of the room, backed by white hospital screens. He examined dogs on a table covered with white paper, which he changed after each patient. He gave the impression he was examining each dog's teeth, then he prodded, petted and praised each pet. After each examination, he took from an apparently empty bag labelled "Dog Treats," an invisible object which he fed to his patient. Behind him on a shelf were several cans of dog food, the oval on the front of the can, which usually housed a healthy, pearly-toothed, smiling dog, was ominously empty.

I was just in time for the awards. On stage, propped against a stool was a blue and white sign that read "Best of Breed." A young boy crouched beside the sign like a ballboy at a tennis tournament.

"The winner for Best Pekinese is Mrs. Maude Fenster of New Westminster, with Ming," an announcer proclaimed.

There was scattered applause, a few low rumblings, as Mrs. Fenster, leading the invisible Ming, made her way up the stairs and across the stage to a spot marked with a chalked X and the words "Stop Here."

The boy inserted the word Pekinese in the slot on the signboard, while Mrs.Fenster took her bows, a number of photos were taken by family, friends, historians and possibly even media. Mrs. Fenster, smiling tearfully, picked up Ming, clutching him to her breast as more photos were taken.

Then, just as the winner for Pomeranians was announced, a dog fight broke out, albeit a silent one, as both owners frantically pulled on their tangled leashes and shouted at their dogs. They were separated by a third party wearing heavy leather gauntlets. The row subsided.

"Wherever is your dog?" a buxom lady asked me. She was encased in a raspberry-coloured dress of a material that might have upholstered a sofa in the 1920s.

"Behind me," I said, turning and looking at my right heel. "She's just spent seven weeks at the Invisible Dog Training School at

Quantico, Va. She can smell out plastic explosives, spot a terrorist at a hundred yards, count to seventeen by slapping her tail on the floor. She understands three languages and has an IQ higher than most hockey players."

"I'm sure she's brilliant," the woman said suspiciously, not properly impressed, "but all dogs must be on leashes. For their own protection, you know. What if she got into a disagreement with another dog?"

I went outside and retrieved my leash, but as soon as I re-entered the raspberry lady appeared again.

"You're a fraud," she cried accusingly, "an outsider. I can tell by the way you hold the leash. No tension. There's no dog there."

I wanted to ask how she could tell, but apparently she could.

"Easy, Ilse," I said ominously. "She's baring her fangs," I went on. "She doesn't like to have her integrity questioned. What have you got in your purse, Ma'am. Ilse minored in drug sniffing at Quantico."

"Hector," the raspberry woman called, and almost immediately the burly man in the leather gauntlets appeared, accompanied by a beefy individual who looked like an escapee from World Wrestling.

"Evict this man," she shouted. "He claims to have a dog on his leash which he clearly doesn't." She pointed at Ilse.

"Let's go, Mac," said the guy with the gauntlets, taking a firm grip on my arm.

"Freakin' looky-loo," said the beefy guy, grabbing my other arm.

As I was unceremoniously escorted from the hall with Ilse, I tripped over a sign reading "Sanctioned by the American Kennel Club."

I walked Ilse home to the Breathing Castle and met Mrs. Illingsworth taking Winston for an evening stroll.

"What a beautiful dog," said Mrs. Illingsworth, smiling broadly and stooping to pet Ilse. "Why she's barely more than a puppy, but German Shepherd, very smart."

"Yes," I agreed, "Ilse is very clever."

CHAPTER 27

Christie in a golden aura of sensuality, clinging to me, devouring me.

"Love me. Christie wants to be loved."

Afterward, she cuddled close to me. We lay for a long time, silently holding each other. She turned slowly from me and, laying on her stomach, tucked her arms under the sides of her body, palms up, in her sleeping position. I kissed the back of her head, her hair tickling my nose. I draped an arm over her and slept. When I awoke she was gone.

An excerpt from another conversation:

"Even though you're wonderful in bed, a psychiatrist would still tell you that you hate your body."

"Christ! You sound just like this chick I knew in the joint. She was always trying to figure herself out."

I watched her carefully as she spoke, but there was never a hint that what she was saying was a contradiction of what she had told me previously. Christie was too smart to get caught in a lie, unless…

I notice a sheet of lined yellow paper peeking from my thesaurus. I pull it out. It is covered on both sides with Christie's looping, innocent handwriting.

"The mailman's unseen hands slip letters through the slot, where they flutter to the floor, quiet as camellias on the dark, polished wood," she wrote. "Letters addressed to my body at this drafty house.

"I look at them a long time – a medical bill, a pink envelope possibly from someone who cares, perhaps a card from someone I used to know.

"My nose quivers like a rabbit's. I smell carrion in this dark hallway. Unspeakable odours flit and claw and attempt to draw my breath from me like the evil cat who hides under the basement stairs and stares at me with wisdom-filled yellow eyes.

"Outside, the wind scuffs across gray-crusted snow sharp enough to slit my wrists and bleed me blue. I pace about our room, a red sweater, like blood on a bandage, loose on my shoulders, the sleeves limp as a doll's leg.

"I hold the letters against my breast but they refuse to become warm. I stroke out my name rather than the address. My heart giggles at this subtle murder as easy as clipping my moist nails after a hot bath.

"My stare is straight and frosty, my hand white and true as I write: Christie doesn't live here any more."

THE KNIFE IN THE DOOR

"I don't care as long as we do something," Nancy said. "I just want to get out of the apartment for a while. I have to get out somewhere or I'll go crazy."

The hardwood floor gleamed bright yellow in the light from the overhead fixture. The apartment and furniture were old but clean. The sofa was blue, the curtains white. Nancy loved blue and white. As she talked, she moved nervously about the room taking short puffs from her cigarette, but careful to use either the ashtray on the arm of the sofa or the one on the oblong coffee table in the centre of the room.

"I just get so sick of the sight of this room. I feel like I've got kittens running up and down inside my arms and legs. The only way I can stop their scratching is to get out for a while."

Nancy's hair was the colour of apricots, cut short and combed back at the sides. Her eyes were blue and the uneasiness that hid behind them allowed them to change from the colour of new denim to that of sky on a frosty winter morning, depending on her moods. Her complexion was fair, her bone structure good. Her lips however, were thin, and there were lines of hardness around her mouth. Her wedding picture still sat atop the TV. Nancy, wearing blue and white, stood smiling beside a sullen youth with wavy hair, so blond it looked like whipped cream. His name was Leroy.

"I couldn't stand him," she said, following the man's gaze to the photo. "But I was knocked up. What choice did I have? It was the little things. He'd go to the bathroom and not wash his hands after. Silly to remember something trivial as that after all the really rotten things he's done. But it's lessons you're taught as a child that you remember all your life. No matter how different you try to be. God help me for the things I remember."

The tall man with heavy glasses sitting on the sofa was trying to separate Nancy's words from the jabber of the snowy show on the television he'd been watching. He had recently been to the bathroom; he tried to remember if he had washed his hands. Perhaps he hadn't. She certainly would have noticed. She listened for inconsequential things like water running in the bathroom, yet ignored her life and her children's lives, which were falling apart around her.

The man glanced again at the ex-husband, who would be frozen forever on his wedding day.

"He was such a mean son-of-a-bitch," she said. "Selfish, selfish, never thought of anyone else."

"Was he mean to the kids?"

"He tolerated them. I'd have killed him if he ever hit them. It was just me. The son-of-a-bitch would have three drinks and start to knock me around. Once, we were going on a holiday. We never had a holiday all the years we were married. I saved two of my pay cheques and we borrowed daddy's camper. I dropped my kids at my sister's and was all packed. You know what that bastard did? He took our holiday money and went on a two-week bender. When he finally came home he knocked me around because there was no food in the house."

While she was talking she was getting their coats from the closet by the front door.

"Christ. I feel so used," she said.

A teenaged girl arrived to babysit. They left the apartment and went to his car. Snow drifted around their ankles and it was bitterly cold. His car was small and old. The starter ground like a dying bee. "God, how I hate this car," she said.

"It's better than walking," he said. The engine sputtered to life.

"We had a station wagon but that son-of-a-bitch took it with him the last time he disappeared, even though it was in my name because he owed money to everybody in town. Why don't you get a decent car? Isn't there a heater in this thing?"

"It takes time to warm up." He wiped fog off the inside of the windshield with his glove. There was so much he wanted to say to her; he could have started a real fight on any of a dozen pretexts she had given him this evening. Nancy was like an animal that had been mistreated, snarling at every gesture, friendly and unfriendly alike. He would wait. Healing takes time. "It's only a few blocks to the bar. The drinks will warm us up," he said.

She was happier in the bar.

"I like to sit and watch people and know that they're happier than we are. Being out of that freakin' apartment is the only way to know that there are happier people in the world."

"They probably think the same about us. People are not really very different."

"You're different. You just sit staring at me like I've got lipstick on my teeth or something..."

"You're a very attractive woman. Why shouldn't I stare at you?"

"I can't get a rise out of you, no matter what I do, can I? I'm sorry, I'll try to be nicer."

She swirled her drink, a tall rye and Coke, and took a long swallow. "God, I love booze."

The man didn't answer.

"Winter before last, Leroy was out of work and he sold the TV set to buy booze. I think I'd do the same thing if I couldn't get a drink now and then. I've always got to have a drink. You don't like that about me, do you?"

"I didn't say anything."

"I can tell though. You don't have to say anything to disapprove. You don't like to get drunk, and you don't think I should."

"This is your night out. I want you to do what pleases you."

"Oh, for chrissakes, don't be so condescending. I'd like to stay right here until the bar closes, get really drunk and be somebody for a change. You're already looking at your watch. You want to get back to the apartment, have a little roll in the hay, and then go back to your goddamn dolls, right?"

"I can't stay too late. I do have dolls to repair tonight."

"You and your goddamn dolls. I wish you wouldn't tell people that you run a doll hospital. It sounds so...so..."

"Sissy."

"Yes."

He laughed. "What if I break a glass on the edge of the table. I'll spit on the floor and maybe the next time the waiter comes by I'll cut him with the glass, call him a son-of-a-bitch and sneer. Would that make me tough enough for you?"

"Okay, I'm sorry. I really don't mean to hurt you. Keep on stringing your dolls."

"Yeah. Seems I've spent most of my life trying to repair broken dolls."

Nancy finished her drink and with a nervous gesture signaled the waiter for another. She took a cigarette from an open package on the table. The man reached across and lit it for her.

"You're a real gentleman," she said in a way that could be interpreted either as a compliment or a put-down. "That son-of-a-bitch Leroy never lit anyone's cigarette but his own in his life." She paused, then looked across at him, smiling. "I'm sorry, I shouldn't talk about him all the time. You're so good to me and I don't appreciate it." She reached across the table and took his hand.

"I try to please you because I care a great deal about you," he said.

Instantly, her eyes were dark and full of tears.

"How can you care about me? You sound like my father. He says he loves me no matter what. And all I've ever been to him is a disappointment."

"What's your father got to do with us?"

"Daddy liked me better than the other kids. It wasn't fair. I was the youngest. The only girl. I could never be what he wanted me to be, because I never knew what he wanted from me. So I became what he didn't want me to be. I quit school because he was a teacher. I smoked and drank because he didn't. I chose Leroy because he was the exact opposite of my father. I've fucked up my life. I'm no good, and yet you sit there just like my father, and tell me that you care for me."

He had met her father, an undistinguished man in a sweater and baggy slacks, who had pale grayish hair that slid down over his forehead, a limp handshake and the small orange eyes of a chicken.

"You don't know me," she said. "You don't know me at all."

"I don't care about the past."

"Well I do, and you should. You've only known me a few weeks. After Leroy left, and before you, there was another guy. He promised me and the kids the world, but I found out after that the bastard didn't even have a job. I screwed around with him too, and didn't have a period for eight weeks. I thought about drinking gasoline, but it turned out to be a false alarm. That's the girl you call sweetheart. The girl you say you care about. Nobody could love me. I know nobody could love me."

Back at the apartment, they sat close together at the kitchen table drinking coffee. There had been much silence, and sobs lurked in the corners of the room. Nancy clung tightly to the man's arm.

"I suppose you expect a little bit," she said, yawning and blowing smoke at her coffee cup.

"I don't want you to do anything you don't want to do."

She stood suddenly as if strings attached to her shoulders had been pulled taut. "You don't understand. That's why it's no good. You haven't listened to anything I've said. Don't you understand, I want to do things I don't want to do. You're too damn good to me and I can't stand it. One of these days I'm going to come crashing out of my skull, and some terrible, ugly, deformed, aborted thing will screech and swing around the room like a monkey."

While she was talking she took a kitchen knife out of a drawer and moved across the hall toward the bedroom. The man followed.

"The kids," she said, as she had said each time, closing the door, carefully inserting the knife in the jamb.

"Not yet. Not yet. Make it last longer." But it was already too late.

"I'm sorry," he said.

"It's alright. It's just that I thought I might..."

"I'm sorry," he said again.

"I've never made it that way. It just seemed so close." She slipped to her side of the bed and took a cigarette from a pack on the night table.

"Could you make it that way with Leroy?"

"Not that way," she said, lighting the cigarette. "He could make me come the other way. But you don't like that, do you?"

"I never said that. It's just that we're always so rushed. So furtive. That knife in the door...I like to take things slow, but you always seem in such a rush, as if you're expecting an interruption."

"Look who's talking about being in a hurry."

"I said I was sorry. I bet if you'd said the same thing to Leroy he'd have slapped you in the mouth."

"He would have. The son-of-a-bitch."

"Do you want me to be like him."

"I suppose I do."

"I can't, you know."

"I know. I don't want you to be. Not really. What was it like when you were married? In bed, I mean."

"She shouldn't have married. Nothing was pleasurable for either of us. It's why we're not together anymore."

"We used to do dumb things," she said, moving closer to him, laying her head on his shoulder, blowing a cloud of smoke at the ceiling. "Dumb things. We'd have pinching fights. I'd have black and blue marks for weeks. And tickling fights, and I'd pull the hair on his chest."

"I don't like that sort of thing. I like closeness, tenderness…"

Swiftly she turned toward him and was kissing him fiercely.

"You're so good to me, but I'll hurt you. I know I will. I'm used and dirty and ugly. Get away from me quickly before I really hurt you."

He could taste her tears. Then she was gone. The knife clattered to the hardwood floor, the sound reverberating. The water in the bathroom began to run.

He sat shivering in his car waiting for it to warm up. The knife shouldn't be in the door, he thought. It should be in her hand. She was like a voodoo doll shoving pins in herself in order to hurt him, her father, her ex. He decided he'd go back, at least until she told him not to, something that seemed inevitable. Starting the cold drive home, his thoughts turned to the dolls waiting in his workshop.

CHAPTER 28

Christie is gone. Emery is dead, and the Oakland Contingent has scattered. Or at least someone is dead, and I don't know what to do. I can no longer be sure what is fact, what is my fiction, what is Christie's fiction, or Christie's reality.

Jones simply says, "I told you so."

There was a murder at a jazz club somewhere in Chinatown, a black man shot on the dance floor by a red-haired girl who disappeared into the night. It happened the day after Christie disappeared. Christie? Coincidence? No connection to my situation? I fantasized Christie, arms around his neck, her belly pressed against his, her tongue...

When I first understood the circumstance, I incongruously thought of something Christie had said months before.

"When a guy's hot for sex, you could amputate and he'd never notice. Whenever I see one of those old movies where they're gonna pry the bullet out of the hero's arm, and they give him a bullet to bite or a slug of whiskey, I always figure that the heroine, instead of looking innocent and scared, should get in there and give the hero a nice, slow blow job. As long as he doesn't come, they could cut off his fucking arm in three-inch sections and he'd never feel a thing."

I imagine Emery's shadow was so large that those around him were perpetually in the shade. I imagine his shadow made it back across the border to the United States. The customs people at Blaine, Washington, briefly considered arguing, but at 4 a.m., when a sleek, silver Lincoln Continental, driven by a giant black shadow dressed in the sinister black and silver uniform of the Oakland

Raiders, demands entrance to the United States, prudent customs and immigration officers ask very few questions.

To my surprise no one came looking for Christie, not what was left of the Oakland Contingent, not the police. No one questioned me.

No one asked me about Christie. In a few days, I became an anachronism. An old man without a chick. Faces change quickly on the street. A chick disappears. She gets replaced. Someone's old man gets busted.

The walk-in closet in my room, with the hollow plywood door that has been immobile all the years I've been acquainted with it because, like a recalcitrant streetcar, it refuses to stay on its track, gapes half-empty. I am a pessimist today. When she disappeared, Christie took the same brindle suitcase she arrived with. As a sort of insurance against her leaving me, I had begun storing notes and manuscripts in it. Now they are scattered like giant feathers where Christie dumped them, banked against the paralyzed closet door.

A litter of shoes and dust demons tumble on the closet floor. A slippery greenish pantsuit that Christie never liked hangs limp as a chicken from a metal hanger. A pair of jeans with a wide black belt and leather lacings down the front, that she often wore because I found them exciting, sprawls carelessly across a chair. The open zipper mocks me. I ache.

We were walking on Gore Street, not far from where we live, past a row of wholesales suppliers. This was just a few days before Christie disappeared. A faded sign on the side of one of the brick buildings read Ship Chandlers, an occupation that seems to no longer exist. I pointed out Girardi's, a food wholesaler where I had worked an occasional day moving pallets of cheese and roof-high boxes of tinned tomatoes with a forklift. Next door was Wholesale Greenhouse Supplies.

A sleek gray Audi glided to the curb, a short Asian woman bounced from the passenger side. She was wearing jeans and a brightly flowered smock. She waited for the driver, a distinguished looking older man with styled silvery hair, to join her, talking happily, leading him by the hand into the store.

"Wow! Characters you couldn't invent," Christie said. "What's their story?"

"A bank president having an affair with the gardener?"

"You can do better than that."

"She's a very wealthy woman. He's her chauffeur."

"There's a connection there bright as neon. This is a love story."

"Perhaps. I'll have to think about it."

A week after Christie left, I sat down to write. It took nearly ten days to get the story into the shape I wanted.

THE LAST SURVIVING MEMBER OF THE
JAPANESE VICTORY SOCIETY

I fell in love with Kimiko because she was a happy person. It was easy. Happy is contagious, especially to me, after a lifetime of too little pleasure. Kimiko was not what I would ordinarily have considered attractive, but joy makes the plain beautiful, as their aura of cheerfulness expands to encompass all around it.

I met Kimiko at the plant nursery she operated. I had recently taken up gardening; I asked her advice; she was very helpful. I found myself returning again and again, telling myself that the trips were necessary. Asking questions just to interact with her, leaving each time with my station wagon crammed with new acquisitions.

I was one of those fifty-something men, recently divorced after a long unhappy marriage, on my own in an ancient Victorian home in an older area of the city. I had no money worries, having practised law for over thirty years. My ex-wife lived alone in what was our million-dollar home. She was and is a terribly unhappy person, something I should have realized immediately on meeting her, had I not been blinded by her beauty, her model's figure, her honey-coloured hair, her large, brilliant blue eyes. If I had not been so enthralled I would have noticed her lack of passion, her critical tongue, her negative attitude toward everything and everyone except me. A concept that changed dramatically after a few months of marriage. My business success that allowed me to provide the best of everything including world travel was never a consolation. I watched beauty become bitter.

What could I have done differently? I tried for most of thirty years, experimenting, failing, blaming myself for failing.

But now I was free, and after numerous visits to her greenhouse, I finally asked Kimiko out. I did it badly because I was truly scared. I had been on my own for a year. My friends were eager to find me a new partner; I tired quickly of the frail women in expensive clothes, swathed in clouds of perfume, bird-like, anxious, talking too much about their ex-husbands. Kimiko was not like other women who I would ask for a casual date to dinner, the theater, or a charity function.

Kimiko was totally different, probably no more than five feet tall, muscular from wrestling tubs of plants and saplings about the nursery every day. Her nose was wide, flat as a baby's, her eyes a hazel blur, behind rimless, Coke-bottle glasses. Her father, who had started the business, was dead. Her mother, who appeared to speak no English, handled the cash register. There were no employees, it was a summer business that closed from November to April.

Kimiko smiled up at me. If she was surprised, she didn't show it. "So, you like Japanese chicks?"

"Uh, no," I stammered. She wore her usual work clothes, black jeans and a flowered smock, today one decorated today with pink geraniums.

"Don't tell me you didn't notice I was Japanese?" She laughed prettily, the sound like the burbling of a meadowlark.

"What I'm saying badly is that I've known a number of Japanese women but have never asked one for a date, until now."

Everything about Kimiko was joyful. She smelled tangy, like lemons. Our first date was at a Greek restaurant. Kimiko ate like what she was, a hard-working woman. It was such a pleasure to watch her devour a fried cheese appetizer, moussaka, a rice pudding, then a baklava with our coffee. I was used to women who ordered salad, then pushed it around their plate, pretending to eat.

"What you see is what you get," said Kimiko, her eyes sparkling behind the thick lenses, as she finished an after-dinner drink. "I'm a big girl, I eat like a stevedore, and I've never watched my weight. Most men find that a problem."

"Not me," I said. "I'm successful enough that I can afford to feed you." Kimiko laughed. "I asked you out because you're funny, and happy, and not the least pretentious. All night I've been longing to put my arms around you."

"Well, let's take care of that right now," said Kimiko. She stood up, walked around the table, and as I stood up, she put her arms around me, stood on her tip toes and kissed me. She was warm, and soft, and tasted lemony.

We never looked back. In the car we couldn't keep our hands off each other. She spent the night at my place. My bed was in a spacious upstairs room. Outside, a brisk wind rubbed birch limbs against the side of the house. The blind was up, tines of moonlight spangled the bed. She was everything I dreamed of, sexual, sensual, loving, anxious to please and be pleased.

"You're a very passionate woman," I said, breathless, as we rested, her head on my shoulder.

Kimiko laughed her wonderful laugh. "When people do something that on the surface appears so ridiculous, it would be a terrible shame if everyone involved didn't enjoy a great deal of pleasure."

That was Kimiko; she felt that everything in life should provide a great deal of pleasure, even work. Particularly work. I had a weakness for annual flowers, brilliant begonias, pansies. Marigolds, which reminded me of a trip to India, where, in some rural areas, rivers of marigolds ran beside the roads, their spicy odour masking the unpleasantness of poverty. It was Kimiko who wrestled the tubs of pampas grass, the potted roses, the flats of brilliants, to my station wagon. "I love customers like you," she said. "Everything but the roses and pampas grass will die in the fall, then you have to replace it all in the spring. You're like a trust fund for my business."

I had guessed I was twenty years older than Kimiko. It was actually twenty-two.

A few months after our first date I suggested that, since I essentially had more money that I knew what to do with, she could sell the nursery if she wanted to and we could travel a lot, do whatever we wanted. She wouldn't hear of it.

"I love my job," she said. "I'd go to fat if I didn't work. I wrestle hundred-pound bales of peat moss, huge tubs of trees and plants. I'm a hundred-ninety pounds of solid muscle. So if you don't treat me right, you better live in fear." And she laughed as she threw her arms around me, and pushed me back onto our sofa. I never again mentioned selling the nursery. It was about that time that Kimiko first suggested I carry her. She was being facetious, but there was a certain longing I sensed. "I'm fifty-eight years old, I'm six feet tall and weigh a hundred and fifty pounds. Do the math" I said in a jocular tone.

"Maybe you should take up weight lifting?" said Kimiko.

As lovers do, we exchanged life stories in monologues. Mine was very short, and as I told my story, I realized I had spent a small lifetime, repeating the same mistakes, expecting different results, trying unsuccessfully to please a woman who couldn't be pleased, though I didn't realize my mistakes until I was distanced by divorce from the situation.

Kimiko's story was much more interesting.

"My father grew up in Hawaii, the island of Maui. But he was the youngest son, their farm was small, there was no life for him there, so he married my mother when she was sixteen, and they had the bad luck to immigrate to Canada a year before Pearl Harbor. They were interned, my father's recently purchased land, in Richmond, where he was establishing a market garden, was seized and sold without compensation. It was part racism, part fear of the unknown. Japanese Americans were treated equally badly, but in Hawaii things went on as normal, because a third of the residents of Hawaii were of Japanese descent, there were just too many of them.

"Virtually all Japanese immigrants were loyal Americans or Canadians; the way they were treated was so unfair. That unfair treatment made many of the Hawaii Japanese choose sides. In all of the Hawaiian Islands there was not one act of sabotage during World War II, but that doesn't mean there wasn't great resentment. They were just too subtle for sabotage.

"They realized any resistance would be small and futile, and put everyone in danger, so they established an underground. The Japanese Victory Society. Mama says it started with my father's family, and some members of her family, and other neighbors on Maui. Eventually, there were cells on every island; they believed without reservation that Japan would win the war. They decided to wait and watch and be prepared. They established a shadow government, had it all in place, ready to take over as soon as the Japanese took control of the islands. They believed that as soon as Japan won there would be a massive exchange of prisoners. On that rationale, my father, Hiro, was to be secretary of agriculture in the occupation government.

"Mama said he joked that he would be secretary of pineapples, for they communicated through pineapples. Incoming mail to the internment camps was censored, outgoing letters too. But a crate of pineapples could be shipped from Hawaii. The paperwork was always immaculate, the attached letters innocuous in the extreme, but inside the pineapples lay sedition.

"I had a brother, Norbu, born in the internment camp in Alberta. After the war, when my father came back to B.C. and started over, my brother was known as Knobby, and was rebellious, hating what had been done to him and his family but not quite knowing how to take revenge. He hung out with rough white boys in East Vancouver. When he was sixteen, he drove his first car into a lamp post and died, at the time when my mother was pregnant with me.

"Mother's small revenge was to refuse to learn English. My father spoke fluent English with just a trace of an accent. Mother claimed her refusal was so I would have to speak Japanese and would not forget it as many teenagers did when they assimilated in white society. I taught her the only word she knows in English. 'Ask.' When my father was alive, no matter what anyone said to her as she tended the cash register, she replied, 'Ask Hiro.' After my father died it became 'Ask Kimiko.' She may not speak English but don't ever try to cheat her at the cash register, she makes change better than a bank teller."

"The Japanese Victory Society did not die with Hiroshima and Nagasaki?" I asked.

"They could not believe that Japan lost the war. The secret meetings continued, at least on Maui, at least within my father's family. Japanese society was highly patriarchal, but because she was a prisoner, mother was considered a member of the Japanese Victory Society. At the camp, the crates of pineapples had come addressed to her – what harm could a teenage wife, with a tiny baby do with a box of pineapples?

"Once, when I was a teenager, mother went back to Maui for a visit. She was guest of honour at a meeting of The Japanese Victory Society. 'Aging men,' she said, 'with unrealistic dreams of Japan ascending to power again,' and a box stuffed full of rising sun flags, folded neatly, stored in a dry place, sleeping until insurrection or conquest called.'

"My uncles are all dead now, and I'm not far from middle age. Mother must be the only surviving member of the Japanese Victory Society."

The war appeared never to have ended for Kimiko's mother. Kimiko introduced us. I bowed clumsily, called her Mrs. Shibayama, tried to smile a lot. The old lady stared stonily at me, with small black eyes, glaring as if I was attempting to shortchange her.

"Mother is hard to get to know," Kimiko said, smiling. "We'll just play around her, as if she's a tree in our yard. By the way, she refers to you as 'White Devil,' not A white devil, but THE white devil. She advises me not to play with you."

"How can I win her over?"

"You can't. But I'm a big girl, I can choose my own friends."

We were married in the winter, at city hall on a day of alternating squalls and sun showers. Her mother, who pretended I didn't exist, refused to attend. We went to Hawaii for three glorious weeks. Kimiko found some cousins on Maui, but though they were hospitable I sensed they weren't comfortable with me, and when Kimiko brought up the Japanese Victory Society, her cousins politely changed the subject.

Kimiko moved in with me in my spacious Victorian home, once again suggesting that I should carry her over the threshold. "And if I put my back out, what good would I be as a husband?" I laughingly protested.

Kimiko and her mother had been living in a drafty cottage shed, at the back of the nursery. It was immaculate in its sparseness. I suggested that the old woman move in with us. "She can have the back bedroom on the ground floor; she'll scarcely have to see me. There's even a Japanese market two streets over."

Kimiko laughed. "Mother says she would rather die than live with THE White Devil. She can still look after herself. Here, she'd slip around the house like a ghost, cleaning things that don't need cleaning, putting her mark on everything like a cat spraying its territory. She'll be happier alone."

I was persistent, "She's had a hard life," I said. "I could make things easier for her."

But she continued to live behind the nursery for a number of years until she took a serious fall. Luckily, it was in July, when Kimiko worked every day, so she only lay unattended for a few hours. Her hip was broken. She was in hospital, then in a rehab center for several months. She could no longer live alone so, against her will, we moved her into our first floor bedroom.

I peeked in one day. The floor was covered with tatami mats, a pallet for a single bed, a wooden pillow with a thin pad for comfort.

The closet door was closed. I assumed everything she owned was inside the closet. I would go weeks without seeing her. She moved about the house like a spirit, emerging to eat only when she was sure I was away or in some other part of the house.

I would sometimes hear her high-pitched voice speaking rapidly in Japanese, like bursts of gunfire, and then Kimiko's softer, slower speech, but sometimes even Kimiko grew frustrated and her voice would rise, then she'd emerge from her mother's room, shaking her head in frustration.

"She says, if something happens to me, you will throw her onto the street."

"Can't you reassure her? First, I'm twenty-two years older than you, I'll die first. If it would comfort her, I'll open a bank account for her. I'll give her a pillowcase full of money that she can hide in her closet. I know the only thing we have in common is you, but there must be something that will ease her mind."

There was not.

But the old lady was more perceptive than I. It was she who first noticed that Kimiko was losing weight and energy. I had noticed the dark circles under her eyes, the constant tiredness, but we had both been lucky health wise, our years together had been blessed. I had gone into old age quite gracefully, scarcely noticing that I was grayer, slower moving, more forgetful. Kimiko was shrinking before my eyes and I had scarcely noticed. I simply thought she too was slowing down.

That was not the case. There were treatments, but they were stop gap. Our world was turned topsy-turvy. It had always been a foregone conclusion that I would die first, but it was not to be the case either.

Even Kimiko's good nature could not forestall the foreboding that seemed to drip from the walls. The nursery was sold within days of being on the market. We waited, none of us quite knowing what to do with ourselves. Kimiko and I shared a love seat in the living room where we watched TV in the evenings. She was always cold, needed to be swathed in a blue afghan quilt; I sat close to her those evenings so she could draw from my warmth. She was still cheerful, still joked that I should carry her to bed. Now, she had to take my hand and lean on me as we walked down the hall and up the stairs to the bedroom.

Sometimes, I watched surreptitiously as the old woman moved about the kitchen, her sandals and cane clicking ominously on the tiles. What was she going through? She had lost her son, her husband, and now she was about to lose her daughter. She would be left to share a house with someone she mistrusted.

One evening, after Kimiko was in bed, I made a pot of the thick green tea that Mrs. Shibayama liked. I had seen Kimiko pour it in a bowl and take it to her hundreds of times. I did what I could, I knocked lightly on her door, waited a few seconds before opening it. I cupped the heavy little bowl with both hands. She was sitting cross-legged on her pallet. How could someone so old sit that way? It would be an impossibility for me, as would sleeping on a pallet on the floor.

I bowed awkwardly, holding the bowl of tea out to her. She stared at me for several seconds. It was her chance to humiliate me as she had seemingly longed to do for all the years I had known her. Then she held out her own hands and accepted the tea. I thought there might have been something like the start of a smile on her face, but it quickly vanished. She drank the bowl of tea, while I stood by awkwardly. When she was about to return the bowl to me I motioned for her to set it on the mat by her bed. I held my hands out to her in a universal gesture. Again, she stared at me for several seconds before letting me take hold of her dry, aged hands and help her to her feet.

"I love Kimiko," I said. "I love her so much." I placed my hands gently on her shoulders and moved her toward me. "I love Kimiko," I said again, my voice breaking. My body shuddered and tears dripped down my cheeks. She remained rigid, her arms at her sides, like sinewy old brooms. She smelled of tea and something like fresh cut grass. Suddenly, I felt her fingers on my back just above my waist, her old hand patted me a few times, very gently, like a cat tapping at a new toy.

As Kimiko's time lessened, we still spent our evenings on the love seat, but several times Mrs. Shibayama joined us, sitting on an oak chair near us, though there was a large comfortable sofa across the room.

Tonight, the TV show is over. The three of us have finished our tea. I stand in front of Kimiko, offer my hand to help her up from the sofa.

"I'm so tired," she says, "I think you'll have to carry me."

Our standing joke.

But this time, I take a look at her strained face, then scoop her gently into my arms, afghan and all, her cheek against mine, an arm tight around my neck. She weighs scarcely more than her clothes. I carry her for the very first time, down the hall, resolutely toward the stairs, my heart so full of love, but bleeding with each step.

CHAPTER 29

Today I am lonely. Ghosts of Christie mirage about the room. Christie naked, standing in front of the dappled mirror, fingering a dark, sea-coloured bruise on her thigh.

Christie atop me, leaning back, pressing, trembling like an earthquake. Christie, sweet and musky against my mouth, convulsing, whispering, "Tell me? Tell Me?"

Christie, jangling like a gypsy, gold bracelets, earrings big as pancakes, bare thighs, suitcase purse, scarlet polish, the ever present green scarf in her red hair.

Christie, soft as a cloud beneath me, pulling me into her, whispering her love...

And Christie, her mood dark as the whiskey bottle from which she pours unsteadily, unstable as the gulps she takes from the glass.

"What am I doing here with you? You're not my kind."

The statement could have been made by either of us.

"I love you very much."

"You know fuck all. I got no right to be loved."

Christie lives on in my memory. "I have no one," she said.

"You have me."

"That's not what I mean. It matters a great deal that someone remembers what you were like when you were young."

"I remember the smell of sour milk," I said. "Vicks Vap-o-Rub. I associate that with my grandfather. The odours of age and death."

"Sun patterns on the floor, like the chalk outline of a body."

"Not pleasant," I said.

"My family is gone. I don't even know where to look for them. I heard rumours that one of my brothers was murdered with a machete over a drug deal gone wrong. The other one was selling Bibles door to door in Alabama, that was years ago. My closest sister was like a careening car – drugs, booze, sex. I'm sure she must be dead. The one I remember as Vanessa got taken away from Mother and put in a foster home. Maybe if she doesn't know where she came from, she stands a chance. If there was just some way to erase memories."

Christie stares at me, insolent, waiting.

"I've given up asking for details." I said.

"Good."

DO NOT ABANDON ME

I don't really know what my husband, Richard, does for a living. I do know that because of his occupation he is one of the loneliest men on earth. The reason I don't know is not for lack of interest, but lack of understanding. Richard – never Ricky, Rick, or Dick – is employed by Harvard University as a sort of one-man think tank. He spends his days in a quiet office in front of a clean desk thinking about mathematics. He has made some breakthroughs in the echelons of higher calculus that only two other men in the world are capable of interpreting, of telling him whether he is right or wrong. One is in Japan, the other in one of those countries, Honduras, Ecuador, Bolivia, where magical thinking is part of the national psyche, a country where it is unreasonably hot and humid and the political situation is terminally volatile.

I know it sounds cruel to say this, but Richard is such a bore. I am so sick of him. He is totally predictable. I know I am being unfair to Richard because, ten years ago, predictable was what I wanted. I was twenty-two, had just come out of a two-year, knock-down, drag-out relationship with a six-foot, eight-inch tall tackle for the New England Patriots. Sex so intense I often felt I'd explode, or at the least cause myself irreversible bodily harm if we continued for one more minute. The bad times were equally intense; to summarize all our difficulties, Karl had no concept of the word fidelity. Women flung themselves at him as if he were a rock star. I travelled with him one fall, road trips to Dallas and Los Angeles. He received FedEx packages and letters at the front desk, hand-delivered letters slipped under his door. Panties, bras, photos, gifts, some purchased,

some handmade, each accompanied by primitive, pitiful letters full
of misspellings and pornographic suggestions. I'll always remember
one from a girl who in her arcade stall, three-for-a-dollar photo
looked about eighteen. She had a long pimply face and lank black
hair. The accompanying note read in part, "I like to due a good blow
job so theres no chance I should get pregnant."

I met Richard at a book signing. There is a monster bookstore
in Worcester and a girlfriend convinced me to accompany her there
one Sunday afternoon where a young author, whose name I had
never heard, and can't recall, was signing his book which had something to do with philosophy and the cultural revolution. I enjoy love
stories and mysteries, and like to be scared by Stephen King. While
we were waiting in line to get her book signed, Richard walked by.
My girlfriend's brother had roomed with Richard at Harvard, where
Richard had attended from freshman to PhD, and then gone into
their esoteric think tank. He looked like a sad puppy. I wanted to
cuddle him and pet him and wipe those laces of black hair off his
forehead. We went for coffee after the signing, and Richard was shy
and looked into his coffee whenever he spoke. My girlfriend was
the one he should have been interested in, she had a degree in psychology from Smith and was about to set up her own practise; she
was as close to an intellectual equal as Richard might find. She was
trying to impress him, but it apparently didn't work, for the next
week Richard phoned her brother and asked him to call his sister
and get my last name and phone number.

After my tumultuous relationship with Karl, Richard was peace,
tranquility, stability. Richard would never have groupies.

We dated for several months. Movies, dinners, concerts, lec-
tures. I had to seduce him. Undoing my bra while he was tentatively
touching my breasts, after about our seventh date, gave him a clue
that I was ready. I compared this to Karl, who moments after we
met, clutching me in an elevator on the way to the parking garage,
asked me if I enjoyed a number of activities, all connected with oral

sex. I was too stunned not to reply. I panted that I did. "Just laying it on the line," said Karl. "There are actually chicks who think they can impress me by holding out."

When we did make love, Richard was surprisingly passionate. I hadn't expected much from this slight, sink-chested man with his uneasy smile and small, pale hands. Eventually, Richard asked me to marry him. I said yes. I longed for stability. But not boredom.

Let me give you an example. This is what Richard considers a significant activity for the two of us. I'm sure he's read somewhere in a magazine that married couples should do things together in order to keep their marriage fresh. He enrolled us in a course on Navigational Codes and Signals.

"We don't own a boat," I protested.

"That's not the point," Richard said. "This is something new to us. I'll bet none of our friends have done this."

"And with good reason," I said, but under my breath.

We do occasionally go out for a Sunday afternoon on a friend's boat, but if they have any navigational flags I've never noticed them, and I certainly don't recall anyone ever flashing them signals. After the first class, held in a musty room in some kind of privately funded community center not far from Harvard Square, I said to Richard "These flags aren't even applicable anymore. They're obsolete."

We had to put a one hundred dollar deposit on the text, a book published in the 1930s, and long out of print. The elderly instructor loaned us a copy held together by glue, tape and fingerprints. "These flags were used by commercial vessels," I complained to Richard. "That kind of communication has been almost completely replaced by radio, radar, sonar, computers. And who is this guy teaching the course? He looks like he's old enough to have sailed on the Pequod." The signals themselves were mainly commands. T: Keep clear of me. U: You are running into danger. Y: I am dragging my anchor. I joked that many of the commands could apply to personal relationships as well as seagoing vessels. Richard stared at me as though I had spoken in a foreign language. His sense of humour is minimal, to say the least.

We attended every Thursday for six weeks. We wrote a final exam, received a little certificate stating that we were qualified in the Communication Aspects of Practical Navigation.

"I'll put this on my resume," I said. I laughed. Richard smiled slowly. I have no resume. My degree certificate reads Artus Generalis or something foolish; I took a few literature courses, some theater, art history, basic psychology. I'm qualified to work as a part-time clerk in an art gallery, which I do when I'm totally bored.

West travels. On a moment's notice, he flies off to Cairo, Budapest, Peking, Madagascar, Zanzibar. He told me a story about being associated with clove smugglers in Zanzibar who risk death to sneak sacks of contraband cloves into Kenya, from where they eventually make their way to the gourmet chefs of Europe, who use them to create exotic sauces.

"My business," says West, "is dangerous antiques and artifacts."

His life is full of intrigue. Albania has only recently become accessible. Last month, he smuggled a dozen silver goblets from the 1300s out of Albania, each encased in a garishly painted plaster statue of a saintly-looking monk. I helped him unpack them from their bed of cedar shavings and shredded newspapers.

"Part of my business is to circumvent bureaucracy," says West, a smile crinkling the lines at the corner of each eye. "Countries make unacceptable rules concerning cultural artifacts. It is my job to stretch, bend, or even break the rules. I can bribe my way through customs anywhere except the United States, Canada and sometimes Great Britain. One has to be patient, in some countries it takes a long time to reach a bribable official."

West has golden hair, the body of a very good tennis player which, at forty-two, has widened until his step has slowed enough that he only plays doubles of a Sunday morning, and only for fun.

He has a golden aura of danger about him. I have to admit, I have a fascination for dangerous men.

"I want us to travel together," West said over the phone yesterday, as we were finalizing this date. West has been married once, has a child to whom he is very good. "My ex," he says, "lost her spirit of adventure."

"Perhaps we could introduce her to Richard," I say. We giggle like children.

I met West at an antique show. "I don't usually do this," he said, after I'd stopped to admire a jade dragon, seamless, seeming to glow with an inner light. "But sometimes rich people go slumming, and they assume that I'm selling at below my regular prices because everything else in the show is so tacky. I usually work by appointment only."

I inquired about the dragon. "Because you're such a beautiful woman I could let you have it for $80,000."

"I'm afraid only tacky is within my price range," I said. West was wearing khakis with many pockets; he looked like a scientist in a Tarzan movie, the one who warns the expedition leader 'The natives are restless, I don't think it's safe to travel any further up this river.'

"I'll give you my phone number," West said cheerfully. "Call me, I'm sure I have any number of artifacts within your price range." He handed me a business card centered with a W in sweeping calligraphy. His hand held mine for a few seconds as the card, and a jolt of sexual energy, passed between us.

I called him the next day. I went to his shop on antique row, where customers are admitted only after ringing a bell, stating their purpose, and sometimes showing ID. "I deal in coins, precious gems," said West. "Browsers aren't welcome here. There are many extremely devious men in my profession."

We went for lunch, three hours with good wine, and food I don't even remember. I spent my time staring into West's aquamarine eyes and longing to touch him. As we slid from the booth in the now empty restaurant West faced me, put his right arm around me, lifted me right off the floor and kissed me. I didn't want him to stop.

Whatever guilt I had drifted away as his tongue filled my mouth and I grabbed the golden curls that extended over his collar and returned the kiss as passionately as I knew how.

Still, I put off consummating the affair.

"I have to be certain," I told West, "about our feelings, about my lack of feelings for Richard. I think it would be sinful to just have an affair. That would be tacky."

We've had lunch almost every afternoon for three weeks. I've lied to Richard about working at the gallery. I've actually told the owner I won't be in for the next few weeks, maybe never again. We've done everything but have actual intercourse. I have only to say the word and West will get us a hotel room for an afternoon, because I can't figure a way to stay out overnight.

One afternoon in his office, after kissing passionately for a long time, West sat me in the huge leather swivel chair behind his desk, knelt in front of me, slipped my panties down and loved me with his tongue until I shrieked and thought I might faint from ecstasy. We traded places and I found myself, still trembling from my own climax, letting myself go completely. I was so anxious to fill my throat with him, to please him, that for a moment I knew what those football groupies (Karl referred to them disdainfully as cum garglers) must have experienced, the chance to give the gift of passion, with a hope, no matter how slight, that it would be received meaningfully, that something like love might follow.

In the evenings, whenever Richard retires to his study to read his texts and treatises on mathematics, I phone West, who lives some fifty miles out of Boston. The calls will appear on our phone bill. I don't know how I will explain them. I don't care.

I think of Richard in his study perusing documents in a language only three people in the world understand. Richard once considered a hobby. "I think I'd like to get a little lathe and put it in the garage," he said. "I thought I could make wooden coat hangers."

The word "opulent" might best describe the hotel room where I will shortly give myself completely to West. There are fresh flowers, champagne, a fruit basket, a wooden bowl of those delicious, foil-wrapped chocolates that are mysteriously placed on your pillow in the late evening. I eat one without even realizing what I am doing. Its taste is so intense I eat another.

I have been in this hotel room once before, this elegant, impersonal space, or at least an identical room on this or a nearby floor. The room was engaged by Harvard, and from it we were able to see the finish line of the Boston marathon. The Japanese genius was visiting Boston, and Harvard had booked the room months in advance because the Japanese mathematical prodigy, a Mr. Nakagawa, postulated that there was a possible mathematical formula that would explain the muscular coordination of trained athletes, something to do with the way they pumped their arms when running.

It was an eerie feeling watching the progress of the race on television where, every so often they would cut to the finish line, which we could see below our window. In fact, once they showed the hotel and if they'd held the shot another few seconds we could have picked out our window. The view was remarkable in that we could read the numbers of the runners, chests heaving, as they crossed the line, and we could see the journalists shoving microphones into the faces of the sweating athletes. I felt disoriented, like a kitten in a room filled with somber monkeys in business suits, their arms folded in privacy across their collective chests.

At 10:00 a.m., a FedEx courier had arrived at my door with a large, colourful envelope. It contained one of those coded plastic cards for opening a hotel room door. There was a hotel business card with the room number scrawled on the back along with the word Noon, and West's large calligraphed W, his signature, the same W that appears on his shirts, in gold on a ruby pinky ring, his key chain.

The ringing phone jars me back to the present. Oh, no. West is going to be late. Worse yet, West can't make it. Some European count is desperate to purchase a Ming vase.

"Madame, it is the concierge. Madame is requested to glance out the window of her suite."

"What on earth for?"

The concierge has a heavy French accent. All American concierges have heavy European accents. He's probably lived all his life in Worcester. I wonder if European concierges have heavy American accents?

"I can only repeat the message supplied to me, Madame. I am informed that if you glance out the window of your suite you will see something interesting."

I hang up.

It can be only one of two things. West is doing something wonderful and extravagant, a banner on one of the nearby buildings that says I LOVE YOU, ESME. A huge floral arrangement – I picture a horseshoe-shape, ten feet high, like those at the Kentucky Derby, or a gangster's funeral, sculpted of white carnations, with my face centering the interior, my cheeks and lips red roses, my eyes blue hydrangeas.

On the other hand, what if Richard has followed me? I can't imagine him doing that. He's never missed a day at his job in the ten years I've known him. I've been so happy the past few weeks, since I've been spending time with West, perhaps Richard has noticed. Has he shown any signs of suspicion? Nothing comes to mind. He left for work at his usual time; he always leaves the house at 7:30 a.m.

I make my way across the room to the window, slowly, as if I am walking in something congealed, each step an effort.

Oh, it is worse than I thought. It is Richard. He is standing across the street, about where the runners crossed the finish line of the Boston Marathon, staring toward me through his thick glasses. He looks so helpless. His colourless slacks are rumpled, he wears a brown windbreaker, a slight breeze blows unruly laces of black hair down across his forehead. His right shoulder droops so unhappily. He is holding a flag. It is on a tiny flag pole. Where in the world would he find such a little flag pole? It is one of the flags from our textbook. I can picture Richard in his study, thinking about, instead of mathematical formulas too complicated for even extraordinary mortals, something he can do to rekindle my interest in him, to make me love him again.

The flag he holds displays the letters CXL. I have to admit I only did a half-hearted job of learning the signals, and after we passed the test, Richard with a mark of one hundred percent, me with fifty-five, a bare pass, I let many of them drift way like notes of music disappearing forever. This is information I will never use again, I thought. Let's see: A = I am undergoing a speed trial. K = You should stop your vessel instantly. What do these combinations mean? CXL sounds like the acronym for a football league.

Oh, my. Oh, my. It comes to me. And I place my hands, palms flat to the glass, arms extended above my head as if there is a burglar with a revolver standing behind me. Tears well up, overflow. I snuffle. Richard looks so intense, so vulnerable, so lonely.

CXL is a command: Do not abandon me. DO NOT ABANDON ME! It is the perfect flag. Richard sees me, raises the flag a little higher with his right hand, waves diffidently with his left.

West's knock sounds at the door. Cheerful, full of energy. My heart flutters. I remain at the window. West knocks and knocks.

CHAPTER 30

Foreshadowing! When I dreamed or imagined losing Christie, it foreshadowed what was actually going to happen. As I predicted, Christie is gone, and as a final, desperate attempt to find her, like tossing hundreds of tangled lines into a stormy ocean, I am tempted to include here an appeal to my readers.

"Help! I have lost Christie. I want to let her know it is alright to come back to me, or for me to go to her."

I have only one photo of her. A Polaroid taken by my philosopher friend Jones, of Christie leaning seductively against the front wall of the Sunshine Bar. She is wearing jeans with a white shirt knotted across her belly, black, ankle-high boots with silver buckles. Unfortunately, the photo is slightly out of focus, Jones standing a few feet too far away from the subject. He probably moved as he was taking the photo. He probably moved on purpose. He never liked Christie. I stare at the photo. I think of a song, "Your Picture Still Loves Me." My fingers seem to feel a warmth from the photo. I imagine Christie in my arms, the sweet odours of her…

My appeal will read, "Christie is a slim, green-eyed woman with short, plum-coloured hair and freckles. If you see her in a teeming bar, or walking straight-backed, wearing a low-cut white blouse, carrying a hand-tooled leather purse, smiling her ironic smile, moving her head every so slightly to keep the smoke from her cigarette out of her eyes, or tossing imaginary strands of hair off her forehead with a movement like a beautiful show horse, or if you hear her say, 'Christie is presently living alone,' then you will know it is her.

"If you see her, I beg you to write me in care of my publisher."

In harsh reality, I can no longer write an appeal like that. Though it might draw some responses, from editors, readers, and academics who are fascinated by squalor. It takes imagination to write a heart-felt appeal like that. Since Christie left, my imagination feels like an egg that has been dropped on the floor. I'm thinking more and more about "The Spaceship That Crashed on a Cattle Ranch."

I can stay here and wait, or I can go back to that other life where I live with Christie in stainless steel surroundings, in a bitter prairie city. Where our bodies touch like glass against glass, passionless.

I would rather be alone, with hope, than together in a lifeless dimension where passion has been spent, or never existed.

"I dream of myself as a sunflower stalk," Christie said once, "with petals large and soft as silk scarves, floppy as dogs' ears. My petals bruise if you yell at them, cower like old ladies in a hail storm. There are, I am told, plants that are meant to grow in isolation, away from sound and sunlight. My foliage goes limp, turns an ugly brown when confronted by bright light and decisions."

I continually reread the last piece I wrote before Christie left, as if it might contain a clue as to where she's gone.

"Someday I'd like to have an Asian baby," Christie said to me shortly before everything came apart at the seams.

"I'm afraid I can't help you there," I said.

"But Asian babies are so cute." We were in bed. She rubbed her nose against my shoulder. Her laugh like a tiny, tinkling bell.

"Sorry," I said.

"You're no fun," she said.

ASIAN GIRL

My wife was very upset when the nurse brought our new baby into the hospital room.

"I'm very upset," my wife said.

"She's incredibly beautiful," I said. "I'm in love with her already."

"Don't you notice?" my wife said. "She's a beautiful baby, but she's...she's...Asian."

"Of course I noticed. Do you think I'm insensitive? What difference does it make?" The baby was perfect in every way, her features were like a doll's, her skin tinted just so, her tiny eyes beautifully abaxial. She had a full shock of straight, black hair.

"We are not Asian," my wife said.

"I'm aware of that," I said. "Now, how should I word this? The fact that she's Asian is certainly no reflection on you."

"Thank you for that," my wife said. "But, I'm going to make inquiries."

"I'll do it," I said.

I explained the situation to the head nurse on the maternity ward, then to the administrator responsible for the orderly functioning of the maternity ward.

"We live in a Global Community," they said.

I accepted their explanation.

I work as an editor for a renowned publisher. Which means I am a failed writer, who now tells other more successful writers how to make their work better. At the time, our renowned publishing house was bringing out a new novel from Stephen King. While Stephen King's editor, also a failed author, was at lunch, I perused his private files, extracting Stephen King's unlisted phone number.

"What do you think of the idea of an Asian baby being born to a Caucasian couple?" I asked him.

"Been done," Stephen King said.

"No. I mean what do you think of the idea?"

"Been done," he said, with considerably more emphasis, and hung up.

My wife was unable to get used to having an Asian baby. She eventually took up with a blackjack dealer and moved to Atlantic City.

I bought a really fancy rice cooker.

Our daughter won a spelling bee in second grade.

"I don't want you to be lonely, Daddy," she told me when she was fifteen.

Four years later, my daughter brought a professor home from college, a beautiful woman in her forties who looked enough like her to be her mother.

"Have a Bovril and a game of Scrabble and get acquainted," she said, leaving us alone. The professor used the word uterus for a triple word score. We fell into each other's arms.

Acknowledgements

Coteau Books gratefully acknowledges that the stories "Do Not Abandon Me", "The Last Surviving Member of the Japanese Victory Society", "Risk Takers" and "Waiting on Lombard Street" earlier appeared in *The Essential W.P. Kinsella* (Tachyon Publications, San Francisco, 2015). Also, the story "Truth and History" first appeared in *Red Wolf, Red Wolf* (Harper Collins Canada, Toronto, 1987).

Used with permission.